INSUFFERABLE BOSS

IONA ROSE

SOME BOOKS

UNTITLED

Author's Note

Hey there!

Thank you for choosing my book. I sure hope that you love it. I'd hate to part ways once you're done though. So how about we stay in touch?

My newsletter is a great way to discover more about me and my books. Where you'll find frequent exclusive give-aways, sneak previews of new releases and be first to see new cover reveals.

And as a HUGE thank you for joining, you'll receive a FREE book on me!

With love,

Iona

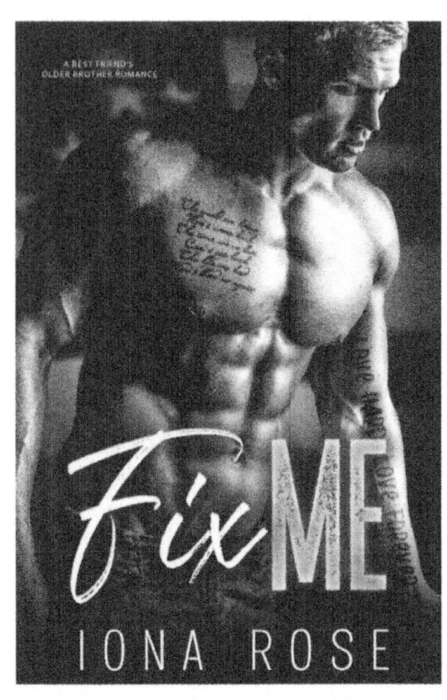
A BEST FRIEND'S
OLDER BROTHER ROMANCE
Fix ME
IONA ROSE

Insufferable Boss

Publisher: SomeBooks

978-1-913990-72-5

PROLOGUE

Lena

LAST WILL AND TESTAMENT OF JOHN MERCER

I, John Mercer, being of sound mind and memory, do hereby make, publish, and declare this to be my last will and testament, revoking all prior wills and codicils made by me.

FIRST: I give, devise, and bequeath all of my estate, both real and personal, to be divided equally between my two children, Lena and Dylan Mercer.

. . .

SECOND: In particular, I bequeath to my daughter, Lena Mercer, and my son, Dylan Mercer, each receiving an equal share of my 50% equity in the Standard Rock Company, as well as the following assets:

(A) MY VACATION HOME IN HAWAII, to Dylan

(b) my personal art collection, to Lena

(c) my yacht, "The Pearl," to Dylan

(d) my beach house in the Hamptons, to Lena

(e) my townhouse in the Upper East Side of Manhattan, Dylan

(f) my villa in Tuscany, Italy, to...

IT WENT ON AND ON... and my mind floated back to a time when he was still alive, the sun was in his eyes and he was laughing. The whole family was laughing with him. Not until my name was called out once again did my attention return to the words that were being read aloud.

"... Lena Mercer as the executor of this will. In the event that she is unable or unwilling to serve, I appoint my son, Dylan Mercer, as the alternate executor."

FOURTH: If any provision of this will is declared invalid...

I ZONED OUT AGAIN. Not until the reading was over, did I look up again. I'd been dragged here, obliged to listen to how my father's assets were to be distributed. However, it was the last thing I wanted to think about. I had been slated to see him in the winter, but I was too busy. "I'll see you in spring," I said. How was I to know it was his last winter? I never saw it coming.

I WAS STILL IN SHOCK, of course, but the torment was slowly beginning to set in.

"I'M GROWING MY COMPANY, Dad. I just need a bit of time. Christmas is our busiest season. I'll see you soon. I promise. Oh, and don't forget I love you,'" I called gaily, as if we had all the time in the world.

IT WAS MORE than two weeks since I last spoke to him, and now all I had from him were the words of this will.

SUDDENLY, I was aware of many eyes turned in my direction.

"ARE WE DONE?" I asked softly. I felt completely drained. I wanted to be on a flight and out of here as soon as possible. There was now a cloud over this city in my mind that I couldn't wait to put behind me so that I could breathe again and begin to heal.

. . .

"Yes, Miss Mercer," my father's lawyer said expressionlessly.

I rose to my feet.

He mentioned something about sending the documents my way and about the execution, but I didn't care. Not now.

My brother was present too, but I didn't look at him. There was nothing we had to say to each other. I just kept moving forward until I arrived at the lobby of the office building in Manhattan. I slipped on my sunglasses, but before I could exit the building, my name was called. I ignored the voice. There was some unpleasant memory attached to the voice and my first instinctive reaction was to ignore it, but the man was relentless.

"Lena," he called again, his voice ringing out authoritatively across the vast space.

I stopped and turned around slowly. The breath slowly escaped from my chest as I watched him stride across the polished granite floor. Yes, he was exactly as I remembered. Tall, broad, and utterly delicious, but an undeniable asshole I would

. . .

"YEAH?" I asked affecting a bored manner, when he stood in front of me.

HIS NOSTRILS FLARED with annoyance at my tone, but his voice was even. "Can I have a few minutes of your time? There is something extremely important that we must talk about."

VAGUELY, I recalled the particular detail of my father's will where he had assigned his 50% equity in Standard Rock to my brother and me. Given that this man was the CEO and one of the other owners of the company, I wasn't surprised he was on the warpath.

"I'M GOING to assume your sudden desire to speak to me is about my share of Standard Rock, but I'm afraid I'm not in the mood to talk about any of it, so speak to my brother or something. I don't give a damn."

HIS PIERCING GRAY eyes narrowed with displeasure, but I didn't care. I started to walk away. To my surprise though, his hand closed around my arm, and the very strength of it stopped me in my tracks. I looked down at his tanned hand. It was a beautiful hand, sculptured like some Greek marble statue, but warm on my skin. For some reason the impeccable beauty and wonderful warmth of it irritated me even more. The hand of an jerk should be cold and claw-like.

. . .

"Excuse me?" I muttered between gritted teeth.

"I understand you want to leave the city immediately, but this will only take a few minutes," he said calmly, as he removed his hand.

The fact that he was forcefully demanding my attention did nothing to make me more tolerant of him, but he did run the company, and as an equity owner myself and to be respectful of my father and his life's work, I forced myself to calm down.

"Go ahead," I instructed coldly.

"I'll get straight to the point then," he said. "I want to buy you out. I don't think you have much interest in running the company, so I'm more than willing to take it off your hands. You're not allowed to sell now, not until two years after you've worked at the company, but...."

His words faded into the background as I stared at him, angry he was bringing this up now. Even so, I understood him since I ran a company myself. Plus, the company was worth over a billion dollars, so of course, he couldn't be considerate of my current emotional state.

. . .

GIVEN my past experience with him, though, I didn't expect him to behave any better, so this immediately drained whatever patience I might have had for him.

"I'VE NOT READ THE WILL," I said impatiently. "So I can't make a decision yet."

I TURNED AWAY TO LEAVE, but he stopped me again. "Can I contact you in the future for an update?"

"NO," I replied. "My father just passed away. Please leave me alone. When and if I'm interested, I'll give you a call." My words sounded relatively calm, but I felt as if I was screaming into the wind.

THANKFULLY, this time he didn't try to stop me. I couldn't wait to get out of New York for all the pain, shock, and hurt it had brought me the past few days. Maybe things would change for the better soon.

1

Lena

"So let me get this straight," Diana said. "You're going to sell your company to them, but you're also going to keep being in charge of it and also use their money to expand it?"

"Yes," I replied as I brought out two blazers from my closet and held them up before her. She considered the choices between the stripe and pattern and went with the pattern.

"I don't know," she said. "That seems... extremely favorable?"

"Yes," I said, smiling.

“Hm,” she said. “And if I feel this way, then there's no way the other equity owners will feel any different right? Especially since you all aren't close, right?"

"Yeah," I replied, all the worries that had plagued me earlier now coming to mind.

“Hm,” she said again, and I sighed.

"We have to figure it out. At least I have to figure it out.

It's my dad's company, after all, and I don't want to ignore it the way I ignored our relationship."

"That's unfair to yourself," she said. "He understood you. He was a businessman himself, and you both were constantly busy and didn't always find the time to spend together."

"Yeah," I said and tried to focus on packing, but she kept going.

"So now since you can't sell your equity before two years lapse, you're going to work there till then?"

"Don't know if I'm going to sell or not even after the two years elapses," I told her. "My original plan was to remain as uninvolved as possible, and since I never had the intention to sell, then I didn't need to work there, but now that he's made this offer to buy my company, I have a reason to consider moving to New York."

"Ah," she nodded. "It's clear to me now."

"Hm," I replied. "What will forever be unclear to me, though, is why my dad gave equity to my brother as well. I mean, he could have just handed the properties over to him instead. He knows Dylan has no interest in it or the ability to run a business. Or even contributing for that matter."

"He's graduated college, right?" Diana asked, and I nodded.

"Yeah, he's been wasting away his time since then, but my dad hasn't had the heart to cut him off."

She laughed. "But you've said that you might be the bigger disappointment to your dad since at least Dylan finished college while you did not."

I sighed as she pointed this out.

"You're right. That's why I worked so hard, but at the same time, it kept me away from him because I always felt that no matter how well I did, he wouldn't get over that disappointment.

Anyway, let's not talk about these anymore. I'm running late."

"When does your flight leave again?"

"10 am."

"Hm, we have four hours more," she yawned.

She continued helping to select and fold items into my suitcase. However, my mind remained in turmoil, so I stopped and laid down beside her on the bed.

"What is it?" she asked.

"I need to clear my head," I said. "It's too cloudy. I feel like I'm not thinking straight."

"Alright," she said, giving me her full attention. "What exactly is the problem?"

I briefly went silent as I tried to sort through my thoughts, but she came up with her own topic before I could.

"Does your cloudiness have anything to do with that... person who's going to be in the picture?"

"Who?" I asked.

"The CEO," she replied, and I frowned at her reminder, and then I sighed.

"Kane goddamn motherfucking Lazarus. He's one of the reasons this move is making me anxious. He was the one who told me about the offer to buy me out, but he can't exactly be trusted."

"You've called him a slime and sleaze ball every single time you've mentioned him over the past few months. Are you still not going to tell me why you detest him so much? I mean, has he done anything so far to cheat you beyond the fact that he offered to completely buy you out?"

"Also, did he make the same offer to your brother? Why didn't he take it?"

"I don't know if he made the same offer to Dylan, but even if he did, why would Dylan sell?" I asked. "Dylan's lazy, but he's not an idiot. Staying connected to the company assures he keeps his wealth and access to resources. If he leaves with a buyout, then he has to manage it himself and grow it. Why the fuck would he want to do that when he can keep doing the bare minimum and ride on the backs of others?"

"Okay, well, he doesn't sound like he's going to be your ally in this."

"I'm not going there to fight," I said. "I'm just there to consider my options with Standard Rock. My father gave almost his whole life to building that, so it's the least I can do."

She nodded. "That's great and all, but can we please go back to Kane? You two knew each other when you were younger, right? I mean, his father owned the company along with yours, so there must have been meetups and gatherings or something?"

I didn't respond.

"Lena," she called. "I need to know why he, amongst everyone else, grates on you. I mean, his sister owns equity, and you've mentioned that she's nasty. Then you're not close to your brother. In all of these, Kane seems to be neutral and maybe even an advocate in your favor, yet you can't stand even the mention of his name."

"It's not that bad," I said, and she laughed.

"I'll hold up a mirror so you can see how your expression changes when he's brought up. Like now."

She began to search for a mirror in the bedside drawer, and I shook my head.

"You're so fucking nosy."

"Of course I am. You're a generally peaceful person, so it makes no sense. There has to be something else that makes you antagonistic towards him, and I need to know what it is."

Sighing, I considered her words, and then I gave in.

"It wasn't a big deal, or anything too serious," I said. "It was just annoying."

"Of course, it's not serious; you wouldn't be so emotional otherwise. What I'm sure of is that it was embarrassing for you, and this is why I have to hear about it, or else you're going to miss your flight today. I'm not letting you leave."

Amused, I continued to stare at the ceiling as I conjured the memory to mind, and she came over to poke me.

"Speak," she said. "You're going to be late."

"Fine," I conceded. "There were many of those... joint festivities you mentioned since our fathers owned the company together."

"Okay," she said.

"So," I continued. "During one of those, I was in the library trying to get away from all the noise when I heard someone come in, so I hid. I thought it was the housekeeper trying to get me to come downstairs to meet the other guests."

"However, I later found out that it was Kane and some woman."

"Oh?" she asked. "And?"

"Well, what else could have happened? He had sex with her right there?"

She gasped.

"In front of you?"

"No," I replied. "There was an inner reading room and he took her there. Took her on my bloody reading daybed! At first, I wasn't even sure what was going on, so I went to take a look."

"Of course," Diana said, and I smiled.

"Well, I saw Kane, and he saw me."

Her mouth fell open. "Really?"

"Yeah. Our eyes met, and when it did, I thought at the very least that he was going to be startled enough to pull away from her, but he didn't. Instead, he had the nerve to invite me to join them instead!"

Her eyes widened to the size of saucers. "You're joking."

"I kid you not," I replied. "I can even recall verbatim what he said. He was like – *hey Tom, rather than peeping, you should come join us*?"

"Was he still fucking her when he was saying this?" she asked.

"Bastard didn't miss a beat, and she was noisy as well. To excited to realize there was someone else in the room. I was so embarrassed I nearly died."

Diana burst out laughing, then covered her mouth. "What did you say?"

I cringed, remembering the scene as if had happened yesterday. "Not even if you were the last man on earth," I admitted with a sigh.

Diana's eyes went wide again. "Oh my! "You really said that?"

"I was young," I replied.

"What did he say?"

I shifted uncomfortably. "He threw his head back and laughed."

"And this... is the guy you're going to work for now."

"I won't be working for him," I frowned. "I own equal amounts of the company as he does."

"But he's the CEO, right?"

"Right," I agreed slowly.

She gave me a look. "That would make him your boss."

I glared at her.

"Correct me if I'm wrong, but you have to work for two years before those rights are vested to you, and before then, you'll be working under him, right?"

I grabbed the pillow and put it over my face. I would have screamed into it, but I didn't have the energy.

She couldn't care less about my sudden realization of the horrid situation that was awaiting and was instead spinning her own fantasies.

"So... you once watched him have sex with someone. And both of you remember this. Hmm... Was he good, by the way? Did the girl look like she was enjoying herself?"

"Way too much," I spat angrily. "I couldn't get her stupid whimpering out of my head for years after that."

"Wow, sounds like he made a massive impression on you?" she asked.

I threw the pillow aside. "No, he didn't. All I remember is that supercilious, arrogant, uncaring smirk on his face when he caught sight of me. I turned around and hurried the hell out of there as soon as I could, but as I was in the corridor I heard her, you know, reach her grand finale."

She laughed. "She was loud, huh?"

"The volume was just freaking ridiculous."

"Is he an attractive person?" Without waiting for my response, she retrieved her phone and started to Google him.

"Don't," I groaned, but she didn't listen.

"I need to put a face to him," she mumbled and continued. In no time, she found his pictures and began to scroll through them, her eyes widening with every passing second.

“Wow,” she gasped.

Shaking my head in defeat, I got off the bed and returned to my packing.

"How old was he when you walked in on him?" she asked, her eyes still glued to her phone.

I thought back to the past. "I was eighteen.”

"He's thirty-one now," she said. "And you're twenty-six, so back then he was..."

She lifted her gaze to do the math.

"Twenty-three," I supplied.

She nodded. "Yeah. Twenty-three. Damn."

"Damn what?"

"I'm sorry Lena, but judging by these photos, and if he is still as delectable as he was back then..."

I stopped and waited for her to complete her statement, my eyes narrowing in warning.

"I’m going to make a prediction right now. You're either going to have a hell of a time there, or it's going to be a complete nightmare of cold showers for two years."

Annoyance surged through me at her words but rather than rage at her for mentioning the possibility, I decided to be rational.

"Ugh... I'd rather cut off my arm," I said calmly.

"You better gauge your eyes out first, because that's the only way you're going to avoid your fate. He looks fucking del-"

Suddenly, she noticed the sour expression I couldn’t

quite conceal and, quietly, she came over and began to help me fold.

"Don't mind me, Lena. I'm just being a silly ass. Sorry," she said sheepishly.

"Don't worry about it. I don't know why I'm being like this myself. I guess I'm just so worried that the trouble of this whole mess will be much more than I want to deal with, but I also joining Standard Rock can help my company expand more. We're lacking in so many aspects that Standard Rock can provide. Distribution channels, an entire new department that can focus more on developing scents and fragrances for a much wider populace. Especially since I want to go mainstream, and they already have a textile and home goods division, which means they're the perfect boost I need."

"Do you have an idea for a solution?" she asked.

I nodded. "I think I'm going to turn down the offer of being bought out."

"Really? Why?"

"There has to be a reason he's offering to buy me out, I just have to hear it from him first to figure it out."

"Yeah," she agreed. "There should be a reason; otherwise, he doesn't have to. Or maybe it's because he's trying to get you to work for him and become involved in operations? I mean, you gave them the impression that you weren't going to abandon your company for theirs, so maybe he's trying to kill two birds with one stone. Buy you out, gain the company, and the owner."

This made a lot of sense to me, but some knots still remained loose.

"Sure," I replied. "But what benefit is this to him?"

"No clue. Maybe he needs an ally?"

I stopped at her words and considered them.

"Makes sense, doesn't it?" she asked, and I nodded.

"Yeah, but why would he want to make me an ally when he has his sister?"

"True," she said. "Is their relationship good?"

"I have no idea, but I don't think it is," I replied and continued with my packing.

"How much is Kane willing to offer, by the way?"

“Ten million.”

She gasped!

“Now it really sounds too good to be true, doesn’t it?” I asked and she nodded.

“Of course, it does.”

“Well, hence why this trip to New York worries me.”

“There’s sure to be a catch,” she said.

I nodded. “Most definitely.”

2

Kane

I ignored the ringing phone for as long as I could, and then I eventually had no choice but to pick it up.

"Sir," Elias said.

"Yeah," I replied, and he relayed his report on Lena's scheduled arrival.

"Alright," I said.

"Give her the option to go to an apartment or the hotel as soon as she lands, and of course, ensure David is on the ground to see to whatever needs she desires. I'll call her afterwards to set up the meeting."

"Yes, Sir," he replied, and I set the phone down.

"You're really not enthusiastic about her visit, are you?" Our resident lawyer Matthias commented from his seat across my desk.

"What's there to be enthusiastic about?" I asked as I straightened and tried to get back to work.

"She's been a pain in the ass from the moment her dad passed away. Uncooperative and fucking selfish. Now that I have to deal with her, what joy could possibly be in that?"

"Not only deal with her, you have to technically buy her cooperation."

"Exactly," I said. "Everything has been going fucking downhill since her dad passed away and left the company to these idiots, knowing that since I'm in charge, I would-n't'have a choice but to manage them. I loved the old man, but this has to be the cruelest thing he has ever done to me, and I deeply resent him for it."

Matthias chuckled. "I understand your pain, but the more things unfold and the more tension arises, I'm beginning to think that your fathers may have had ulterior motives with equally dividing the company between the four of you.

"What do you mean?" I asked, and he explained.

"What was their favorite game to play together?"

"Chess."

"So what if all of this is nothing more than a chess game. Your father, in particular, always used to say that even if you distributed resources equally amongst the masses, it would all end up going to the person who was the most qualified in the end. So, I don't think he wanted you four to just possess equal equity and run the company in harmony. They wanted the best man to win since obviously they didn't want to just hand it all over to you. I mean, you're obviously the best one, but they needed to I guess, show your partners that so that they'd believe it."

I listened to his words and smiled.

"You're quite confident that I can get back the equity from all three of them eventually."

"Why wouldn't you be able to?" he asked.

I went silent after this and shook my head while he became curious.

"You'll be able to, right?" he asked, and I was amused.

"Why the fuck wouldn't I be able to?" I asked. "I've long suspected what you just mentioned, so of course, I'm going to annihilate their diet asses."

"Exactly," Matthias agreed. "You've been working here for a decade, and you've single-handedly generated more than 60% of the company's profits. What other proof of competency does anyone need to know how this is going to end?"

I sighed. "Sometimes, though, I get the feeling that they did this for entertainment purposes. To put us against each other and see who would win solely for their enjoyment. They probably just didn't know that they'd both pass way before the plans came to fruition. If this truly was their idea and intention, then I am deeply offended. If I put much thought into this now, I truly might just leave and toss the company to them to burn."

"You'll never do that," Matthias said. "It's not just about money for you now, is it? It's about impact and legacy, and of course, you enjoy this."

At his words, I had nothing to say in response because, as unfortunate as it sounded, he was a hundred percent correct. I sighed and began to sign the stack of documents that had been presented to me.

"So..." Matthias continued. "On to legal matters. You're going to tell Miss Mercer about the dividend increase battle, right? And where you want her to stand on it?"

"Well, knowing her personality so far, I don't think anyone can tell her where to stand on anything," I said. "But at least she's coming here, which means there's an opening and she has considered my offer. I'll see how she responds tonight and how things go."

At this, Matthias went silent for a little while and then he spoke again.

"Any possibility that she won't be offended when she finds out that what you actually want is to buy her vote?"

"I'm paying extensively for it."

"Hm," he said. "That is also another bone of contention. The others still don't know that you put ten million on her table."

"Exactly, that's why there's still relative peace. After I get Lena to agree to it, then we can finalize it, and by then it'll be too late for them to have a fighting chance at stopping it."

"It'll still be two against two," he said.

"Two against two is better than two against one. When they asked for dividend payout increase last time, I gave in because I had too many other more important things to deal with. Things that were generating the money that they were so eager to get a bigger cut out of. The morons.

I didn't want to fight then, but clearly, this has made them even more greedy."

"I'm not surprised," Matthias said, and I nodded in agreement.

"Neither am I, but now that it has come to this, I'm ready to fight this battle, and they're going to lose. They've already lost. And afterwards, I'm going to kick each and every one of them out of the company."

"Big plans," Matthias said, but I didn't respond.

"Lena too?" he asked, and I set my pen down.

"Why do you keep mentioning her?"

"Because she's not a moron," he said. "And if you're

buying her company now, then you most definitely won't be able to kick her out."

"I might be. I mean, she has her own thing going on, but everyone and everything has a price. I just need to know what hers is."

"It's hefty, that's for sure," he said. "She refused to come to New York for any reason over the last few months, but as soon as this ten million was offered, she complied."

"She's a businesswoman," I replied, "so I'm not surprised by this. Plus, I don't think it has to do with just the money."

"Sure," Matthias said. "But when she finds out that, despite the bylaws stating that major decisions have to be made with the four of you, you ignored this and gave in to their demands last time without her input, what do you think her reaction will be? Wouldn't she be offended and become uncooperative?"

"She better not be," I replied, "because that is completely her fault. Her brother claimed his share as left by her dad in his will, and my sister, of course, jumped at the opportunity to have hers when it was issued. She's the one that was difficult and stayed away rather than contribute so what was I to do? I'll be sure to emphasize all of this to her directly and then I'll see how she responds. She's a businesswoman herself not an idler, so I guess the outcome will depend on how mature she is."

Matthias smiled. "I truly wish I could be a fly on the wall during your meeting with her. She's never in the spotlight, but I have heard impressive things about her, and it doesn't hurt as well that she's a stunner."

"If you were on the wall, I'd smash you. Or she would before I even got to you. I'll provide you updates tomorrow."

He laughed while I shook my head.

"Alright," he said and rose to his feet, very clearly receiving the cue to leave and get back to work.

3

Lena

"So..." Diana said on the phone. "What are you wearing for dinner with Mr. Edgy?"

"It's not a date. It's a dinner," I groaned as I held up the plain halter-neck black dress I had brought along, as well as the power suit in my hand.

"So, what is it?" she asked. "Isn't it to welcome you to the Big Apple? Or are you two going to be discussing business straight away?"

"Who knows what it's for, but whatever it is, it's not a friendly dinner. More like a meeting between..."

"Enemies?"

"That's extreme. Not getting along with someone doesn't make him my enemy."

"But you have assumed that you won't get along with him, even though you haven't seen him in so long or even interacted with him."

"I've had enough indirect interactions with him over the

course of the year to know that I definitely won't get along with him," I replied.

"Really?" she asked dryly, and I rolled my eyes.

"Yes, really," I said as I made the final decision to choose the halter-neck dress.

"I have come to the conclusion that I absolutely do not like him."

She was amused while I busied myself with changing.

"Which outfit did you pick?" she asked as I looked at myself in the mirror, taking in the way the soft fabric clung to and hugged my every curve. The outfit was decent, but it was equally as provocative. Not suited to a business meeting at all, but I didn't want to go in there looking as though I had something to prove. I wanted to appear unapologetic, and of course, drop-dead gorgeous was my chosen strategy for taking control from the get-go.

"The dress," I replied, and she laughed again.

"This is gonna be a great show."

"What do you mean?"

"That's a fuck-me dress," she said, and I smiled. I was about to counter this when I decided to just admit it.

"You're right," I agreed.

"So... is that your message?"

"Part of it," I admired how it hugged every bit of my hips.

"And the rest?" Diana asked. "What's the full message?"

"Fuck me, but on second thought, no, thank you."

"Mn, the ring to that is a bit off," she commented, and I shook my head as I let my hair down.

"It's the best I can do for now," I said. "And I'm running late, will talk to you later."

"Sure, have fun," she said. "And don't wear any underwear."

"What?" I had to stop on this one.

"You know what I mean. Not wearing underwear, and with all that material rubbing against your skin, you'll have quite the experience tonight."

"Don't wear any bra as well, and you'll see what all that stimulation and blatant provocation will do to him. It'll drive him crazy, especially because he won't be able to make a move. Now, that's power."

I was silent for quite a while as I truly considered this and then I shook my head at her obscene ideas and ended the call. Just as I grabbed my purse and took one look at myself in the mirror however I eventually decided to do as she had suggested. My bra was never going to cut it in this halter-neck style and the thoughts she had put in my head already made my nipples hard.

So, what was wrong in completely going all the way out and enjoying myself? I wanted to feel myself drip wet from the sight of him or not and what better way to test it?

None of these frivolities were my reason for being here but I was going to put in as much excitement as I could into it.

Plus, the way he had taunted me years earlier still rang in my head and haunted me as well as the way he'd been fucking that woman. The way he had taken her with so much strength and dominance. All I could still see in my minds' eyes when I thought of that scene was her eyes rolled into her head which had completely fallen back as she rode him with abandon.

Till today, I still doubted that she had even noticed my presence as she had been too overwhelmed by her euphoria. He on the other hand had seen a teenager to taunt and hadn't held back and so I was so eager to see what his reaction would be this time around nearly eight years later.

I was confident of this stance as I headed down but the closer I got to the restaurant, the more uncertain I became.

All of this was for every serious business and yet I had these thoughts swirling through my mind. For a moment I considered heading back to change but then I looked at myself in the mirror once again and decided against it. I looked great and felt great and so I was going to stick to it.

The nipple thing was definitely over the top but as long as I didn't get turned on by him in any regard or the room wasn't too cold then I would be fine. Or perhaps either or both would happen, and the latter explanation would work.

Our appointment was at 8pm, since I was given ample time to freshen up and relax after the flight and I was right on time. About five minutes to eight.

Not too late and not too early either.

The moment I got to the hotel's restaurant and was led to my table, I saw that he was already seated and on the phone. He faced me and so all the way his eyes were on me as I walked over, however he didn't say a word. Not till I arrived, and he rose did he send me a light nod of acknowledgment.

I pulled out my own chair and took my seat, not even offended. This wasn't a date but a business meeting and if anything, I was the one inappropriately dressed. He on the other hand was in a suit along with a vest, but there was no tie. He looked dashing and I was quite surprised by how much bigger and handsome he had gotten. The pictures we had found on Google truly didn't do him justice and I had been too grief stricken the first time around to notice him properly.

Now I could look my feel and had to admit that his eyes were striking, they appeared to be even more gray than I remembered them being and the longer he stared the more uncomfortable I became.

When his sly remark from years earlier came to mind as well as his curt behavior so far with getting me to join the company, I reminded myself that he had the looks and that was it. I was dealing with a brute and shrewd person, and I had to act accordingly.

My nipples, however, I soon found didn't share the same sentiment because in no time I couldn't help but notice how they jutted out against the soft fabric.

Sighing and after setting my purse down I grabbed the menu and got ready to deal with the consequences of my actions as professionally as I could.

4

Kane

I couldn't take my eyes off her breasts. I didn't think I'd actually seen any recent photos of her body, only her face, and given the recent circumstances, there had been no thought on my mind beyond the best legal moves to make to prevent her stubbornness from making my life difficult. But now, as I watched those full, heavy mounds bounce in that sin of a dress, creamy shoulders exposed, as well as her impossibly long legs, I realized that I hadn't been paying much attention. But now I was, and I couldn't stop staring at the hardened peaks as they jutted against the fabric, and just like that, I was hard.

I also went deaf since it took me a while to hear that Matthias was still on the phone with me, talking me through the material of the agreement he had dropped off for me to show Lena. Eventually, and after settling down, soft tendrils of her hair making her look much younger than she actually was, she met my gaze. She was bold, always had been, as I especially recalled how she had watched me fuck that woman years earlier at one of our endless family gatherings. I'd been surprised to see her there, but at the passion in her gaze and her refusal to leave, I couldn't help but taunt her. I couldn't remember how she had shot back, but I did know that whatever she had said had made me laugh and come. Hard. I'd been on the lookout for her then but had eventually lost interest, especially when I found out that she was eighteen. I wasn't much older myself, but older women then had been my forte and preference at the time. Now though, this woman before me, coupled with all the stubbornness and feistiness I now knew her to hold, was indeed my forte. However, nothing could happen between us. I didn't mix business with pleasure and given how serious-minded I am, I was certain she was, I didn't think she did the same either. But then, what was this dress about? She wasn't exactly provocatively dressed, but I was immensely provoked. I couldn't get the picture out of my mind of sucking every part of her skin and then fucking her on the closest hardest surface I could find. This table was a great option, and as I lowered to peruse it, my eyes finally left hers.

I closed the file that had been open before me and straightened.

"Sure," I told Matthias on the phone, for whatever he had said and ended the call. Then I linked my hands together and looked at Lena.

"Long time no see," I said, and she gave me a sort of confused look which made me wonder if she was thinking of the last time we'd actually seen each other months earlier at the hotel or eight years earlier in her father's library. It didn't seem likely that she'd forgotten the time in her father's library, but for the benefit of the meeting, I chose to proceed as though she had.

"How are you?" I asked, and she nodded in response.

"Good." She held out her hand for a handshake, and I could see that she was intentionally trying to be as businesslike as possible, but not in that fucking dress. She had to be joking.

"So... what's this meeting about?" she went straight to the point, and I couldn't help but smile. It was going to be very interesting relating with her, especially if our communications went beyond tonight.

"A lot," I replied. "As agreed, you're coming to the office tomorrow to discuss and review the terms of our agreement, but before then, I wanted to touch base with you to try to get our interests to align."

She smiled at my words and at that moment my heart skipped a beat. She was gorgeous, but there was something about that smile... about the boldness of it... the confidence of it that instantly reflected all that she was now and the incredible strength that she now possessed.

She was no longer eighteen and scurrying away from a most improper scene. But she was now a grown fucking woman, ripe for the taking and astute to boot. Her strength, I was beginning to suspect, could rival mine and that was something that I could handle.

I sat up even straighter and gave her all of my attention.

“Sure,” she replied. “Let us indeed see if our interests can align.”

I understood every single word she was saying and not saying and couldn’t wait to begin.

“But first we should eat,” I said, and she nodded as she picked up the menu.

"Sure."

I called the waiter over and couldn't help but watch her as she perused the page. She bit down on her bottom lip, and whether she did this on purpose or absent-mindedly, I would never be able to know, but it didn't matter because once again I found my entire body reacting.

The blood began to rush away from my head, and I couldn't believe how attracted I was to her. I couldn't recall ever feeling this instantly attracted to other women, even in my younger, more promiscuous days. Perhaps I had been too busy in the past several years and completely removed my attention from dating or relationships, and so my body was hyper-aware and paying rapt attention.

She lifted her head just as the waiter arrived, and I watched her send him that smile once again.

He nodded eagerly, and I watched the effect she had on a man that wasn't me. He was practically drooling over her, answering her questions and completely abandoning, or rather forgetting, the notepad and pen he had in hand.

He was young and impressionable, but still, he was so mesmerized that he forgot to ask me if I had any interest in eating. He started to walk away, and only a few seconds later did he return, apologizing profusely.

"I understand," I said, and relief came to his eyes.

He took my order and finally took his leave, leaving us both together.

"That's quite the effect you had on him," I said, and she met my gaze once again.

And as usual, she didn't disappoint me with her comeback.

"What do you mean?"

I stared at her as I wondered whether to go down this

line in our relationship. This was the moment where we would set the tone and given all that I wanted to accomplish through her cooperation, I ultimately decided against it. I wasn't here to pick around, and neither was she.

"Irrelevant," I said and sat up. "So, Miss Mercer," I called. "Do you mind if we casually speak through dinner, or would you prefer that we wait till we're done eating?"

"Speak through dinner," she said. "I have somewhere else to be as soon as our meal is concluded."

This was a surprise to me, but I guess it made sense now as to why she was dressed this way.

"Alright," I said.

"As a compliment, we''ve provided you with round-the-clock services in everything from a chauffeur to an assistant and personal shopper and so on. Just say the word, and it will be done."

"Yeah," she replied, sounding unimpressed. "They've already told me all of this earlier. Let's get to the business at hand."

I was somewhat offended by her curt tone, but she was right, so I just went straight to the point like she wanted.

"Have you considered our offer of ten million?" I asked.

"I have," she replied. "But as you mentioned, there's more to the agreement that we need to talk about, and I, of course, have many questions."

"Please go ahead," I said, and she picked up her glass of water for a sip.

Just before she began, however, the waiter brought the wine that we had ordered, and we got started with that.

"So first of all, I find it hard to believe that the other owners are okay with this. I mean, I am aware that I do hold equal equity in the company but still..."

"'This is correct," I replied, and she continued.

"So, what is their stance on me not only receiving this payout but also working in the capacity of head of the purchased scent brand? What exactly will change and what will not?"

Sharp and astute, just as expected.

"Well," I replied, "my goal is to align our interests, which I am certain was the intention of our fathers when they divided the assets equally between the four of us."

"Okay, so what do you require of me?" she asked.

"Well, for starters, I would like you to start contributing to the operations of the company in the capacity of part-owner."

She didn't seem surprised by this request but given who she was and the progress she had made so far with her own business, I didn't expect her to be. She remained attentive and nodded, somewhat amused because none of this came as a surprise.

"I'm assuming that your willingness to consider this is why you made the trip over?" I asked, and she nodded.

"Yes."

"Alright. I understand you mentioning earlier over the phone that you couldn't serve two masters at the same time and that you chose to serve one, which is your company. But if you do accept this purchase offer, we will all be under the same roof, so I hope that you can participate then. Is this an assurance that we can explicitly receive your cooperation?"

Her response was straightforward.

"No," she said. "I am seriously considering the acquisition, but only if I am put in full managerial control of my company."

I stared at her. "So this means that you still hold no

interest in participating in the major decisions of the company."

"No, I do not," she replied. "They're bound to be extremely severe, especially since it affects so many people's lives, so I'd like to stay out of it and focus on what I know how to do well."

I watched her and then took up the baton to convince her.

"What if we upped our offer?" I asked. "Would you be willing then to participate in the major decisions made?"

"Ah," she said. "So this is a bribe of some sorts?"

I was amused.

"Even if it is, there is no doubt that it thoroughly benefits you. There is absolutely no drawback to it."

"Except my time and focus on the things that I actually want to do myself," she said.

"Mn," I replied. "I guess you could say that, but purchasing your company will make it a subsidiary of ours, which means that whatever benefits us would benefit you as well."

"True, but you have run the company exceptionally well so far, and the last thing I would want to do is interfere."

I nodded.

"I agree, but the problem is that other people now also have just as much right as I have to interfere, hence the need to establish some form of order."

She stared at me, so I continued.

"Do you have a price, then, that will make you consider interfering? I have asked that you sell your rights to me, but you haven't expressed any interest in this. Plus, the terms of your father's will state that the sale of any sort is only eligible after the rights have been fully vested in two years and after you have also worked in the company for two years. So, I'm hoping that by then, you would have a more suitable response for me."

"True," she said, and I nodded.

"But I do have a question for you."

"Go ahead," I replied.

"Is it true that the bylaws state that no major decision can be made without all owners in agreement, right?"

"Sure," I said.

"So am I to believe that no major decisions have been made so far because my input hasn't exactly been needed. You all have done well so far without me so I'm not sure why I need to explicitly be involved now. I mean, I haven't protested, have I?"

"No, you haven't. But, Miss Mercer," I called, trying to control my temper. "We're no longer all in agreement as I'd hoped we'd continue to be. The particular issue at hand now, for instance, is major, and we have been unable to resolve it consensually as done in the past. This leads me to believe that if some measure of control is not exerted, things will only get more difficult in the future."

"What are you talking about exactly?" she asked, and I dropped the inferences.

"Dividends. The other members are looking to increase the percentage paid out to them annually, and I can't allow it."

"Why?" she asked.

"Well, because they made the same request a few months earlier, and in order to move on to other more pressing matters, I allowed it. But as the last two quarters were wonderful, and the annual payouts are around the corner, they want another increase. I can't let that happen again. However, I am only one man against two others, my sister, and your brother, so I'm going to need you on my side to fight this one because it is an incredibly dangerous habit that shouldn't be encouraged."

"Hm," she said. "Even if I were to join you, though, it would bring the decision to a tie, so it doesn't exactly resolve the issue, does it?"

"No, but having you in my corner is a first step. And being who you are, it may be all we need to resolve this. Two of us, I believe, can be quite formidable."

She considered this, and through it all, she stared at me.

"There is no way that buying my company won't look like you're buying my vote," she said.

"I'm not bothered about how it looks," I said. "I just need this resolved so I can focus on actually running the company, which both of them are a severe hindrance too. You're not close with your brother, are you?"

"No," she replied. "Especially not since our father passed away."

"Yeah, this is apparent."

The waiter brought our food then, and we began to eat. I watched her, refusing to interrupt throughout the meal as she considered things quietly, and midway through, she set down her fork and responded.

"You don't have to buy my company," she said.

I set down my fork as well, completely unsure as to where this was leading to.

"What do you mean?" I asked.

"You don't have to buy it, but in return, with having me join operations as well as the board, then I want the company to branch out into a new industry."

I watched her, and then I smiled because, although I

wasn't surprised, I truly hadn't seen this additional request coming.

"What division?" I asked, and she replied.

"Fragrances," she replied.

"Fragrances?" I asked. "Isn't this the same as what you're currently involved in?"

"No," she replied. "Mine is perfumes, and they're released in small collections. I want to go mainstream and branch out into fragrances for the market and use them in makeup and home products. Standard Rock already has a significant market share of the home goods industry, so I want to capitalize on this. "But in order to do this, I need the company's backing and market reach," she said.

I looked at her for a while as I considered the offer, and then nodded.

"It's something we will be willing to take into consideration."

"You should," she said. "In exchange, you'll get my contribution and support."

"Just to be clear, what exactly would you be requiring for this new proposed division?" I asked.

"Everything," she replied. "Support for the current scent lines that we have and support to expand. A new or added office space, staff, research labs, the works. And this support will be guaranteed for the next five years while we find our feet and get off the ground."

"And if it fails?" I asked, and she smiled.

"It won't fail. If it fails, then it fails. That's business, and that's why I'm not selling my company for ten million dollars. That's a lot of money you'll be saving Standard Rock. Instead, back us up and provide funding."

I leaned back then and took a sip of my wine while she resumed eating.

"I have a question for you," I said, and she nodded.

"Go ahead."

"You never wanted anything to do with the company earlier on when the equity stake was assigned to you. So why the change of mind now?"

"Well, you've been hounding me, haven't you?" she asked, but I wasn't going to make light of this as it had been infuriating me from the beginning.

She sighed and responded.

"First of all, my father died. My heart was broken, and it took me a while to recover, so the stake he left me of his billion-dollar company wasn't exactly my priority. The company wasn't in dire straits... you've been running it excellently for years, so why did I need to be involved? Plus, as stated, we can only transfer or sell the rights after two years of contribution to the company. I had my own company, I was very busy and familiar with it, and my father had never exactly supported my own path. He was always disapproving of it, even though I had managed to make it decently successful."

"Hence I didn't want to make my grief worse by thinking about things that didn't need to be thought about. I'm not trying to gain the whole world, so the equity could be ignored until I could see how it served me, and now that I do see how it can be beneficial, here I am."

"Hm," I nodded because I could relate to everything she had just said. We finished our dinner, both of us remaining more or less silent and contemplating, and then the plates were cleared away. I picked up the agreement I had brought with me.

"Given your new demands, now it's clear that I have to head back, discuss with the other equity holders, and reach a consensus. Only then can I revise this."

"Sure," she said. "You know where to reach me, but how long is this going to take?"

"We will call a meeting first thing tomorrow morning, but as always, you're welcome to be present. In short, since you're in town for this very purpose, I'm extending the invitation to you to participate in the meeting so that we can resolve this."

She sighed then, and it almost made me smile because I understood all that was not said in that expression possibly more than anyone else.

"Sure," she said and pasted a smile at the corners of her lips.

"What salary compensation would be suitable for you?" I asked, and she looked surprised.

"I'll still be paid?"

"Of course, you would need to be. If you're assigning your company over to become a subsidiary of ours, then of course, you're no longer in control of the finances regarding it."

"True. But just to be clear, I will keep a percentage of it. I'm only assigning a part of it."

"Ah," I said. "A very important almost missed point. So, what percent would you like to keep?"

"The majority, of course. I propose 60-40."

I stared at her, and she smiled.

"Too low? Okay, then I propose 65-35."

I laughed out loud, my voice ringing out across the room. I truly enjoyed speaking to her more than I had expected. It made me wonder then what else about her I could enjoy. My gaze lowered down to her nipples again and found that they were beginning to harden. What a delight it was to watch her.

"I'll take all suggestions under advisement and present them tomorrow. How does 10 am sound?"

"I'll be there," she replied, and I nodded.

5

Lena

He was bold. Either that, or he was completely shameless. Throughout our business discussion, he kept his gaze directly on mine, but now that the basics had been resolved and we were somewhat on the same page, his gaze kept going once again to my chest. I could feel the weight of them, especially without any bra on, and the more he looked, the harder my nipples got. At some point, it was as though he was playing a game with them, and I didn't know whether to be amused or offended. I wasn't uncomfortable, though, which I understood, and that was because if I could outrightly stare at him as provocatively as this, I probably would, so he could have his feast. It made the dinner all the more interesting, especially as my clit continued to throb in response to his attention.

I wondered what he thought, and then the waiter came to take our dessert order, and I decided that I didn't want to know. With Kane, I was sure that not knowing was always the better option.

He suggested and ordered the "Chocolate Trilogy," which was a dark chocolate tart with a cocoa nib crust, a milk chocolate and caramelized hazelnut dacquoise, and a white chocolate and passion fruit mousse. It was served with a scoop of vanilla ice cream and garnished with gold leaf. It was fascinating to look at, and as soon as it arrived, we dug in.

The first taste was heavenly, and although I didn't intend it, a moan escaped my lips as my tongue ran down the spoon. He looked at me, all traces of amusement disappearing from his face. It was still technically a business meeting, so I refrained from making any such sounds, but apparently, the damage had already been done.

"You said you had somewhere else to be after this," he asked, and I nodded, though I didn't give any more details because I absolutely did not have anywhere else to be. I had acquaintances in the city since I had spent a year after college here interning at Bond No. 9. After this decadent dessert, I was going to go to the gym and work it off so that I could sleep in peace.

"Where?" he asked, and I looked up, a smirk on my face.

"Why do I have to reveal that?" I asked.

And he smiled.

"You're right, you don't have to. If you do need a personal chauffeur or

"

"I know, I know," I cut him off. "It's provided for me. Got it."

He went silent then and kept watching me.

"You don't want this?" I asked. "I can't finish it all on my own."

"I'm not into sweets," he said. "Eat what you want, and we'll dispose of the rest."

"Too delicious to be disposed of," I said. "I'll take it to go. All the more reason to work it off tonight."

"How exactly will you be working it off?" he asked, and I looked up to glare at him.

"I'll find a way," I said. "Hence why I have plans."

He smiled, his gaze once again going to my heavy breasts.

"I look good, don't I?" I asked. "Think I'll be able to find what I'm looking for?"

At my words, he lifted his gaze to me, somewhat surprised. I, too, was surprised at what had just left my mouth, but I wasn't taking it back.

"What exactly are you looking for?" he asked, and I responded.

"Just a way to shed the dessert weight off. If I don't find what I want, then I'll report to the gym."

His gaze was now lowering to my lips and then once again to my breasts.

"My face is up here, sir," I said, and he looked at me.

"I thought you wouldn't recall how we last ran into each other the last time we met," he said. "But it seems to me that you do."

I smiled but refused to respond.

"No point going down that hole," I said. "Let's keep things professional between us."

"Hm," he said. "I think that ship sailed when you chose to wear this dress."

I cocked my head then and almost sighed. The door had been opened, and I had no interest whatsoever in backing out.

"What's wrong with my dress?" I asked, and he shook his head.

"Absolutely nothing, it's fucking fantastic."

I knew where this was headed and decided to nip it in the bud before it got too out of hand.

"Alright," I set my spoon down. "I think we can leave now. I'm running late."

He smiled, and then he nodded.

He called the waiter over and even when I offered to pay for the bill, he gave me a look and declined.

"This is not a date," I told him. "I should pay for my own meal."

"You're company guest," he said. "The company pays for our guest."

This made sense to me, so I nodded and rose to my feet.

"I'll walk you outside," he said, and I nodded in response.

We headed over to the curb, and there we stopped in the dark but cool bustling New York City evening.

"You're going to take a cab?" he asked, and I turned to look at him.

"Yes, I am," I replied.

"A chauffeur is safer," he said. "Especially at this time of the night."

"I'll be fine," I said and began to look out for one.

I could feel him staring at me, and suddenly I felt self-conscious, especially as the breeze began to blow my hair into my face. I tucked it behind my ears, and eventually, the taxi arrived.

"See you tomorrow," he said. "The chauffeur will be ready to pick you up at any time you prefer."

"Sure," I said and got in.

I shut the door behind me, and soon we were off.

It took a little while, but eventually, I was able to completely settle down, and then I met the driver's gaze.

"Where to, ma'am?" he asked, and I opened my mouth to reply but realized that I had no clue.

"Just drive around," I replied, feeling quite ashamed.

A few blocks and then back to the hotel for some fresh air.

He gave me a strange look, and then he nodded.

I turned to look out of the window and watched the city. Things were so bright and busy, much more fast-paced than LA, and it made me wonder once again if I was ready to make this new move. Things were about to change all around, and since I had made the physical move here, then I was sure that my heart was fully open toward it. However, from what I had heard at dinner, things could get quite ugly, but I was up to the challenge.

We went around a few more blocks simply because I enjoyed the ride, and then we returned to the hotel.

I was exhausted and itching to go to bed so that the day could start, so I headed in and called it a day.

6

Kane

The next morning, as I headed down to the conference room, I could tell that something was wrong. My secretary, Madison, was unable to meet my gaze and was more nervous than I had ever seen her. When the elevator stopped and she got out on the wrong floor, then got back in with her papers scattering all about, I tried to be patient despite feeling irritated.

"What's wrong?" I asked and she tried to force a smile, but I wasn't buying it.

"Madison," I called, and she winced.

"The meeting is supposed to start in ten minutes, Sir, but only Miss Mercer has arrived."

I frowned at her words but remained calm.

"Why?" I asked.

"Well, Sarah called in this morning to say she wouldn't be able to make it and would be out of town till next week, while Dylan, I'm sure, is just running late as usual. No word from him yet if he'll be there."

I could understand her nervousness, especially as a surge of annoyance rushed through me. This meeting had been set up a week prior as soon as Lena's visit to New York had been confirmed. Its main purpose was to discuss the terms, and yet they had chosen to disregard it for whatever reason.

I didn't say a word until I arrived at the meeting room and indeed found that Lena had arrived.

She looked much different from the previous night, now dressed in a striped pantsuit with her hair pulled away from her face.

I gave her a nod in acknowledgment, took my seat, and decided to wait a few more minutes until the clock struck ten. By then, she had perused the document I had sent over to her, so she looked up and met my gaze.

"It seems we are missing a few members," she said, and for a moment, I was certain that her gaze softened in understanding.

"Let's proceed without them," I said.

"Can we?" she replied.

"Yes," I said. "We will, and the first order of business will be to fire your brother. Do you have any objections to this?"

She stopped then, her eyes widening in shock.

"Um..." She looked around at the secretary taking notes in the corner, who absolutely refused to raise her head.

"Can you do that?" she asked, and I nodded.

"Yes, I can. I'm the CEO, and I maintain the right to employ and discharge employees as I see fit."

She gave this some thought, then shrugged.

"Go ahead."

That settled, we moved on to other matters.

"I was going to bring up your proposal for the new

fragrance division today. Actually, we already have a few members of staff who proposed the idea a little while ago and have been researching it. This happened after we launched our collection of diffusers, but it was quite difficult to find the right fragrance for them. So, I'm thinking to refer you to them, and they can be a preliminary team so that we will be able to do all the pre-market research and analysis needed before the final decision is made."

She looked at me.

"So basically, I should get a detailed plan ready and then present it for consideration?"

"Yes," I replied, and she nodded.

"Got it."

"If things go according to plan, then you can get started and officially come on board."

"Got it," I replied again. "I'll set you up with an office in the meantime, and get the team to you, and let's give this one month."

She said nothing more about her brother's dismissal until I started to leave, then she stopped me once again.

"Got it," she said, and I looked around at the empty seats once again. She didn't miss my gaze.

"My brother's going to throw a fit when he hears that he's been fired," she said, and I rose to my feet.

"He's been given several warnings before on being late to meetings and being lackadaisical with his work, so he deserves this."

I started to leave, but she stopped me once again.

"Can it be overruled?"

"Of course, it can," I replied. "If the majority of board members interfere, then it can be."

I started to leave, but she stopped me once again.

"And what direction do you want me to lean towards?" she asked. "Supporting you or..."

I stopped then and turned to face her.

"I'd like you to be on my side."

"It'll come to a tie," she said, and I nodded.

"Then we'll settle in court, and I'll make sure to drag it out as long as possible. It doesn't matter if he's able to return, but it won't be without any significant loss."

She stared at me at this, and then she nodded.

"Understood."

7

Lena

I watched him go and didn't know what to think. He irked me to even think of myself as his ally in any way, but in this case, I could understand his annoyance. Firing my brother was brutal and would be detrimental to his lifestyle, but the message was clear, and all I could foresee ahead was a lengthy battle in trying to get back into Kane's graces.

Shaking my head, I rose to my feet and was excited to see the office that had been prepared for me. A meeting was scheduled for the following hour with the team he had spoken about, so I headed over to get started. It was sizable, but more importantly, the warm hues of colors and fabric made it quite welcoming. I had absolutely no complaints.

I sat down and began going through the documents that had been left on my desk. It was as I did, that I saw the terms of acquisition for my new company, and it left me flabbergasted, to say the least. He had boldly and unapologetically proposed a 40-60 percentage term when I had clearly stated the previous day that I wouldn't be accepting this. I looked up then, frustrated but wondering if I should waste time on a call with him or just go to his office. Both would be a monumental waste of time regardless, but I still had to resolve this. In the end, I picked up the phone and called his office. The phone disconnected the first time, and then the second time around, he picked up.

"What?" he asked, and I looked at the phone. Anytime he did something that made me want to consider him as a decent human, it was ruined immediately after.

"This is Lena," I said.

"Go ahead," he replied and scoffed.

"What is this joke of an agreement? 60-40?"

"Yes," he replied. "This is what we are proposing."

"And you think this is fair?"

"Why would it be fair?" he asked. "You're asking for a significant amount of our resources to be invested in this, so it's only right that we have a say in the way things are run. You'll get your rewards, but we should be able to control our investment."

I scoffed.

"You're all about control, aren't you?"

"Shouldn't I be?" he asked, and I had no response to this, but I didn't however have a response about our agreement, and it was a complete no.

"I'm rejecting this," I said. "It's unacceptable, so tell me if you are ready to revise it or if I should walk out of here right now and call it a day."

At my words, he went silent for a moment and then he gave me instructions.

"Come to my office," he said and hung up.

I was so exasperated that for the first few minutes of the

call, I could only stare ahead. I didn't know if it was because I was so shocked that I was annoyed or because I was so annoyed that I was shocked. Eventually, I got up, straightened my jacket, and headed to his office.

His secretary was at her desk when I arrived, and she immediately got up with a smile for me, but I didn't care about any of that.

"Miss Mercer, Mr. Lazarus is in a mee-" I ignored her and pushed the door to his office open.

"Don't ever summon me to your office again like I'm some-" I stopped mid-sentence as I noticed that truly he wasn't alone. There was a man standing before his desk while Kane's gaze was buried in the open file before him. Both men looked up as I walked in, and at their arresting gazes, my annoyance went down a notch. However, when I noticed how Mr. Lazarus in the distance didn't even bother acknowledging my presence, my annoyance came back with a vengeance. But before I could speak, his visitor did.

"Miss Mercer," he had a smile on his face and started to head over to me. My eyes, however, remained on Kane, and not until the man had arrived before me did I turn my attention to him. I accepted his handshake, wondering who he was, but he soon introduced himself.

"I'm Matthias Wilson," he said, and I nodded.

"Lawyer," I said, and he nodded too, a smile on his face.

"Yes," he replied. "It's great to finally meet you."

One glance behind him, and I could see that the man I had come to see was still working on his desk and ignoring me. Matthias immediately and thankfully got out of my way.

"I'll leave you both to it," he said. "Kane, let me know what you decide on," he said but didn't bother waiting for a response. He left the office without any further word, and then it was just the two of us.

I headed over to his desk, and when I arrived, he finally lifted his head. He stared directly at me, and I could tell that he was in an even worse mood than earlier.

"Is there a reason why you barged into my office?" he asked, and I had my response ready for him.

"Is there a reason why you hung up the phone so abruptly?"

He watched me, and then he straightened.

"I thought we were done conversing."

I scoffed. "Well, I thought you were expecting me, so what was the need for knocking?"

He rose to his feet then, and I watched as he rounded the desk. I faced him when he arrived, and then he stopped right in front of me.

"I understand that you own this company just as much as I do," he said. "But you need to understand that there is a pecking order. All of you need to understand this. I cannot do my job as CEO if I am constantly having to cater to everyone's moods and demands."

I smiled.

"If you're not capable of such basic duties, then perhaps you don't deserve to be CEO," I said, and he cocked his head.

"Maybe we should include replacing you as an item in our next meeting agenda. I'm pretty sure we might be able to find someone else just as capable or even better."

His gaze lowered to my lips as I spoke, and I was thrown off. My mind completely went blank as I watched him and then he looked back into my eyes again.

He didn’t say a word. Didn't even try to remind me of where I had left off and it frustrated me to no end.

“Stop doing that,” I said, and his eyes narrowed.

“Stop doing what?” he asked.

“Stop looking everywhere you're supposed to fucking look but my face.”

At this humorless smile came to my face.

“You're a gorgeous woman Lena,” he said. There’s a lot to look at,” and just like that I was thrown off once again.

8

Kane

I had been mad.

But now, as I looked at the fire in her eyes and inhaled her scent of vanilla and something even sweeter, I could barely think. Yet, that annoyance that I had gotten up to address still burned in the pit of my stomach, and I needed to let it out somehow. Fucking her mindless would do the trick, but I didn't imagine that it would be an easy feat, so I sighed and turned to return to my seat so that I could think clearly.

However, just as I moved, her arm closed around my bicep. I turned, ignoring the heat I felt at her touch, and watched her plump, full peach lips once again as she took another shot at me.

"I'm not done talking to you," she said, and I grabbed her wrist. I saw fear flash in her eyes, and it gave me deep satisfaction.

"Don't put your hands on me," I warned her. "Ever,

unless you want this to take a very, very different turn than what you'd probably want."

She stared at me.

"What kind of turn would it take?" she asked, but I didn't respond, so I took a step closer to her.

She stood her ground and didn't retreat. I stared deep into her eyes.

"On second thought, I think you do know."

She didn't say a word afterward, so I tapped the table and then returned to my desk. She also didn't take her eyes off me, but for the life of me, I couldn't read her. Because she soon spoke, and her voice was much calmer than before.

"I won't accept the terms you stipulated. If you're going to insist on that, then you better throw in the ten-million-dollar acquisition check as well."

"If we throw in the ten million dollar check, then we get full control. 100-0. However, if we're to provide you with all the resources needed, then it's just as I proposed."

"I don't accept it," she said, and I nodded.

"I understand." She glared at me then and returned to her office.

9

Lena

I was close to losing my mind from the meeting, but you wouldn't have been able to tell just by seeing me. As I headed over to my office, I returned every nod and smile I received, and soon I was within the safe glass walls overlooking the gorgeous skyline of Manhattan.

Once inside, I took my seat, turned around to face the glass wall to ceiling windows, and shut my eyes. It was time to head back, alright, but that didn't seem like a reasonable solution. In fact, I was sure it was what he expected, so I cleared my head and came to terms with how I had just majorly messed up.

Frustrated, I called Diana, and she picked up immediately.

“Uh oh, it's just 11 am in New York. Anything exciting happened yet?” she asked.

I sighed, then frowned again.

“I lost my cool,” I said.

"Uh oh," she said. "That doesn't sound good. How exactly?"

"I was too emotional. I got mad over the stupidest shit, and now I just look unprofessional and emotional, like a..." I couldn't find a word, but she supplied it.

"Like a woman?" she offered.

"And he made suggestive sexual statements to me. In the midst of my true anger, he said all that, and I just wanted to punch him in the face."

"Just punch him in the face?" she asked, and I sighed.

"I'm not admitting to anything else. Having those stupid ideas in my head is what is currently throwing me off. Now I'm all flustered, furious, and irritated, and just..."

"Horny as well?" she asked, and I sighed again.

"Please stop, this is serious."

"I'm sorry," she said, and we both went silent.

"I just..." I began again. "I just don't know if I should pack up now and leave or go running back to him with my tail between my legs."

"Well, you definitely can't do that," she said. "So what should you do then?"

"You need to, as you said, let go of your emotions and approach this like the brilliant businesswoman I know you are," she said.

I listened to her words.

"Go on," I said, and she laughed.

"Well, you need to ultimately put the needs of your company above everything else. Your company and your assets should be your top priority, because like it or not, you significantly own Standard Rock, and I think it's quite easy for you to gloss over that fact now, but you shouldn't do that."

She was absolutely right.

"Yeah," I said, and she went on.

"So do you need this expansion as much as you say you do, or is it just something that might be nice? If you're fine with the way your own company is going right now and want to keep just managing that, then your decision on whether to proceed or not will be easy. Plus, the dividends accruing to you from Standard Rock with your 25% ownership aren't small, are they? They might just be able to fund the expansion that you want to make."

At her words, I couldn't help but smile.

"If this is the case and the way that I should go, then I might as well leave Kane's side and join the other members to oppose him. I mean, the higher dividends I get, the better for me, right?"

"Yeah," she said, and I nodded, but at the end of the day, a baseline that spoke to my heart appeared.

"I think I know what to do," I said. "Or rather, I know what I want."

"The dust has settled," she said. "Let's hear it."

"Okay."

"I love him... lov-" I stopped, my heart hurting.

"I want to be a part of what he built. He loved this business and... mine is quite... mine can be aligned with his to make it even better. I can't do it all alone and I don't want to. I don't have to."

"Great," she said. "Now we're getting somewhere."

"Isn't this an emotional decision as well?" I asked.

"Emotional decisions are bad. Logical decisions are bad. A mix of the two is perfect. That's what makes us human. The logical path is to succumb, emotional is to leave, so why don't you find a way to get him to meet you halfway... in some way. Unless he's just an unreasonable person through and through, then that is a problem, and you probably won't fare well being there anyway."

"So... give the both of us a chance... a true chance."

"Professional? Yes. Personally? I'm not sure yet, we still don't know his actual personality. What do you think?"

"I'm hanging up," I said and she laughed. "Why?"

"Stop putting these strange ideas in my head."

Fine," she said. "I'm sorry."

"No need to be, and thank you. I think you just helped me clear my head. Thanks a lot Diana."

"Of course, sweetheart," she said and the call came to an end.

After the call ended, I sat in my office, thought a bit further about my options, and made notes.

By the time I was done and sure of the direction I wanted to take, I looked at the time and found that it was past 12 pm, which was lunch time. An idea came to mind then, and despite the antagonism from earlier that morning, I pushed my emotions aside and picked up the phone. A few seconds later, I was connected to his office; however, what I heard was that he was in a meeting that was running late. I gave the instruction that he was to call me back, and then I went back to work.

My secretary came in multiple times to ask if I wanted to eat something, but I told him that I hadn't decided yet. It was 1 pm and my stomach began to hurt. I hadn't yet received a call back from Kane, so I got up and headed out. I needed to think a bit further, plus it was a good chance to explore the new city, so I decided to have lunch outside. I waited at the elevator as I looked through my emails.

However, a familiar voice soon came over to me, and I turned to see who it was.

Turned out that it was the devil himself, Mr. Kane Lazarus looking dapper as always but this time around quite expressionless as he watched me. He had his phone to his ear and was listening to the call but didn't say a word until the end.

"Sure," he said when he arrived by my side, and then he ended the call. We both turned to face the elevators, and neither of us said a word to the other.

"These things are quite slow," he eventually said, to my surprise. "We should do something about it."

I turned then to look at him, and even though everything inside of me was screaming for me to give into my emotions again, I tried my best to remain logical and unemotional.

"You didn't get my call?" I asked.

"I was just told," he said, "on my way out. It's something to be addressed when I get back. I need to eat."

"I need to eat as well," I said, and he slightly cocked his head.

"Do you have a lunch meeting planned, or are you just going to eat?"

He smiled.

"Lunch meeting," he responded.

"Can you cancel?" I asked. "We need to talk."

He looked at me intently, and then he added.

"Yeah, I will."

10

Kane

There was no way that I was going to reject a lunch invitation from her. I knew that it wasn't going to be anything personal, but she was just the person I preferred to spend my lunchtime with. The stuffy businessman I was going to meet compared to her was a much lousier decision, so for once, I took a page out of her emotional book and went with what I wanted.

I deeply suspected that I would regret it, but she was a sight for sore eyes. I took her a bit further away from the office than I would have liked, but any closer, and we were sure to run into prying eyes, which was the last thing that I wanted. Soon we arrived at Gramercy Tavern, and I asked if she wanted to have lunch in their outdoor seating area or inside.

"Inside," she said, and I led her in.

We were soon seated, and although I didn't outrightly watch her, I could feel a certain change in her from the morning. However, I couldn't quite tell what it was, so I waited for her to speak. Or maybe there wasn't a change whatsoever, and this was just a part of her persona. I couldn't quite tell.

I couldn't tell anything about her. As she sat down, I couldn't take my eyes off her. There was so much I wanted to know, but the curiosity in itself was alarming. However, I didn't look too much into it since it was probably because she was a new character in my life, a brand new one to boot, so I couldn't tell but wanted to figure her out.

We soon placed our orders, and as the waiter left, we were once again left alone.

She met my gaze and then smiled.

"We got off on the wrong foot today," she said, but I didn't comment. She went on.

"Well, first of all, I want to extend my apology. Things definitely could and should have been handled much better than they were when I came into your office earlier."

"And I the same," I replied. "I think we actually can get along, and so I'm willing to approach our relationship in a better way that can be beneficial for the both of us."

Her eyes slightly narrowed at this, and I couldn't blame her. It sounded as though I was once again hinting at some sexual proposition or something, but that wasn't the case at all.

Nevertheless, I didn't dwell on it and proceeded to pour myself and her a glass of water.

She watched it fill up, and then she lifted the glass to her lips.

Afterwards, she smiled, and our first course of roasted carrot soup was brought over.

"I've thought about things further," she said. "And I truly want to make our partnership work. I don't want us to approach this as a way to strong-arm the other party into doing something they don't really want to do. So, how about we approach this from a logical and mutually beneficial angle?"

"I'm open to this," I said, and she nodded.

"First, let us lay down what we both need the most. You need support to facilitate your control of the company and ensure you're able to do your job. I understand this, and in response, I'm willing to offer you my full support."

I listened as she spoke, and then I nodded.

"I, on the other hand, truly want to branch out into the scents division, and I know that this can bring significant increase to the company and the value of our brand."

"We're on the same page," I said, and she nodded.

"In the end, this is my company. It's both of ours, and we have a legacy to uphold, so why not work together instead of going our separate ways?"

I continued eating, a bit impatient with her speaking in bits and pieces, but I told myself to extend the same courtesy she was giving me and to learn to walk at the pace of others, so I let her continue.

"Change the terms of your offer, and you'll not only get a valuable asset but also my cooperation and backing for the future."

I looked at her then, and maybe it was something in her eyes, but this offer didn't exactly sound as pure as it should have.

"And if I don't?" I asked, and she smiled.

"Then naturally, you'll lose all of the aforementioned. You're a shrewd businessperson, such as I am, so I don't think you'd expect anything less."

I considered her words, and then I nodded.

"Fair enough. Maybe we can come to a more favorable agreement."

"How does 61-39 sound?" I asked, and she gave me a look, but to my surprise, she smiled.

"You do love to jest," she said, but I was no longer joking.

"Let's do 55-45," I said, and she sighed again as she continued calmly eating her soup.

"I can't do that," she said. "This is a company I built from the ground up, and I would hate to feel like I was cheated out of it."

I studied her, and then I set down my fork.

"You know this isn't about money, right?" I asked, and she nodded, giving me her full attention as well.

"Of course it isn't. I can foresee that murky days are ahead, and only those with control will be able to survive."

I listened, and then I went straight to the point.

"You won't, for any amount, completely give up full control of your company, will you?"

"No," she said.

"This is my final offer," I said. "51% for us and 49% for you. As you said, it's not about money but control, and as the subsidiary that you will become, you cannot have autonomous control over that company. Otherwise, it won't feel like ours. This will not only bring further conflict between Standard Rock and your company but also between the two staffs."

She listened, and then she nodded.

"I'll take this into consideration," she said, and I couldn't help my smile.

"Maybe the 2% you're taking away from me will come at the cost of my support for you among the other owners."

At her words, I couldn't help but laugh because I had actually expected her to say this.

"If that is the cost, then that's fine with me. As you have just said, you do care about the company, and so do I. So, I don't believe that at any point you'll support decisions that will harm the company. That is more than enough for me. So please feel free to not support me at any time if you feel that my moves or interests are not in any way for the good of the company."

She stared at me and then she nodded.

"I think we've gotten somewhere."

"Yes, we have," I replied, and we continued with our lunch.

11

Lena

As I watched him eat, I couldn't quite believe where we had come to. I had expected this conversation to go a little bit more left field and take much longer to resolve, but to my surprise, he was quite reasonable about it, and I was just as surprised as I was impressed.

I was also unhappy, though, because ultimately, I had lost, but it was a loss I found I could handle as I pondered over the matter as we ate. Diana said this would be majorly for the sake of the company, my dad's company, so there was truly no loss. As a subsidiary, Kane would be in charge most of the time, but given his track record of running the company excellently so far, I didn't think there would be any danger coming from him. He'd want it to succeed just as much as I did, and he'd be someone I could go to for the difficult decisions as well.

I could stomach this, so by the time we were done with the light cheesecake dessert, the atmosphere between us was a little bit more harmonious. I looked at the time and was impressed by how we had both eaten quite quickly, and we were right on time. Lunchtime would be ending in about twenty minutes, and it was more than enough time to spare in heading back.

"Let me pay the bill this time around," I said as I pulled out my wallet, and to my surprise, he didn't stop me.

"Please, go ahead," he replied.

Shaking my head slightly, I handled things with the waiter, and then it was time to leave. However, he stopped me.

"Before you leave, can I ask that you consider one more proposition?" he asked, and I wondered what it was.

"Let's hear it," I said, and he said it plainly.

"Are you open to a more personal relationship between us?" My heart skipped a beat, or perhaps several.

"Um, what kind of personal relationship?" I asked.

"There's chemistry between us," he said. "We don't have to act on it and can choose to ignore it. It's up to you, but I would be remiss if I didn't at least make the offer. I've never really looked away from something I wanted, so why should I start now?"

I looked at him and then decided to be bold as well.

"You want me?" I asked.

"I do," he said, and his words from earlier in his office came to mind.

"Well, Mr. Lazarus," I replied, "as you well know, we all want many things, but that doesn't mean we're going to get them."

"For the right price," he replied, "we can always get what we want."

At this, I slightly frowned, but once again, I reminded

myself to be logical about this in order not to feel insulted right off the bat.

"Okay," I said. "And what do you think my price is?"

"Well, that depends on what you feel you need right now," he replied. "I, for one, am not open to a relationship of any sort, but a woman like you and an arrangement where we could get exactly what we want from the other could be incredibly beneficial."

I smiled at his words.

"Given the nature of our relationship, wouldn't this generate multiple conflicts of interest?"

"We're intelligent people," he responded. "And a point of appeal for me with you is the expectation that you will very clearly be able to separate the two."

I didn't respond and instead took a sip of my glass of wine. The glass that I had been planning to ignore but now I could very clearly see that I needed it. He watched me and then he asked.

"What do you say?"

I so badly wanted to say yes, but that would be an emotional decision. Saying no would be purely logical as well, but somewhere in the middle? I shot for that.

"I'll consider it," I said, and he smiled.

"I respect that."

"You should," I said. "In order to go that far with someone, with anyone for that matter, I have to at least like them, and currently, I really don't know if you fall in the category of people that I can like enough to have intimate relations with."

His chuckle was dry.

"This has nothing to do with whether we like each other or not. Actually, not liking each other might be a barrier to what we do ultimately want. What I am sure you ultimately want."

"Which is..." He stared at me.

"Permit me to be vulgar?"

"Go ahead," I said, and he did.

"What we both want is to experience ultimate levels of pleasure bordering on the extreme. I want to fuck your brains out, literally, and I think you'd also like that as well." I smiled.

"And you think you're up to the task?"

He smiled, and then the smile left his face. Without a word, he then rose to his feet, arranged his jacket, and started to walk away. I wondered what was happening and if I had offended him with my words. It seemed to be the case, and a part of me couldn't help but be just as nervous as I was amused about this. I didn't call out to him, but when I arrived at the front of the restaurant, I could see that the car had just arrived.

"You weren't offended by my question, were you?" I asked, and he gave me a look...

"Why would I be? Someday we'll get the opportunity to prove if we are capable of giving the other what is needed, so until then..."

I kept quiet for a moment, but the junction within my thighs was already wet.

"Until when?" I found myself asking, and then he stared at me.

Soon, the car came around, and he got in. I watched for a while as the driver got out, and then he opened the opposite side of the door.

"You're not getting in," he rolled down the window just enough to ask, and I had to ask myself if I wanted to get in.

Eventually, given the time, I accepted the ride offer and got into the car.

"The Park Hyatt, Henry," he said, and my eyes widened.

I looked at him and then at the driver and then back at him.

“We have to head back to the office. Why are we going to the Park Hyatt?"

"We have ten minutes," he said, and I counted.

"Park Hyatt is what, eight minutes away?"

"Six, to be exact," he said, as he scrolled nonchalantly through his phone. I sat back, exasperated, unable to quite believe that this was happening, and yet not exactly willing to bring it to an end. And so, I sat back and waited to see if we truly arrived at the Park Hyatt.

He got out, and I followed, watching silently and all the while questioning myself as to if this was what I truly wanted. If this was a bad idea. If, dear God, this wasn't going to end up badly and blow up in my face at the end of the fucking day.

This man was not to be trusted in any way but then as we got closer to the room, I had to ask myself if he wasn’t right? If the fact that I was wary of him and didn’t quite like him was the perfect anecdote to what we were doing? After, it would guarantee that I didn’t start to develop any attachment or bothersome feelings for him, and it would in turn get my needs met as well as his. Zero strings attached, no hassle or fuss.... I mean there was no other man I had met in my life that I had even remotely considered this with but before me was a competent and breathtaking specimen of a man and yes, I indeed wanted him to fuck my brains out.

When we eventually arrived at the door of the room and

he pulled the key card out, it was very clear that he was giving me the chance to back out.

"This location is somewhat close to the office but yet just far enough away. If it's to your fancy, then I could leave the room open just for us."

"I haven't agreed to this," I told him. "I told you that I was going to think about."

He chucked loud and clear.

"Sure, and that's why we're here."

"What do you mean?" I asked as he unlocked the door and pushed it open.

"I'm going to give you exactly what to think about."

His words irked causing me in that moment to almost change my mind from even considering anything because God, he annoyed me with his dominance and bravado but as I stared up at his chiseled face and overbearing aura, I had to admit that he had the right. He infuriated me but God was I more turned on than I'd ever been by anyone else.

I gave him a harsh look and walked into the room.

"You are right" I said as I took in the space.

"You do need to give me something to think about, so I hope that you won't be disappointing but, in the meantime, I hope that –"

The words died in my throat as I was suddenly grabbed from behind.

"What are you doing?" I tried to ask but before I could process much I had been flattened against the door.

"No talking when we get into these walls," he said directly into my ears and the words reverberated through my body.

I went silent then, not by will but truly because I felt the bulge of him against me and I truly didn't know what to say. My heart was beating so fast that at the heat and scent of him that I had to work to catch my breath. His hand went to the front of my pants and in no time the button was undone, and the zipper pulled down. He took his time and every sound made was pure torture.

"First of all, I need to know the truth," he said. "I need to see just how much and how intensely you hate me."

I had no clue what he was talking about but when his hand slipped into my underwear, and he grabbed me, his intentions became clear.

I gasped out, as although I expected the intrusion, I really didn't expect that it would come so rudely or feel so good.

I could feel myself leak even more now onto his hand and my clit throbbed with a fever. The length of his middle finger was pressing hard against the greedy knob while two were practically inside me.

I tried to stop it, but I couldn't help the groan that escaped from lips as my head fell back.

This was just the relief I needed after the recent stress that I had been overwhelmed with in trying to make the decision to move here and to of course navigate my way.

I deserved this ... I wanted this. As he pulled his hand away and pulled my pants down with him... I completely gave in.

He jerked my thighs apart and I held the door for support, wondering what he was actually going to do to me. I didn't have to wonder for too long because before I could think further his mouth was on me. And then there was nothing gentle or careful about it.

He ate me like he had been starving forever till I had to

cover my mouth to keep from screaming. His tongue... his motherfucking tongue did something to my sex that I couldn't quite explain. It felt as though it was everywhere, like he was everywhere, and goosebumps broke out all across my skin.

He ate me up till I was dry and then I was wet again and then he grabbed my ass and seemed to almost lift me against the door. His tongue returned to my sex, this time sucking and devouring my clit and I couldn't hold back anymore. I moaned aloud and endlessly as I completely lost control of my hips.

I began to writhe against him hard and desperately grinding to the fast desperate rhythm he had set for the both of us. I was seconds away from coming at this intensity of the sound and the heat but then he rose to his feet, and I almost screamed in frustration.

I didn't even realize that I still had my panties on and that he had simply shifted them to the side until they were ripped from my body. I wanted to complain but before I could say a word, his finger was inside me. He stroked in and out of my wetness added another and then his left arm came around my midriff. I held onto him, trying my best to hold on for the ride, and then he finger fucked me so hard that my toes curled off the ground.

By the time he was done, I had spilled everywhere and completely lost my breath. Before I could recover, and as my body kept spasming, he lowered himself once again and my sex was in his mouth. I lost complete self-control, holding onto the door and grinding mindlessly into his tongue. That was how I found myself coming again within a few minutes. All the strength left my body, forcing me to hold onto the back of his head for some sort of stability. He got up quickly before I could tumble over, and all I could do was lean against him as I tried to catch my breath.

However, I wasn't done. Thankfully, my brain hadn't kicked in enough to stop me from asking. I turned around to face him and saw the smile on his face as he licked his lips.

"I love the way you take it, Miss Mercer," he said, and I couldn't speak.

He adjusted his jacket, ensuring that nothing was out of place, and then sent me a smile.

"See you back at work."

I couldn't believe him. I was so shocked that it wasn't until he exited the room and the door slammed shut behind me that I came back to my senses enough to produce a single coherent thought.

"Fuck," I swore aloud as I took in the dampness of my thighs and the pants still bunched around my legs.

“Fuck,” I said again and shut my eyes. “What the fuck have I just gotten myself into?”

12

Kane

I tried to act as though I was not shaken, but as I exited the room and headed down the elevator, it took everything inside of me not to head back to the room to finish what I had started with her. However, I couldn't give in now to everything I wanted and to everything I was sure that she wanted. This was the first time, and it was enough. However, as I headed back to the office, all I could think about was the taste of her that still lingered on my tongue and mouth. I couldn't believe this, but I wanted even more of her, and it made me wonder if I was going to be able to think coherently for the rest of the day.

"A stack of work awaited me in the office; however, if all I could do was think about the next time, which was when I was going to, without fail, put my dick inside of her, I didn't think that I would actually be able to focus."

"What about Miss Mercer, Sir?" Henry asked as I got into the car, and I realized that I had truly left her to her devices. She could make her way back; however, I couldn't get myself to instruct Henry to leave, and so I waited. A few minutes later, I saw her emerge from the hotel. She looked flawless, and it seemed as though nothing had happened, but when her eyes turned, and she caught me waiting for her, I could see the turmoil come back into her eyes. She stared straight at me, and then she headed towards the car.

"I can make my way back," she said, and I shrugged.

"No harm in waiting after all; I brought you here."

"I thought the goal was to make me hate you. Leaving without caring how I got back would have been a perfect move."

I considered her words, and then I nodded.

"You're right. Lesson learned. See you back at the office then, I guess," I said, and for a second, she didn't believe I was going to do it. Even I didn't believe I was going to do it as this very behavior was not in my nature, but then I rolled the glass up and gave the instruction to Henry...

"Back to the office," I said, and even he hesitated. He looked at me and at Lena outside, but he had no choice but to obey. Without any further words, he started the car, and we pulled away from the curb, leaving her right by it and staring at us.

13

Lena

I didn't know what to say as I watched him leave. I didn't understand even what the fuck I was doing by telling him to leave me there, but the fact of the matter was that I saw him and the waiting car by the curb as I walked out of the hotel, and I got scared. It felt like I had just made a mistake, but at the same time, it didn't. Not as I recalled everything that had just transpired within the last few minutes. I couldn't even recall agreeing to it. At some point within the last hour of conversation and interaction, my brain had stopped functioning, and now I could barely put two and two together.

All I knew was that I had loved every second of the moments in the room, and he hadn't even fucked me yet. But the force and the intensity... my heart was racing in my chest, and my clit was still throbbing, looking for more.

I continued to stare after the car until it disappeared, and then a loud honk out of nowhere brought me back to life in New York.

Sighing, I got a cab for myself, and soon enough, I arrived at the office. My secretary David got up immediately to deliver messages of welcome that had come in from the other company staff and I collected them all but when I sat at my desk, found myself distracted and unable to focus on anything for the first few minutes. That was until I heard a loud rap against my door. It was so startling that I was immediately annoyed wondering who was barging in so rudely.

For a few seconds my mind went to Kane and as it did, I found myself moving from my previously slouched position and immediately straightening up.

However, when the door was pushed open, I met my secretary's confused and apologetic gaze, and then I met the gaze of my younger brother Dylan. He looked stressed and pissed, but I could understand all of this given that he had just been fired. Of course, it would be extremely difficult to fully enforce, but it was sure to frustrate Dylan in the meantime, which I was certain was Kane's entire intention.

"It's okay," I said to David so he retreated as respectfully as he could manage, and soon I was left alone with my beloved brother.

"You came to New York, here, and you didn't tell me?"

I sighed thoroughly, not ready to deal with this now, but what other choice did I have?

"I haven't heard from you since the last time I called you two months ago," I reminded him. "Was I supposed to call you royally to inform you of the changes in my life when you didn't care to ask?"

He stared at me, and then he took a seat.

"What are you doing?" he asked. "I thought you didn't want to be involved in the company."

"You're not happy to see me," I noted.

"Why should I?" he asked. That spawn and you—"

"Please leave," I cut him off. "If you are here just to whine, then I really don't want to hear it. I'm having a bad enough day as it is."

"What exactly is bad about your day?" he asked. "Did you just get fired for no reason?"

"You missed the scheduled meeting this morning," I reminded him, and he gave me a dark look.

"He had an agenda this morning that neither Sarah nor I were looking forward to, so we decided to give ourselves a bit more time to consider things."

"Ah," I said. "So you two planned it together."

He gave me a look.

"I'm not saying that, but I can understand that it may look that way. However, I heard that he rescinded the proposal he presented to you to buy your company. Instead, you'd actually become active in this company. I'm so incredibly curious as to why you would agree to this. Did he buy your loyalty in some other way or..."

I gave him a look.

"That's what the meeting was for this morning. The meeting that you didn't attend."

"We knew what it was for," he said. "He was going to strong-arm us into losing our case somehow, and we needed to get ready for that."

"So, you are admitting to intentionally boycotting the meeting?"

"I didn't boycott it. I was late."

"Intentionally?" I asked, finally noticing the exhaustion and strain in his eyes he tried to hide.

"What were you busy with?" I asked. "Partying overnight on your yacht?"

He laughed.

"Don't sound salty now. You handed that over to me, hoping I'd sail away most probably and never come back. Unfortunately, here I am, and I really don't know what you two are planning but kicking me out the first day you came back is a very, very bad move."

I looked at him and sighed.

"What if my coming back wasn't a move? Have you thought of that?"

"I have," he nodded. "I tried to give you the benefit of the doubt, but who are we kidding here? You ignored all of these gifts for months, and suddenly you're back when he's about to lose an argument? How convenient."

"An argument?" I asked, and he shrugged.

"He's too fucking uptight. The company's doing well so why will a measly percentage in payout increase do? Stingy fucker."

I no longer wanted to speak about this and had a team to touch base with, so I gathered the files on my desk and moved to switch on my computer.

"That's it then?" he asked and I replied.

"Yup, I have to get back to work."

"You're still not going to tell me how he got you to come here?"

I considered this and refused.

"Nope. Attend the next meeting and you'll find out."

"I've been fired," he said. "How exactly am I supposed to attend?"

"You're accepting that? You're not fighting back?"

He glared at me and then he rose to his feet.

"Glad to have you back Sis," he said in the driest tone in existence. "I'm elated."

I ignored him and went back to work.

Thankfully, his visit brought me back to reality, ensuring that I understood that I was quickly distracted. So, I was able to completely focus, even meeting with the team that had been researching towards this division for a bit, as Kane had informed me. However, afterwards, what I realized was that there was no division or standing. I wasn't yet employed here.

I had every right to be with the company. It was all blurry, and by evening time, I had a headache. Mostly because I had forced the possibilities for building the scents division, but also because I needed to speak to him once again about my status in the company and what exactly I was to be working towards.

Calling him was unsavory, given the prior experience of doing so and going over to his office. There was no way to prove that I was just asking for it. And so, I sighed and picked up my phone to call someone else. She answered immediately, almost as though she'd been waiting for me to contact her.

"Twice in one day," she said. "That's a new record."

I leaned against the chair. Then I turned around to look at the gorgeous sunset seen over the skyline of the city.

"Don't make it weird," I said. "I'm already uncomfortable as it is."

"Alright," she said. "What's the update?"

Wanting to talk yet not quite wanting to.

"How was class today?" I asked her.

She stopped for a moment, and then she laughed.

"Alright, let's say you need to talk about something else

before you warm up into what you actually want to say, but just so you know, I am incredibly curious."

I smiled, and she went on, talking about the cutest kid that was beginning to top the others.

"I was so surprised when he came up to me and offered his juice pack," she said. "He's never done that before. Never even considered it. Children are just so moldable; it's amazing."

I was happy at her report and wanted to hear more; however, she stopped me.

"Nope, that's enough," she said.

"Knowing you're still at work, you better spill now. I have a feeling you just called me to be some sort of band-aid, but no, let's go deeper. What's happening, or rather, what happened?"

I sighed, and then I responded.

"It's no big deal..." I began the lie echoing in my head, but then I really wanted it to be a lie, but I couldn't quite convince myself of this.

"I mean it's not a big deal, is it?"

"What happened, ma'am?" she asked, and I went on.

"So, we had a meeting... and we went to a restaurant."

"A date?" she asked, and I rolled my eyes.

"No, and stop, I'm trying to remove any personal connotations from this. It was a business lunch between two very serious-minded business owners."

"Okay," she said seriously, and then she messed up again. "Until..."

I was about to get upset, but then the humor caught on and I just smiled.

"Until?" she asked, and I finally gave in.

"Fine. We went to a hotel afterwards. And... he um..."

"He did what?"

"Stop," I said.

"Just get to it. There's no good way to say it. You guys fucked?"

I sighed.

"Wow," she said. "I mean, I have no complaints though. I almost even expected it, but on the first day?"

"Miss ma'am," I said. "I didn't say that we didn't do that."

"So, what did you two do at the hotel?"

I let it go, though my tone I noticed, went several pitches lower than ever. Still, she heard me loud and clear.

"He went down on you?" she asked, and I nodded until I realized that she couldn't see me.

"Yeah," I said, and she laughed.

"Oh, that had to be good. You don't do that easily."

"Tell me about it."

"So now what's the plan? Is that why you called me?"

"There's no plan," I groaned. "I just..."

"You just what?"

"I want to move past it, put it behind me, but I really don't know how to do it. Maybe if I ignore it long enough, he'll do the same and-"

"Wait, what are you trying to put behind you? What happened at the hotel? Why the hell would you do that?"

"It's the first day," I told her. "Things are so unstable and yet I'm already letting the CEO eat me out?"

Suddenly, there was a knock on my door and my heart nearly left my chest. I immediately sat up, groaning, and then I excused myself from the conversation. A few minutes later, my secretary walked in.

"Mr. Lazarus is here to see you," he said. "He wanted to know if you were busy and had a moment or two to spare."

I listened to his words with a straight face and almost shook my head. If he truly wanted to know how I was settling in, then he could and should have just called. But then here he is.

"Just a moment," I told him, and with a smile, he walked back out.

"I'll talk later," I told Diana. "It seems I have a surprise visit."

"Who?" she asked. "Kane motherfucking Lazarus?"

I ended the call and straightened up in my chair.

A few minutes later, he walked in with his hand in his pocket, but then pulled it out the moment he was in my space, and I couldn't help but notice that perhaps my office was a tad too small because he seemed to instantly shrink the entire space by two as he walked in with his hawk-eyed stare.

It seemed as though he was trying to see right into my soul with how directly and intensely, he stared at me. As the seconds passed and I began to squirm, I was sure that he was succeeding.

“Please take a seat,” I said, and he nodded and did so.

Then he stared at me, and I truly, at that moment, couldn’t believe just how handsome he was. It was glaring, but now, and somehow, he seemed even more attractive. Perhaps it was the evening glow or whatever, but I really wouldn’t have minded if in that moment a repeat of this afternoon, and perhaps even more, occurred. The very thought though filled me with hate, and I didn’t know if it was for him or myself.

“I wanted to stop by to see how you were settling in,” he said, and I nodded.

"Thank you, that's very thoughtful. I was going to come see- to speak to you as well."

"Well, I'm here now," he said. "Go ahead."

I looked at him and knew with the way he stared at me, head slightly cocked to the side, undistracted, he was thinking about that afternoon, and as a result, it took me longer than it had ever had previously to put a sentence together.

"What do you want to speak about again?" he asked, and I slightly lowered my gaze. And then I remembered.

"Where do I stand here?" I asked. "I've met with the team... we've shared our ideas and vision for where to go with the new division, but it hasn't exactly been approved yet, nor have I been employed."

He looked around the office and then he nodded.

"You're right. You're right."

"I can go ahead to employ you now, but approving funding and eventually getting started towards the new division is another feat. We need to bring this to the equity holders and somehow be able to get the other two on board."

I looked at him because that statement... if he had mentioned moving Mount Everest, things would have felt more plausible.

"Sure," I said and picked up a pen to twirl around. "And how do we do that?"

"That's another reason why I'm here," he said. "We should be on the same page as to how to handle things since the other parties are both our siblings. We should understand them a bit, right, and be able to know how best to handle them?"

I was amused.

"You fired my brother today, I don't think he's going to be wanting to be handled by you in any way for the foreseeable future."

"Yeah, I figured, but that's where you come in. I don't have to handle him, but I'm pretty sure that you'll be more than up to the task."

I watched him, and then I sighed.

"I don't know," I said. "He seemed pretty pissed. In fact, I deeply suspect that a lawsuit for wrongful termination is coming your way."

"I suspect the same as well," he replied.

"But I didn't just fire him because I was mad. His lackadaisical attitude has indeed been slowing down his department. He's in charge of logistics, but I think he assumed that it would take less work than it actually does. It requires his presence, especially when tough decisions need to be made, but he's never around. He more than anything relinquished complete authority to the deputy head there, which is fine, but when tough decisions need to be made, and your brother is unreachable, guess who they call? Me."

"They need a leader. Someone who can help them grow in a specified direction but it's not happening, and that is a crucial part of our company. We need innovation and speed, and it needs to be fixed. I have a man for the job, but I know your brother won't just allow me to replace him, so I needed to find a way for him to. Not sure yet if this will work but let me see if he will bend to my will in exchange for his job back."

I smiled.

"You don't have to work too hard. It'll take him a while because of his pride, but I'm sure that he would have accepted whatever terms you gave in return for his job. He needs to work to get his dividends. And if he doesn't get those, then how does he afford his exuberant lifestyle?"

"True," he said and nodded.

"Still, a man's ego is a fragile thing indeed, so better to manage this than to truly earn an enemy for life."

"You're scared of enemies?" I asked, and he gave me a look.

"Not scared," he said. "I just know when to make one an enemy and when to make them a friend."

He watched me closely once again until I had no choice but to turn away.

"Got it," I said and continued twirling the pen in my hand once again.

His gaze went to it, and to my disappointment, I stopped. Afterwards, I put it down because it showed more than anything my inner state currently at his presence, and it was embarrassing too, to say the least.

"So," he said. "Let's get back to you."

"Me?" I asked, and he nodded.

"Yeah, truly I am a significant way on board with what you're trying to do, but I need numbers. I need data, and I need projections. So, while we wait for the other owners to stop throwing their tantrums, why don't you work on a proposal? Go all-in: office space needs, staff, budget, plan... I want to know all the details of how you plan to execute. Afterwards, and if things look good, then we can present it to the others. They're reasonable, so let's hope that we can all put our personal differences aside and objectively assess the project. But in order to do that, we need to know more than the idea."

I nodded in agreement with what he was saying and was finally relieved because I had finally received some clarity.

"Alright," I said. "That sounds good. I'll get started on it with the team."

Afterwards, there was nothing further to talk about, so I half expected him to just leave. However, when he remained seated, I knew that there was more.

I gave him a look filled with my question, and he heard it clearly.

"Working late today?" he asked, and my heart skipped a beat in my chest.

This was it. This was where I had to decide what exactly I wanted and how I couldn't tolerate this partnership going forward. And so, I took the time to formulate my response in my head as I watched him. And then I responded.

"Umm... yeah," I replied. "There's a lot to catch up on, as you have just pointed out."

He watched me again, and then he rose to his feet. He began to come around my desk and I leapt up, but to my surprise, he didn't approach me. Instead, he headed over to the window behind me, and I sighed in relief.

But then, at the same time, I felt disappointed. All in all, I now felt like prey, ensnared, and it annoyed me to no end.

"I've always wondered something," he said.

I so badly wanted to turn around to look at him, but I had to feign as much disinterest as possible for my sake, so I kept my attention on the laptop and files I had been reviewing before he had come in.

Sure, here's the edited version:

But then, at the same time, I felt disappointed. All in all, I now felt like prey, ensnared, and it annoyed me to no end.

"I've always wondered something," he said.

I so badly wanted to turn around to look at him, but I had to feign as much disinterest as possible for my sake, so I kept my attention on the last top and date files I had been reviewing before he had come in.

"Go ahead," I said uninterestedly.

"I've always wondered back then... when you walked in on me-"

"Correction, I didn't walk in on you. You walked in on me."

"Oh," he said and turned around to face me. "So you do remember?"

"Why the fuck would I-"

It made sense for me to respond, but once again, as I noted his calm demeanor, I couldn't help but suspect that he was just riling me up for no reason. It didn't seem so, yet I felt so, and it annoyed me to no end. I forced myself to calm down and relax against the chair.

"You walked in on me," I told him. However, that didn't sound right, so I corrected myself.

"I mean... I was already in the library when you came in."

He cocked his head. "You were? Why didn't I notice you?"

I stopped and wondered about this too. And then I recalled that I had hidden when I heard someone come in, but I wasn't going to readily admit that. It was the truth, but I didn't need any more reasons to feel weak before this man than I already did.

"I don't know," I said. "Maybe you were too caught up in the moment."

He shook his head and returned his gaze to the window.

"Anyways," he continued. "You lingered," he said.

"So?" I replied, and then smiled.

"That's why I taunted you the way I did."

"Wait, were you really expecting me to join in or something?" I asked.

"Not really," he said. "But it was sure entertaining to see the look on your face."

"What look was on my face?" I asked, and he replied.

"Interest... curiosity... disgust?"

"I want to know what you really think," he said.

"Are you asking me now to give a review of how you fucked when you were twenty-three?" I asked, and I gave him a look. Then he smiled.

"You're feisty."

"No, just reasonable," I responded. "And for the record, these are working hours, so I would like it if things were kept purely professional between us. Otherwise, anything else, and I'm afraid that being here will become quite difficult for me."

I returned my attention to my computer, but there was no way in hell that it could distract me from the fact that he was still present and probably watching me. I soon got my response.

14

Kane

She was icing me out. I wasn't in the least bit surprised, but I wondered exactly why. When it came to her, I was extremely curious. I turned around to watch as she pretended to get back to work on her computer. I wanted so badly to know how her mind worked, how she processed things, her fears, and why she reacted the way she did.

I also didn't want to leave just yet, even though she wanted me to, or at least told herself that she wanted me to. But before then, I needed to know why she was holding herself back.

So, I headed over, and slowly caged her in. She instantly went stiff as I lowered and placed my hands on the desk.

"In what ways exactly will being here become difficult for you?" I asked.

At first, she didn't respond, and then she turned to the side to meet my eyes. I stared into them, but then my gaze lowered to her plump peach lips, and my libido stirred. I had wanted to know what those lips tasted like for so long, but I held myself back. I returned my gaze to her eyes, then I straightened and went around the desk. I straightened my jacket and then turned around to face her, her sweet scent still lingering in my nostrils.

"We should finish what we started, shouldn't we?" I asked, and she looked at me.

"Finish what we started, and then what?" she asked. "That'll be the end of it?"

"Would you want it to be?"

"Yes," she replied. "I would want it to be. Or more specifically, I would prefer it if it should end right now. We already crossed a very dangerous line earlier this afternoon and I don't see how anything good can come out of this if we keep going."

I listened, and then I responded.

"How do you know that something good can't come out of this?" I asked, and she seemed taken aback and confused all in one.

"You're pretty arrogant to make such blanket conclusions, don't you think?" I asked, and again she seemed not to be able to find a response. I waited, and eventually, though, she had one.

"I don't care for anything good to come out of this," she said, and I was downright amused.

"You really don't fancy me much, do you?" I asked, and she folded her arms across her chest.

"No, I do not... which is why-“

“Suck my cock,” I cut her off and the rest of her sentence died on her tongue in her instant.

“Excuse me?” she asked as though she couldn’t quite believe what I had just said. However, I meant every word.

"I want you to suck my cock," I repeated and began to head toward her desk. And as she watched me approach her eyes widened even further.

"I ate you out at lunch time," I said. "And you enjoyed every moment of it. I enjoyed myself immensely as well. Now that you abruptly want to nip this in the bud before either of us are able to discover the depths it can take us to then isn't it only fair that you repay the service? So that we're even."

She continued to stare at me even as my belt buckle was loosened, and I leaned against her desk.

"This is a simple and fair transaction Lena," I said. "Repay what you've been given, and the playing field will be leveled once again."

An incredulous expression came over her face.

"Shouldn't this constitute as sexual harassment?" She asked and I almost laughed.

Then my hands went even further and began to undo the button of my pants.

"Sexual harassment by definition is an outcry for unwanted sexual advances. I've seen the way you look at me so far when you think I'm not paying attention. Am I to ignore it and believe that you want nothing to do with me?"

She stared without blinking which made me wonder if she was even breathing. I hadn't planned to go this far at all... couldn't even believe that I was acting in this way but something about how stuck up and cautious she was being made me want to taunt her just a bit more.

After the button had been released from the hole, I began to pull my zipper down and then my briefs were exposed.

"Kane," she called in a warning tone, but I ignored her.

Reaching into my briefs, I pulled out my already hardened cock and the moment she saw it she couldn't look away.

I watched her eyes as I began to stroke and then she got up and went over to the window to shut the blinds.

She leaned her head against the window slightly and then she turned around to face me.

"What are you doing?" she called, her voice lightly rising, however I didn't budge.

Instead, I continued stroking my cock, watching as her lips parted and her chest began to heave. She kept her gaze on mine for as long as she could and then her attention lowered down. Mine lowered as well to see what she saw, and it was the thick member in my hand pulling back and forth to reveal the wet, flush pink head. Veins were strained along the length, and I was oozing from the tip and just the fact that she was taking in every bit of this action did something to me that I hadn't quite experienced before. Suddenly though there was a small knock on the door, and I stopped. Her gaze shifted to it and then she responded.

"What is it?"

"Do you need anything Miss Mercer?" her secretary called out.

"No," she said her voice nearly a croak and then she hurried over to the door.

"No," she said. "I'm fine. We're fine. I'm in a meeting with the CEO."

Of course, he knew that. He had ushered me in. Shaking my head, I continued to stroke shutting my eyes briefly as the pleasure began to set my veins on fire. I needed her on her knees and before me and so I rose to my feet and turned around. She was facing me, watching, and then she locked the door behind me. Her voice was low as she spoke.

"You shouldn't be doing this," she said. "You can't be doing this."

"Come here," I said, and she started to head over.

"Stop telling me what to do," she said, and I smiled.

"Get on your knees," I gave yet another order and could see the aggravation darken her features.

Then she pushed at my chest causing me to fall back into her chair.

"Don't fucking tell me what to do," she said.

I controlled my fall and landed smoothly in it then I parted my legs.

"Potato, potato," I said, and she gave me a very dark look before lowering to her knees.

She watched my cock, and I could see the raw hunger in her eyes. She truly didn't want to do this but as the head pulsed and leaked, I saw that she was unable to resist it.

She slipped her tongue out and then she kissed me across the wet slit. She shut her eyes savoring it a bit and then she licked her lips and reopened her eyes.

"I'm going to bite your cock off," she threatened, and I chuckled silently daring her to try.

She pushed my hand off and then she grabbed the root of my cock. With her gaze on mine she licked up and down the hardened length once again the tip of her tongue tracing the engorged veins and then then she pulled the entire head into her mouth again. I leaned back against the chair as my pleasure intensified, the heat and suction from her mouth, just what I needed to release all the pent-up frustrations and stress from the day.

I felt relieved and anew as she began to suck, the pad of her tongue and her throat savoring me with feverish abandon.

I had to give this accolade that she knew exactly what she was doing because I'd never actually been a fan of blow jobs. They were fun when given but nothing and no one had ever made it feel like this. At first, I was sure it was a fluke but as I watched her head bob up and down my length, all prior doubts from earlier completely disappeared.

The pleasure zinged through my blood as her stroking became even harder and I couldn't help my excitement. My hand itched to go into my hair to grab at the roots so that I could control this, yet I didn't want to look away from her for even a moment. Her eyes were shut but from time to time they would flutter open and connect with mine.

And they were mesmerizing to say the least. More than anything though, I loved how she couldn't get enough of sucking my cock. She took me as deeply as she could, and then she pulled back out with more grace than I had ever seen from any woman. She was beyond talented, and I was beginning to see that it was in more ways than I could ever have imagined.

I was about to pull away unable to contain any delayed release but then she licked down my length and then to my surprise went even further down to pull my balls into her mouth one after the other. My head fell back then as a long and guttural, groan escaped my lips. I couldn't have muffled it if I tried, and I didn't give a rat's ass about who the fuck heard. I couldn't in that moment because giving that she was stroking me as she sucked on my balls was way too much sensation to keep me coherent. My eyes went shut as all I could do was accept and try to contain the barrage of feeling that overwhelmed me.

It took no time then.,. in seconds I was coming. At first, I attempted to pull out of her mouth so that I could spill out but then she caught me hard by the root and directed me to her mouth. This I couldn't miss for the world, so I watched as she took every bit of my release and then some.

She continued to suck me until every drop of ecstasy was pulled out of me. I wanted to punch something to contain the rush of excitement and extreme satisfaction rushing through my veins. She was wonderful but given my enjoyment of her from earlier in the day I couldn't wait even further for us to take things all the way to the end. But first I wanted to do something with her.

I couldn't believe how badly I wanted to do it but seeing how she had just taken all of me with so much delight I wanted to feel as intimately close to her as possible. Even if it was a bit dirty. I liked dirty and as I kissed her, the taste of my cum intertwining with the taste of her mouth. I decided that I also liked her. Immensely.

15

Lena

I was still shaky on my feet and quite disoriented when I left my office and headed over to the elevators. I had been planning on working late, but none of that was going to happen after what had happened in my office. I didn't know what to say, or even think for that matter. My mind remained blank as I arrived at the ground floor, walked across the lobby, and to the car waiting for me.

I didn't think he had left yet, so as we drove away, I couldn't help but lift my gaze to the very top of the building. That was where he would be, and I wondered if he had been affected just like I was. This was a very dangerous game we were playing, and no more than now, after that kiss he had given me, had I become aware of it.

We had become quiet afterwards. No more taunting, just deep contemplation as we tried to catch our breaths and return back to earth. What we found, however, was that the earth was no longer all that interesting. What we wanted was to completely bask in each other's essence and presence. Or maybe I was wrong, and it was just me. Either way, it felt both good and terrifying at the same time, so I returned straight to my hotel.

What I soon found, however, was that the buzz of excitement that had begun inside of me from the moment he pulled his cock out and started stroking himself still remained. It had been such a brazen move, so shameless, and yet he had looked so confident and attractive doing it that it had immediately gotten my clit throbbing and sent me to my knees. Any man who could do that so effortlessly was a massive risk and was not to be trusted around me.

Even I have my guard up, but how long until he pulls another brazen move like that once again and sucks me in like a willing puppet.

I needed to relax...to let go a little, so I headed to the hotel's bar. Thankfully, it wasn't crowded, given that it was a work night. I quickly found a stool at the very end of the bar and took a seat.

After placing my AirPods in my ears, I called the one person that would listen and perhaps talk some sense into my head. Or not. I just needed to talk about this, and Diana seemed to be my only solution. However, from her very first words as she answered, I started to harbor deep regret.

"The third time the same day?" she asked. "I don't know whether to laugh or pat myself on the back because I was motherfucking right." I sighed at her gloating and rolled my eyes.

"Hello?" she called. "Hello, miss."

"Don't gloat," I said. "My head's about to explode."

"Tired from work or..."

“I wish it was from work. I know how to decompress from that. Instead, I'm in a bar drinking on a Monday night."

She laughed out at this.

"Alone or-"

"Alone, of course," I replied. "Who else would I be with?"

"Just checking," she said.

"So, what happened?" she asked.

It took me a long time to respond to this.

"It's less about what happened and more about what I did."

"Uh oh," she said. "Did you hit his head with a phone or something?"

"No, but I'm sure someone hit my head with something."

"Jesus, you're making me frustrated and curious all at once, spill it out already."

Remaining silent, in my defense, that afternoon had already happened.

“Did you go all the way?”

I lowered my tone and my head.

“No,” she started, “he started stroking himself in my office. Instead of me kicking him out-”

“Wait what?”

“I’m not going to repeat that.”

“Oh,” she said and I knew she was holding back her laughter with all her might. Eventually, she was able to swallow it down and then she cleared her throat.

“Go on...” she said.

“This is not a joke,” I replied. “At first, I thought he was joking that he wasn’t going to do it. I kept rejecting him and then he did, and the way he looked at me, and the way he looked while doing it... God. He was slow, deliberate... and fuck... I would have probably set anyone else on fire, but as I watched him, it felt like someone had set me on fire. I’m still on fire. I don’t even know if I can go to sleep. It’s either I call him now to release me from my misery or I go after someone else in this fucking bar."

"Uh-oh," she said. "I do hear it in your tone."

I sighed.

"He is handsome," she said. "I understand."

"No, it's beyond handsome. No handsome guy could pull off what he did in my office today. I couldn't look away. I wanted him like..."

"He must have been a pretty one then."

"Fucking beautiful," I exclaimed. "Right length, unbelievable width... just... I'm in fucking trouble. I think I have to move back to LA."

She laughed out again, and then she apologized.

"I'm sorry, I know this is serious, but I'm just so giddy because I predicted this."

"Well, I didn't," I told her. "He fucking aggravates me to no end with his pompousness and arrogance. Always has, so why the fuck am I now a sucker for it and going on my knees to-"

I stopped myself, but I didn't have to complete it.

"Oh my God, you..."

"Don't, please."

"Oh wow... he's got you by the fucking neck. You don't like that."

"No, I do not, but with him... and because of this afternoon..."

"Well, in my opinion, you both definitely have self-control because I can't imagine doing all these in a day and still going home separately."

"Well, I'm two seconds away from calling him up now. Maybe that's why I'm truly here at the bar, to give myself the courage to."

"Don't do it," she said. "You'll hate yourself if you do tomorrow."

"I already hate myself," I told her. "Shouldn't I just give myself a proper reason for this now?"

She laughed.

"No, you're just horny and it happens to the rest of us. Go to your room, take a shower, and call it a night. Your head will be screwed back on by tomorrow."

She was completely and absolutely right, so I drained my final glass of wine, ended the call, and returned to my room.

In there, I turned on the warm inviting lights, and they cast an ambiance that was warm and inviting and ultimately sexy.

It was wonderful, to say the least, but it just made me antsy and even a little bit sad. I didn't even bother going to bed because I sure as hell wasn't going to sleep despite the alcohol in my system. So, I headed straight to the bathroom and ran myself a bath.

I managed to light some candles all around, and then I stripped down and got into the hot soapy water. I left my eyes open for a bit as the day I'd just had ran through my mind, and then I shook it as the memories started to bring that buzzing back. It was now intense, and unfortunately, it made nothing about this bath relaxing. Instead, all the stimulation made me even hornier until my eyes went shut, and my head began to fall back. I leaned completely against the porcelain, and then began to move my hands down my body. I imagined him kissing every bit of it, and then I stopped because it wasn't supposed to be that way. It was never supposed to be that way between us. Rather, it was supposed to be hard, rough, and quick. Pure stimulation and release. I started to feel a bit sad about it, but quickly snapped myself out of it. It was the best way, the safest way. Otherwise, at the end of it all, I might have gotten more than I bargained for. But as my hands went between my thighs, and I continued to think about him, I couldn't imagine how any further affection could possibly develop between us. I couldn't stand his guts and probably never would, and that was all the assurance I needed.

However, now I had to make the decision as to how to proceed from this. Go all the way and possibly get hooked or avoid him and begin to carve a different path for myself in that company that didn't involve him. However, it wasn't too late. And if I ran into him, was there the possibility that he pulled one on me like he did tonight that I would say no? He was beginning to feel like sugar now, and I had long learned from experience that the more I deprived myself of it, the harder the cravings. Yet, I couldn't just give myself the permission to indulge, or else it might never stop.

"Today was the last," I promised myself. There were huge challenges ahead of me, and I needed all the focus that I could get.

Plus, I could very well take care of myself. It had been the preferred way most of the time in the past, so my hand returned once again to the junction between my thighs. Just thinking about him already incurred my reaction, so it didn't take long to get into the slick, slow rhythm. But then, as I thought of him, of how his mouth had taken me to the heavens and back that afternoon, I went even faster. His name and his face, however, were all that permeated my mind. That evil smirk he had... his broad and sinfully muscular physique and that sin of a mouth of his. I ached to dig my hands into his hair and grab at the roots. A smile came to my face as I imagined pulling so hard that he complained. It would probably be the closest I ever came to inflicting some kind of pain on him, and this unsurprisingly turned me on even more. My body began to tighten and writhe in the water as my finger went inside of me. I recalled the way he had handled me, and in no time, I was moaning and releasing into my hands. It didn't take much or long at all. There was enough pent-up sexual frustration I had to get rid of, and at the end of it all, I was exhausted, but thankfully not as horny. I was able to climb into bed a little later and get an actually good night's sleep.

I found the next morning, as I woke up early without headaches, that it had worked. I felt light and ready to move, even though it was much too early, I instantly got up and began to get ready for work.

There was much to do and sort through, especially regarding the proposal that Kane had made the previous day, so I was eager to get started. Just as I arrived at the building, I took in the magnificent views and thought of my father. He had seen this building so many years earlier and had wanted to have his office here. Against all odds, he had pulled it off and now it was my turn to manage it. I felt honored and was even more pumped to do this, so I hurried across the lobby until I got to the elevator.

What I saw, or rather, whom I saw, was more than enough to stop me in my tracks. Kane Lazarus was leaning against one end of the elevator and gazing at his phone. I was surprised to see him and found it quite peculiar that he was just standing there. However, as the elevator doors began to close, I had to make a decision: open them if I wanted to hop on with him or take a different ride. I had a split second to make the decision, but since he hadn't looked at me and had probably not noticed me, I decided to step away. I was fully prepared to face temptation, but what was the point of battling it first thing in the morning? It was truly too much of a hassle, and I needed to conserve my energy for all the very important things that I had to handle.

I walked over to call for another car. However, barely five seconds had passed before I heard the doors I had just abandoned slide open again.

My heart leapt into my throat, but still, I didn't budge. But then, when I heard his voice, I had no choice but to turn around or risk looking like a coward.

"You're avoiding me?" he asked, and I sighed.

"Isn't it for the best?" I asked and smiled.

"The best for whom?" he questioned.

"For the both of us," I replied. "A hassle-free morning can never be underestimated."

16

Kane

Given the day ahead, I was truly not receptive to any amusement in any form, but I had to say that she was quite the jester.

"A hassle-free morning."

I let go of the elevator button and headed towards the back to lean against the car, waiting. Then I pulled my phone out of my pocket and ignored her. The elevator doors began to close, but just as I had suspected, she stopped it and got in. However, she remained as far away as possible. Since it was quite early, there was nothing to bring us closer together, so I continued checking my appointments and emails from the previous evening. Soon, we arrived at the top floor, and without a word, I got out and began heading over to my office.

When I arrived, I walked in and got on with my tasks, but a little bit after eight, Matthias came in.

"I have an appointment at 8:30," I told him. "Make it quick."

"Yes, Sir," he replied and placed the envelope on my desk.

"What's that?" I asked, and he replied...

"Lawsuit. Served on a golden platter to you this morning. I would have actually brought it on a golden platter, but I couldn't find one in the kitchen."

I frowned and accepted the document. After realizing what it was and who it was from, I flung it away.

"Nope, you can't do that," Matthias said as he got up to pick up the document. "You can't fire an equity member. At least not without telling me and having the proper grounds."

"I had the proper grounds," I replied. "He was an asshole."

"Well, I share the sentiment, Sir, but that doesn't constitute proper grounds in a court of law. On the streets, most definitely, but..."

"I'm really busy," I told him. "What do you need from me?"

He sighed, noticing my somber mood and got straight to the point.

"He's suing you for unlawful termination, and it's serious. We need to find a way to settle this thing now and make it go away before more members of the company hear about it, or he could use the chance to screw you and start making requests for compensation for bullshit claims like emotional distress or whatever nonsense he can cook up."

"I want him to make up whatever claim for whatever nonsense he can cook up," I said, and Matthias was taken aback.

"What?"

"I want to frustrate and humiliate him. And if it's possible to fire him too, then why not?"

"The board will bring it to a vote."

"Then we'll vote," I replied. "But for now, drag it on as long as possible until it begins to leave a visible dent in his pockets."

"Hm," Matthias said. "That's going to be fairly difficult since this is also going to leave quite the dent in your pocket."

I looked him in the eyes, a brow raised.

"Why? Aren't you the one representing me? You work for the company."

"Technically, yes, and he is suing the company and not you, so I am available at your disposal. The problem, however, is that I should also be representing him as ownership trumps management. So..."

"So what?" I asked.

"Well, I have to sit this one out. Conflict of interest."

"Meaning?"

"You have to get your own lawyer for this, just as he has."

I looked at him, and his gaze lowered.

"What are even the details of the lawsuit?" I asked, trying to get back to work, most definitely fuming.

"Well," he picked up the folder and began to rummage through it again.

"It's the usual. He's suing you for an exorbitant amount, except of course, if you both settle, and you give him his job back."

"What amount?"

"250 million."

"What?"

"Yeah, his exact share of the company."

I smiled and shook my head but kept working.

“He's trying to override the stipulations of his father's will?"

"He doesn't want to work, and he wants the money, so I'm sure he'll find some way to do it. This termination being one of them. Anyway, I know you want to inflict pain on him, but there is no way you can do that without hurting yourself as well."

I kept working but eventually looked away from my screen and up at him.

"Do you have a lawyer to send my way then?" I asked, and Matthias gave me a look.

"This could become really messy. Rumors are already spreading through the company."

"I considered this," and then I frowned deeply. "Then let it become really messy."

"Should I get you a lawyer to waste his time or one to actually ensure he's stripped of everything?"

"The latter," I said without further thought, and he went silent again.

"Yes, Sir," he said and turned around to leave, and I shook my head at him.

"For a lawyer of your caliber, you sure do like to avoid conflict."

He shot back immediately.

"A lawyer of my caliber did nothing but resolve conflicts for the first fifteen years of my career. That's why I took a position here, not at a law firm. For some peace of mind."

I was amused.

"It hasn't exactly been peaceful here."

"Sure, but we don't get sued every day."

"Please leave," I said. "And find me a good lawyer."

"Not the best?"

I didn't respond. But then, just before he left, an idea came to mind.

"You know what, send me a beginner lawyer."

"What do you mean?"

"Get me someone wet behind the ears from any firm to handle this. That's what he deserves."

"Wow, you don't even respect the guy to take his claim seriously."

"No, I don't respect him."

"You should respect the lawyer he's working with, though."

"And who's that?"

"Emerson."

I looked up.

"David Emerson?"

"Yeah."

I shook my head then and went back to work.

"Still, get me the associate, and if you run into Emerson, send him my condolences on behalf of his wasted time."

"No, I'm the one who should be consoled because, of course, I'm going to have to direct the bloody rookie."

"Well, you will be involved?" I asked.

“I have to protect the interest of the company as a whole. Not directly though so I'll be acting as a consultant.”

“Thank you,” I said. “And as a token of my appreciation the yacht is yours to use for the entire weekend. Take anyone you want. Full catering-"

"That's bribery."

"So, sue me," I groaned, and he gave me a look. Then he shook his head and opened the door.

"Two weekends," he told me, and I smiled in amusement.

17

Lena

One of the perks of living in a hotel was that I didn't have any cleaning whatsoever to do, so I could wake up on a Sunday after the most stressful of weeks and have nothing but the day ahead of me. I was beginning to truly embrace the idea of truly living in New York. It was a much different place than LA, and I didn't exactly have any friends as close as Diana was to me, but it was a new start, and it was what I had been craving for so long, so I was open to it.

The first thing I did was go for a run in Central Park, and after that, I heard of a farmers' market close by that I could check out if I wasn't too sweaty. I didn't expect to be anyway since I hadn't worked out for so long, so I was sure to be famished in no time. I started early, around 7 am, hoping there wouldn't be too many people and I wouldn't get lost.

I put in my AirPods, turned on some motivational track from YouTube to get me through it.

When I was much younger and just leaving college, I

had considered moving here to start my career, but then I listened to some video about taking risks and doing what I wanted instead, and I chose to remain in LA. Plus, my relationship with my father then had been extremely rocky, so I was certain that moving to New York would ensure that we clashed more times than was needed.

I thought about him this morning, or rather, I allowed myself to think about him, and it was painful. It didn't take long for me to become upset, so I paused whatever had been playing on my phone and slowed down because my heart was about to jump out of my chest. However, when I spotted a bench and realized that I would think even more if I stopped, I kept running.

I went a bit further, but then I couldn't take another step forward, so I walked to the nearest bench with a deep frown on my face and sat down. I took a deep breath and tried to collect myself, then I shut my eyes. I'm fine now. I could think about him more often now, unlike the earlier months, but it still hurt like hell. Diana had told me to replace the hurt whenever I thought about it with a happy memory, something... anything that would bring a smile to my face, but it never worked. Because even though we were similar, because even though there had been good times, and despite all our differences, I still believed he loved me. However, these good memories were few and far between. They were difficult to conjure up or even recall, and so by the time I could put this in effect, my eyes were burning. I shut them and buried my head between my knees, but then I heard my name.

At first, I ignored it, but then it became peculiar to me that someone here was calling my name. So, I lifted my head and tried to see who it was. At first, my vision was blurry, so it wasn't until he was almost in front of me that I realized who it was. He was shirtless, all slabs of his muscles dripping with sweat, and strands of his hair sticking to his forehead. As my gaze moved up from his torso to his face, all I could feel was attacked.

"What's wrong?" he asked. Kane. Kane motherfucking Lazarus.

"How are you here?" I asked, and he took a brief look around.

"It's a public park," he replied.

I was in no mood for his antics, so I quickly stood up and started to walk away, but I couldn't get rid of him. He ended up by my side, strolling leisurely, even though I was walking as fast as I possibly could.

"Could you stop following me?" I asked and turned to see him drinking from his bottle of water.

He licked his lips, and my attention began to shift.

"It seems like you're in a bad mood. It's not my business, but you're an employee, so I wanted to make sure you're alright."

He continued to stare at me, but I kept walking.

"I'm fine."

"Sure," he said and turned and began to walk away. I couldn't stop staring at him as he left. I hadn't really seen the strength and build of his body underneath all those suits and vests, but no one was blind to the fact that he was all muscle. Broad, strong shoulders, not an inch of fat anywhere in sight, defined abs...

I began to pick up my pace without even thinking twice. I tried to stop myself, to think with my brain instead of my clit, but the more the warnings came, the faster I ran until I truly couldn't catch up to him. If I didn't know any better, I would have said that he was the one avoiding me, but this wasn't the case at all since when I eventually called out to him, he stopped.

I stopped and lowered myself to catch my breath, and then he watched me. However, he didn't come over. Instead, he headed over to a bench close by and took his seat, then he waited for me to approach.

Dick.

"What is it?" he asked, and I gazed at his sweaty body once again.

"People usually work out with shirts in public places," I said, my gaze going to his dark nipples. I wanted my teeth around them, and I couldn't believe that this was what was coming to mind.

But the fact was that it wasn't just his nipples; it was every bit of his wet and glistening skin.

I wanted sweat and heat and filth, and this, I decided, was how I wanted to spend my Sunday morning.

"Let's take a cab to my hotel," I said, and he went still. Then he looked at me before picking up his bottle once again.

"Why?" he asked, and I almost rolled my eyes.

"Do you really want me to spell it out, or do you just want to humiliate me?"

"I thought you said, 'A hassle-free morning can never be underestimated' or some shit like that."

"This is hassle-free," I said. "Or rather, it will be hassle-free. It should be quick, and it will be fun, and I'm pretty sure it can be the perfect completion, however long you were intending to work out for."

He gave me a once-over, and then he rose to his feet, and without a word, began to walk away.

I couldn't believe it.

And then he stopped and looked at me.

"Aren't you coming?"

I was confused.

"My hotel's the opposite way."

"My apartment's closer," he replied and continued on his way.

I stared after him, wondering if this was truly what I wanted to do, but as I stared at the sweat once again glistening off his back, I made up my mind.

Using sex to distract myself from grief was valid enough. Unhealthy, but valid, and this was the mantra I recited to myself as I headed over to his place. However, as the reality of what I was about to do began to dawn on me... of what I had promised myself I wouldn't do, my head began to clear up.

His residential building extended up into the sky and they had to be extremely familiar with him because even as he walked by bare-chested, he received kind greetings along the way. I received some greetings too. Confused little nods and smiles, and of course, raised eyebrows and assumptions. We weren't even walking side by side, so it was obvious what I would be there for, but what I had expected was that they would ignore me. After all, this couldn't have been the first time.

We got on his elevator, and this thought made me even more queasy. Perhaps my hotel would have been much better. It was my space, and it would definitely feel like I was the one in control. And no, I didn't think it was closer at all.

This had to be some sort of power thing for him. As I stared at him, I couldn't help but roll my eyes. I wouldn't go through with this, but still, I wanted to see where he lived and then disappoint him. Call me nosy, and I would agree. It was exactly what I was, and he deserved it.

Soon we arrived at his apartment, which was on the penthouse of the building, of course, and I started to roll my eyes again. But then I walked in, took in the view, and almost had to pinch myself. It was similar to the view at the office, but this was in a home. Surrounded by the perfect blend of coolness and warmth, it was absolutely magical. I loved it, and for a little while, almost lost myself in admiring his surroundings until he came over and handed me a bottle of water.

"I'm going to take a shower," he said and started to turn away. "Make yourself at home,"

I watched him leave and felt a bit sad, but I also didn't want to have to wait for him to come out of the room before I left, so I stopped him.

"Actually, I'm going to be leaving," I said, and he frowned.

"Why?"

I was almost pressed to give an entire explanation, but then I decided against it, shrugged my shoulders, and started to head towards the door.

"You got me off my run," he said, and I thought of a response.

"I'm sure you can find other ways to work it out,"

I gave a smile and almost wanted to turn around to see the disappointment on his face.

"Stop," he said, and something about his tone made me automatically obey the command. It wasn't harsh or threatening, it was just spoken with the same cold intensity and authority that he used to address all his subordinates, including me unfortunately, at the office.

"Why?" I asked and turned around, only to see that he was already heading towards me. His strides were leisurely, yet he seemed once again to be walking faster than should have been normal. In no time, he was with me. I should have cowered and run for the hills, instead I stood my ground and met his gaze.

"I'm a very tolerant person, Miss Mercer," he said. "I hate it, particularly when I feel like I'm being toyed with."

I wanted to mouth off some tease that was exactly what I had done. However, at the look in his eye, it suddenly didn't feel very flirty.

"I just want to leave," I said, and he took a step back.

"Do you want to leave because you're no longer interested, or because this is some sort of joke to you?"

"Simply because I want to," I said. "I was in the mood then, and now I'm no longer in the mood."

He stared at me, and then he smiled.

"Okay, have a nice day," he said, and I didn't know exactly what to think. I was a bit taken aback.

"You're not going to try and get me to stay?" I asked, and he didn't respond.

He disappeared into the corridor, and now I didn't want to leave.

I looked around again, and since he was no longer there, I began to take a proper look around, at the artwork on the walls and the polished steel, marble, glass, and leather of the apartment. It was sophisticated, with plush soft carpets thrown everywhere, and it made me even more excited about my own apartment.

I headed down the corridor, curious to see where he had gone, and it didn't take long for me to hear the running of the shower in the distance.

As expected, he was indeed cleaning up, and it was time to go. I was in such a weird mood where I had wanted to somewhat leave to spite him, but now that he had acted so nonchalantly about it, I wanted to stay and at least take a peek at that body he worked so hard for.

I thought of knocking on the shower door, but that seemed weird. Being here in general was weird, but I didn't let that stop me. I pushed the door open and met one of the most magnificent emerald-green-tiled bathrooms I had ever seen. For a few moments, it felt like I had walked into a jewelry box, but with the gold accents of the mirror and the steam emanating from the shower stall, it seemed more like a foggy and extremely eclectic dream. And then there was the man... completely naked and running his hands through his hair as the heavy cascade of water descended upon him. Everything, for some reason, played in slow motion in my head, and by the time I regained some element of my senses, I realized that he had noticed me and was watching me.

"This is a violation," he said as he turned the water off. I panicked slightly, wondering if he would be getting out to kick me out, but he didn't. Instead, he grabbed some body wash and began to lather it all over his skin. I found myself moving closer.

"What kind of violation?" I asked and only stopped when I was right against the stall.

"Imagine if I walked in on you this way, in your own apartment."

"Well, I was invited in," I said, my eyes running down his glistening body. "I didn't break in or anything."

He met my gaze, shook his head, and began to run his hands around. I watched his huge hands as he glided across that skin, and my mouth began to water. I wanted my own hands to be doing it... to feel every hard plane and slab of muscle. It felt as though the man himself had been carved from marble, and it was mesmerizing, to say the least.

Suddenly, he opened the door, and I tried to step back, but then I stopped myself when I reminded myself that he was harmless. I wanted to be here... I chose to be here, and so I folded my arms and met his gaze. With one hand, he swiped the water away from his face along with his hair, and of course, I was greeted with several wet drops.

"Thanks," I said as I wiped it off, but he didn't respond. Instead, he issued another command.

"Come in," he said, and my eyes went to that heavy cascade. I could use a shower, but I wasn't exactly dirty enough yet. Not as dirty as I wanted to be. My clit was throbbing, my breathing getting faster, especially as my gaze went down, and I could literally see the semi-hardened rod curving upwards. I knew how far his delicious width could go, way past his navel point, and once again, all I wanted was to have him in my mouth. My jaw still kind of hurt from the previous time, but it was the kind of hurt that I wanted to feel. I looked into the stall and could imagine my hands plastered against the glass and my entire body bent at the waist as he fucked me senseless.

The image was so vivid and intoxicating that when suddenly he grabbed the zipper of my shirt and began to pull it down, I had no complaints. I watched him almost as though this was some out-of-body experience, and then midway through, he grabbed me.

18

Kane

I was fuming. However, I had managed to keep my cool. I had learned to keep my cool. It had taken every ounce of restraint I had not to push her against the door and take her right there, but somehow, I had walked away and thanked the countless times in the past where I had to push my emotions aside in order to perform. But now, here she was, and it was clear to me that she was playing with me.

"Watch your step," I said but didn't give her enough time to adhere to that as I pulled her into the stall with me.

"Hey!" She complained, but my focus was on bearing her weight so she wouldn't fall. And then she was against the tiled wall.

I stared into her eyes, and she stared into mine. Then, I pulled the zipper down all the way until it revealed the sports bra she had on underneath. I started to shrug the shirt off, but she wouldn't budge. She didn't protest too deeply, but the resistance was there.

"You don't want this?" I asked, which was rhetorical because I was fucking hard and way past caring if she wanted this or not.

It took her a while to answer, but the words fell out of her lips.

"No," she said, but they were barely audible. She was lying to herself and torturing me in the process, and I was fed up with that.

I had seen the way she had looked at me back at the park, so even when she had called me back, I hadn't been the least bit surprised. It had been the same at the office throughout the week, especially after that morning when we ran into each other at the elevator. I don't know what she had told herself, but she had assured herself not to be in a private space with me. And even when we unavoidably were in the same room, meetings with her team and the rest of the senior staff, she never met my eyes. It had all annoyed me to no end.

My strength was incomparable to hers, so before she could register what was going on, she turned around and I pressed her against the wall.

"Hey!" I heard the breath whoosh out of her again at the impact, but I didn't care. I pulled the jacket down despite her protest, and then I pressed my body hard against hers.

"I've been in a bad mood the last week," I told her. "And your antics have only served to antagonize me even further."

"What antics?" she asked. "I just don't want to be here."

"Really?" I asked as I flung the jacket aside.

I had wanted to touch her breasts from the first moment I had watched them bounce around in that sinful dress of hers the very first night we met in the hotel. They were so full, they completely filled up the material, the swell peeking out at the sides, and that's when I knew I had been in trouble. I had come with my knives sharpened and irritated, but only after I left and in the frequent days later, did I realize that they had now been incredibly dull when relating to her. But not anymore. I would get what I wanted, and then I would put an end to this frivolous aggravation. I had always prided myself on being able to completely control my body and whatever desire it stirred up. But not this time. Not this time around with her, and it annoyed me to no end.

I wasted no time in pulling down her pants. Everything was stretchy and elastic, so they peeled off her without any hassle. However, she kept squirming and became even more restless, perhaps eager to leave, but the hand I had pressed solidly against her back wouldn't let her.

I parted her thighs once again hungry for her and then I went from behind towards her sex.

"Ah," she immediately cried out as my tongue slid in and licked her.

She attempted to jump out of my hold, but I grabbed her full ass holding her in place and went on.

"*Kane*," I heard the palm of her hands smack against the wall as she struggled for balance however, I didn't respond.

I kept eating her up as my hands kneaded the fullness of her ass and she couldn't contain it.

Eventually though, I needed more so I turned her around and parted her legs even further. Her hands went to her clit to massage the throbbing agitated bud, but I smacked it away and instead replaced it with my mouth. I sucked her hard and got my reward from the release that flowed onto the fingers I had slid into her.

Grabbing her hips, I licked my tongue as deeply as it

would go in her and then I rose to my feet.

She met my gaze, and I could see just how glassy they had become. She was wobbly, her eyes slightly unfocused and completely restless.

"Stop," she breathed but I smiled and kissed her, just as I slid two fingers into her.

I stared into her eyes and saw how she fought to keep them open as I fingerfucked in and out of her. She threw her arms around me then needing to hold on for dear life. Her hands began to rub all over my back and even further down till they grabbed my ass, and I felt my skin prickle with a warm sensation that I hadn't felt in so long,

My fingers went even faster inside her, and I watched as I began to completely unravel her. I couldn't however bear to hold her gaze anymore, so I turned her around and slammed my hips against hers.

"Ah," she breathed as she attempted to reach out for me once again, to hold me.

"Are you on birth control?" I asked.

At first, she didn't respond beyond incoherent as the pad of my middle finger stroked her clit. My rhythm was hard and fast, and it made her knees tremble.

I grabbed her and heard her gasp as I repeated the question.

"Yeah," she said, her hand going over mine. At first, she pressed harder and then she pulled away.

I couldn't resist reaching forward to kiss her jawline and tracing the kisses down her neck. I loved the taste of her skin, combined with steam and sweat and ultimately the feel of her breasts in my hands as I finally gave my attention to them. However, my dick was throbbing and my patience waning and so I reached down and parted her cheeks. Her entrance was soaking wet and pulsing with anticipation and I couldn't wait finally to be inside of her.

I grabbed my cock and then I began to slide it through her sex coating me with her release.

"Stop," she tried to say. I heard her and was sure that whatever had held her back previously was doing it again.

"You sure," I asked, the palm of my hand I pressed my cock even harder against her sex as I thrust my hips back and forth.

"*Ahh*," her fingers dug into the sides of my thighs and then my arm went around her waist to hold her in place. I could no longer wait but I would still give her one last chance to back out. I position the head of my cock at her entrance and then I circled it... watching her as she tried to catch her breath.

"No?" I asked and she swallowed. Before she could respond I pressed in just a little bit, and she melted into my arms.

"No?" I asked again and her head fell back in frustration.

"Just fuck me," she cried, and I was amused.

This unraveled side of her was amusing and thrilling to say the least. I didn't waste any further time anyway because feeling how she would completely sheathe me had been something that I couldn't get out of my mind. I slid in and thought of turning her around so that I could watch her eyes, but I couldn't. My own eyes shut tightly closed as I felt her walls expand and then contract around me, gripping me hungrily.

Up till then I had somewhat been able to control my excitement but not anymore. She was warm and so fucking tight that my knees went weak. And knowing it was her... just knowing it was her...

I went as deep as it was possible to go, and she cried out. As a consequence, I was certain that I was going to find scratches all over my body after this was done, however I didn't care.

"You feel so good," I whispered into her ears as I grabbed her breasts, and she responded by rolling her hips against me. My gaze lowered down to her thick curvaceous ass, and I couldn't wait to see it slamming against me as I railed her.

However, I wanted to savor every moment of this... to commit it to memory because knowing her I was almost certain that she would concoct some new moral reason in her mind for why this wasn't the best of decision. I on the other hand didn't give a fuck.

All I knew was that she was the first woman in probably forever that had made me come unhinged at just entering her. The pleasure was ethereal, soft but intense and with the promise of so much more to come.

"Fuck me," she cried out as she continued to writhe restlessly.

I obliged her, no longer able to drag this out any longer.

My hands went to hers and then I began to move. I began somewhat slowly to get the feel of her and then my pace began to increase. With every thrust she let out a little gasp, and it spurred me on as I slammed into her over and over again hitting the very core of her. I couldn't get enough. I lost control, my groans endless and the sounds reverberating off the tiled walls.

Her moans were like music to my ears and the contact of flesh against flesh... I committed every bit of this to memory. I fucked her until her legs began to tremble and then I was forced to stop because I could feel the pain of her grip.

I pulled out then, but she seemed even more pained. It

would have been amusing if I wasn't nearly losing half of my mind as well at the loss of contact.

But in no time, she was pushed back against the wall and then my hands went underneath her thighs to lift her up. She held onto me tightly and then she slanted her head to kiss me. I was momentarily lost in it at how sweet it was until she pulled away and began to position my cock at her entrance. We watched each other as she guided me in and then her eyes could no longer stay open. A long deep moan escaped her as I was completely sheathed all the way in and then her head fell back. I began to slide in and out of her once again, watching her every expression.

She clenched around me and breathed into my mouth, and I couldn't look away. She was mesmerizing in the way she kissed me in one minute and then threw her head back with a moan and bit down on her lips. She was absolutely wonderful. I didn't even realize that I took on a steady pace more than a faster one and I felt it deep in my bones. It wasn't about the chase, but the moment and I savored the electric sensations on my skin and the pleasure that surged through my body like wildfire.

We came together and at the long cry that escaped her lips I leaned forward and kissed her. She kissed me back even harder, and I continued to fuck her. I had planned to pull out but, in this moment, I didn't think I could even if a gun was held to my head.

She called out my name over and over as she spilled all around me and as I felt my seed fill her.

It was effortless and heated and intimate and eventually we collapsed onto each other, completely spent.

19

Lena

I ached everywhere. And yet I had never felt so good. I almost didn't want to separate from him... and so I held on under the pretense that I needed to be stable. Eventually, though, he began to move away, and I had no choice but to let go.

I gripped onto the faucet and focused on meeting his gaze, even though every part of me wanted to look anywhere but there.

"Are you okay?" he asked, and I nodded. I even managed to work up a smile.

"Why wouldn't I be?" I replied.

He gave me a peculiar look, and then I looked down to see the mess. It was arousing and unbelievable at the same time, and so damn sexy. I wanted to do it again on every surface in this goddamn apartment until I got him out of my system because as he pulled even further away from me, I could feel the guttural loss.

"Clean up," he said. "I'll be outside."

And with that, he left the stall. I was still more or less dressed, with my yoga pants and underwear puddled at my feet, and my shirt bunched around my shoulders. I couldn't possibly imagine how unattractive and ragged I looked right now. It frustrated and aggravated me that this was where my thoughts were going. I wanted to leave here immediately, so I didn't even bother with the shower, even though my clothes were wet and a mess. I couldn't exactly walk back to my hotel looking so ridiculous.

Eventually, I gave in and sighed as I completely stripped and turned on the faucet. The warm, heavy cascade was a remedy, to say the least, and pretty soon, as I explored the selection of shampoo and body wash, I came out smelling like a rose. I knew I could borrow something from him to wear and send him brand new replacements, so I wasn't too worried. My only concern was getting out of here as fast as possible and returning to my hotel.

When I got out of the stall, he was unsurprisingly nowhere to be found, so I headed over to the mirror. What I saw before me was a girl who was somewhere she wasn't supposed to be. But as I thought about how I had just been nearly fucked out of my mind; I couldn't help but shrug. All that ended well was well, and if I walked out of here with my head held high, then all would be fine. We had gotten what we wanted from each other. It had been a transaction, and nothing else, and no one had lost. This was what I told myself over and over until my hair was decently dried.

I grabbed my clothes and walked past his magnificent walk-in closet and into his bedroom. It was a perfect mix of warmth and darkness, both domineering and cozy at the same time. The wooden accents were polished luxurious oakwood, the sheets and carpet warm in varying shades of beige. There were no paintings here... very minimal color, and I could understand it. Even though the space was big, it was something of a sanctuary and needed to be as minimalist as possible to foster restfulness. I loved the room, but it most definitely wasn't mine.

I immediately saw him seated in a corner and turned to address him.

"Can you show me the washing machine and dryer?" I lifted my clothes. "I need to get these taken care of so that I can leave."

"No need," he replied as he set his phone down and then got up. He turned around to face me, and I really wished he hadn't. I truly wish he hadn't. He had only his towel wrapped around his waist, but he might as well not bother with wearing anything at all.

It was loose, riding incredibly low on his hips, and of course, that smooth smattering of hair and the bulge below reminded me explicitly of the dick that had just been inside of me. The dick I was still trying to recover from. I still felt wobbly. My strength was depleted, and although it was easy to see that I had extended too much emotional, physical, and mental energy on the same morning despite having no nourishment whatsoever besides water, I still understood and accepted, especially as I looked at him now, that the majority of my languidness had to do with how he had just fucked me mindless in the bathroom.

He was shameless, I had to say. Either that or he was just completely oblivious and selfish because how the fuck did he expect me to get my bearings when he looked like that and yet still faced me so blatantly? His skin was glistening once again, cleaned, oiled... veined... muscled. It was as though he was cut from marble, and I wanted to trace every dip and curve with my tongue.

"Lena," he called, and I finally pulled my eyes away to meet his. I should have been embarrassed because I was sure I had fallen into some sort of trance as I shamelessly ogled him, but I was past that now. He had turned my ass around and eaten me from behind. Any pretense of shyness now was just ridiculous.

"You can have any of my shirts and shorts from my closet," he said. "They're arranged in one section. Just look around and pick whatever you feel the most comfortable with."

Now he was offering me his clothes. I frowned because this was definitely not where I wanted this to go, and it was definitely not the idea that I wanted to have in my head.

"No need," I told him. "I don't need to wash my clothes. Just drying them quickly and heading home will be alright."

"Home?" He cocked his head, and it was then I remembered.

"Oh... I'm still living in a hotel. Still, they have a laundry service. It's excellent. I'm meant to send in my clothes to them this afternoon anyway, so it's great."

He gave me a look, ignored all my words, and walked past me and back to the closet. I sighed and wondered if I should even bother responding to him. The clothes weren't too wet, and even if they were, so what?

It was better to just leave now to maintain that anonymity and even awkwardness. I didn't want to wear his clothes, and I most definitely didn't want to engage in any light banter of any sort afterward. This wasn't even supposed to be happening... all of this was an error, and I wanted to remind myself of that even though it felt so unbelievably good.

"Do you want something to eat?" I heard him ask before me. His voice, though low and stoic, was sudden enough to make me jump. This space was big, and it was just the two of us. My hand remained against my chest. He gave me a look that was very unfriendly, most probably wondering why I was startled; however, I wasn't inclined to explain myself.

I thought of his request and decided that this time around I was going to stick to my admonition. I didn't need to remain here any longer. I had already broken too many rules.

"No need," I said. "I just want to head home." I watched as he reached for coffee and quietly began to brew it in the pot. Then he turned around to look at me.

"Why are you still here?" he asked, and I frowned.

"Don't I need a key of some sort to leave?" I asked, and he pulled out a stool as he took his seat at the island.

"No," he replied. "Only on your way up."

His hair was still damp, but it was brushed away from his face... sleek, shiny... fucking attractive. He had thrown on a t-shirt now and jogging pants, and yet he looked as though he had just walked off the fucking pages of a magazine.

I knew he was trouble. Diana had known it too, and I thought that I was prepared. I was sure that I had been prepared, but then here I am falling and making a fool of myself every day, and I was completely powerless to stop it. I watched him, and it was then that I got some insight into my deep, genuine dislike for him. He was brutish and pompous, but he couldn't be ignored by anyone, whether they liked him or hated him, and the same went for me. I had tried to ignore him, and I failed, so he was a threat to me. There was no way I could be comfortable around him, and yet he seemed not to care, not to be affected. I felt like I was the one being controlled, and he was just letting me believe that I was the one in control. I felt condescended to and scrutinized every moment I was in his presence, and he didn't even have to say a word. Or even look at me, for that matter. Right now, I was standing in the middle of his apartment, lost, and he sat there scrolling through his phone.

I might have as well not existed. Even a fly would have gotten more attention. Or perhaps he is just pretending and preferring to act as inhalant as you are? That troublesome voice came to my head again however I didn't care.

I truly didn't care. I was ready to leave, and so that was exactly what I did. Without engaging in further conversation with him, I headed to the foyer, changed my clothes, hung the towel on a hook by the side, and was ready to leave. I also found my phone on the gorgeous console by the wall, as well as my shoes neatly arranged at the entrance. I quickly put them on, and without a further word, I pulled the door open, shut it behind me, and just like that, I was gone. I heard the click of the door behind me but didn't stop to think. True, there was no need for us to be hostile with each other in this way, but it was the only way that made sense to me now. Any other way just felt like a mistake, and I couldn't care anymore, not until I was somewhat stable.

And he was right. Turned out, I didn't need any special keys to head down, but I was certain that without his permission, I would never be able to come up on my own. Soon, I arrived on the ground floor, and I was on my way in my damp clothes, headed back to my hotel. It would take about twenty minutes to reach there. It wasn't too far, but I didn't mind. I had had more than enough exercise today, but since I was going to need another shower anyway, there was no issue. Plus, the walk was sure to do me immeasurable good since I needed to completely get out of my head and think.

But life never went my way, especially regarding what I was supposed to be thinking about because just as I was exiting the lobby, I ran into the last person in the world that I wanted to see.

"Lena?" he called, and at first, I ignored the voice, even though it sounded familiar. But when he called again, it became virtually impossible to deny that I knew exactly who that was. And so, I froze, weighed my options, and knew that I would be completely stripped of my pride if I didn't respond. Forever. And so, I stopped and turned around.

Dylan stared at me from across the room, dressed in a blazer and slacks, while I basically looked like a wet dog. A wet, frivolous dog. He was my brother, alright, and for this reason, my shame could no longer be measured. Immediately, a humorless smile came to his face.

"This can't be real," he said as he began to approach.

I turned to face him, squared my shoulders, and brushed my hair behind me.

"What are you doing here?" he asked.

I stared at him and then shrugged.

"I was running in Central Park and ran into Kane."

"Kane? You ran into Kane?"

He was incredulous with wry amusement.

"Well, welcome to New York, dear sis, but Central Park's

quite big, so forgive me for thinking it peculiar that you ran into Kane. And I guess... it rained as well?"

His eyes ran down my appearance.

"What the hell is this? Are you... are you sleeping with Kane? Like, did you take a shower at his place, or did he just happen to dump a bucket of water on your head?"

I decided then that there was no point in listening to any of this. He could think and believe whatever he wanted, but I wasn't going to stay here and entertain it for a moment longer. People were beginning to stare at me as though I had broken into the place and had been caught stealing red-handed or something.

But before I left, I did have my own question.

"What are you doing here?" I asked. "Aren't you suing him?"

"I'm here to lobby for a settlement," he said without any shame, and I cocked an eyebrow. I started to leave then, but he caught my arm and stopped me.

"I was going to bring this to some kind of vote eventually with the other owners, but now that I've seen you here, I completely understand that I'll never win. You'll back him, won't you? He's completely bought your loyalty and opinion in every way."

"I understand that you're trying to annoy me," I said. "And it's working. So let go now before I lose my temper on you."

"I only speak the truth," he said but did let go of me. "I'll be sure to let the others know the reality of the situation."

"What others?" I asked. "And what situation? I can see you want to get sued again."

"Wait, you're threatening to sue me if I reveal this?"

"Reveal what?" I asked. "Did you see me in any compromising situation? Am I half-naked? I am in exercise attire, and because my hair is damp, you're jumping to ludicrous conclusions. One word about this, and you'll have two lawsuits to worry about."

After this, I turned around and exited the building.

20

Lena

"Lena, why did your relationship with your brother get so bad?" Diana asked.

I stood at the kitchen counter, her voice echoing through the speakers of the suite. I was pouring myself a very decadent drink that I had had no choice but to order the moment I had returned to my room. So far, and especially after the shower I had, my nerves were now stable, and I could think clearly. Somewhat. I drained the glass, refilled it, and then headed over to the seats by the window so that I could stare out and watch the city.

"It's been bad for years," I replied. "Actually, we've never really been close. We never had the chance to."

"How come? You two aren't far in age, are you?"

"No, we're not," I replied. "Just about four years, but we weren't raised the same way. I was more or less always with my parents, but he was being shipped away. In short, he grew up in boarding schools, so of course, he would completely take on the personality of the kids he met there.

I used to cut him some slack because of this. In our home, it always felt as though my parents had completely satisfied their curiosity about parenting with me and so wanted little, if anything at all, to do with him. It was the case with my mom, though I was sure, but my dad, not so much, since he was always just working."

"And so, you kind of grew up as strangers?" she asked, and I nodded.

I sighed again and continued to stare out of the window.

"I wish it weren't the case. I wish we were closer. I wish during the most difficult times of our lives; we had drawn strength from each other. Instead, we went our different ways, and now here we are, against each other's throats for no fucking reason."

She went silent.

"Any plans to rectify it?" she asked.

"Who knows," I replied.

"You could take this chance and back him up," she said. "When and if you and the others decide to go through with a vote, then you'll be on his side. A crucial first step."

"Yeah," I replied, now deep in thought as I contemplated her words.

"Alright," she said, life suddenly coming back into her voice. "Now that's out of the way. I need to know how you ended up in Kane's apartment dressed like that. Why was your hair freaking wet?"

I continued to stare out of the window. This I didn't really want to respond to, especially given the last time we talked about this, but how else was I to make sense of the struggle in my head?

"I ran into him at the park," I responded to her.

"And?" she asked.

"Well, I was in a bad mood and..."

"You went home with him?"

"Yeah," I set my glass down. "I know, I know, I wasn't going to do this... I wasn't going to cross any lines with him, but I couldn't-" I stopped myself; however, she urged me to carry on.

"You couldn't what?"

"I couldn't help it. It's not even just because of sex, it's just... him. Everything he represents... the courage, the confidence... I was going to leave his apartment, but then everything just got out of control."

"He kissed you?" she asked.

"Nope, I walked in on him in the shower. Actually, I went in... anyway, I just-"

"Why had you even gone to his apartment in the first place?" she asked. "I mean, how did it even come up, or do you two just have this kind of banter now?"

"No," I replied as my mind went back to what had actually happened. "I thought... I felt a bit gloomy because of my dad. And then I ran into him, and I just wanted to forget."

"I thought you used food for that," she said, and I laughed.

It was a long and hard one, and much needed.

"Yeah," I said. "I had to stop that habit and lose all the weight. Not going back there again. Plus, after our lunch a few days ago, it has been pure torment to get him out of my head."

"You mean his tongue?" she said and blushed red.

"Exactly."

"And today? You two finally went all the way, right? Tell me it was a disappointment, or else I will be jealous."

I shut my eyes, the pangs of our time in the shower stall

vividly coming to mind. I still felt quite weak in my bones, the satisfaction from our time together so intense that I knew it was going to be stuck in my mind for a while to come.

"I haven't had sex like that... ever," I told her. "And we were standing. Through it all. Well, he was standing; I was wrapped around him."

She laughed at this, and although it truly didn't seem to be doing me any benefit to talk like this to her, I didn't feel terrible about it. Perhaps if I let it out rather than bottling it up, it would dissipate and be easier to forget, along with the lightness we were speaking with now. The entire morning had been tense, and I decided that this was what I needed.

We spoke a bit more, and by the time we were done, my entire bottle of wine had nearly been emptied. I drank the rest from the bottle and crawled into bed, worried about how I had consumed it as though it was nothing. I was a lightweight, so the effects were already telling on me, and in no time, I was soundly asleep.

21

Kane

At the sound of my ringing phone, I wondered if she had returned. It had been so sudden, the way she had left, that although I had expected it, I had still not exactly expected her to leave in that way. But she had, and I had forced myself to continue on with my day as though she hadn't even shown up at the apartment at all. It had been a feat, especially since our time in the shower stall wasn't something that I could easily forget. But it had put me in a rare mood to actually take advantage of Sunday to relax, so when the incoming call came, I wasn't exactly thrilled.

But then, as I got up and headed over to the counter to pick up my phone, my heart skipped a beat at the thought that it was probably her.

I found, however, that it was from the concierge, and this made me wonder.

"Hello?"

"Mr. Lazarus?" the elderly concierge called.

"Harrison, how are you?"

"I'm doing great, Sir," he replied, and then he stopped briefly. "There is someone here to see you."

"Who?" I asked.

"Mercer," he said, and I cocked my head. This was Lena, or her surname, but they were one and the same. She was coming up again.

I wanted to speak to her, wondering why she didn't just come up, but then I changed my mind, refusing to give her any reason not to return to the apartment.

"Let her up," I said, and before Harrison could say another word, I ended the call.

In the time she had left, I had a quick breakfast, but now I couldn't help but wonder if it would make sense to start with some actual cooking in order to give her a reason or something to stay longer. However, the idea reeked of distasteful desperation that I wanted nothing to do with, so I instead returned to my couch and continued watching the car race. A little while later, the doorbell rang, followed by a knock, and I turned to the door.

I was very willing to taunt her for a bit and ignore her for a bit, but in the end, I got up and answered the door.

I didn't look through the peephole. I didn't think there was a need to, so when I pulled the door open and saw that instead of her, it was her distasteful brother, I didn't quite know what to think.

I stared at him, the smirk on his face, and I didn't move aside even when he sought to come in.

"What are you doing here?" I asked, and he smiled again.

"Guess who I ran into in the lobby," he responded, and I sighed. Of course, it was Lena he was referring to. No wonder he had used only the surname Mercer because otherwise, I might not have paid any attention whatsoever to him.

"What do you want?" I asked.

"You're not even going to offer me a drink or something?" he asked, trying to look inside, and I resisted the urge to push him out of the archway so that I could shut the door. I did inform him that I was going to, however.

"C'mon," he said. "I mean, I know I'm not my sister, but there has to be some sort of courtesy due to me since you're sleeping with her, no?"

I went silent, and he stared at me.

"I see why she came to New York," he said.

"I truly was wondering how and why you had been able to get her to come when she absolutely hadn't even considered it for months prior. I thought you had something on her, but now I see that wasn't the case at all. More like you had your thing inside her."

"I'm going to break your face if you don't watch your mouth," I said, and he made a face.

"Who are you mad at?" he asked. "It can't be yourself, so are you trying to tell me that you're offended on her behalf? Why?"

He stared at me, and then his eyes widened.

"Oh, are you two... are you two dating? Is this why you brought her in to side with you? You two are really romantically involved? You're not just hooking up? When the fuck did that happen?"

I almost threw a punch then, but he raised his hand and once again stopped the door from closing.

"Fine," he said. "Fine, I won't speak any more about that. But I do have to talk to you, though, about that exciting lawsuit brewing between us. So now, can I come in?"

"Say what you need to say and leave," I said. "Otherwise, this is surely going to make the lawsuit even more difficult for you."

He sighed then and lowered his head dramatically in defeat.

"You're right," he said. "It is hard for me. Immensely. And this is why I'm here. Let's agree that we both lashed out. Emotions were high, so you fired me. Things are not any better now, and we're both reasonable people, so let's get things back to where they were before. For the benefit, especially, of the company. Rumors are flying all around, employees are taking sides. It's a distraction and an unnecessary one. You were mad, I get it, but so was I, and it's been a while now, so what do you say? Water under the bridge?"

I looked at him and furrowed my brow deeply. He aggravated me, always had, especially with his propensity to take everything as a joke. But not anymore. Not this time, especially with the fact that he had seen Lena leaving my place, and so he was sure to use this as some sort of weapon against me if he even got a whiff that it was something I wanted to conceal. I knew that Lena didn't exactly want whatever was between us to be revealed, even to herself sometimes it felt like, but she especially didn't want it coming from her brother. But then again, I reminded myself that this moron before me was her brother and no one else, and so if she wanted to stop anything, they could sort it out. She was a big girl, and I was sure that she knew how to protect herself. However, I couldn't quite tell if they had actually seen each other, so I asked.

"Of course, I saw her," he said. "And I said hello. That was quite a shock for her because unlike you, she is astute enough to know that people finding out about this wouldn't bode too well for how people perceive your ability to run the company unbiasedly."

I almost let out a laugh then because truly, he had to be borderline insane.

"How do you come up with these ideas?" I asked and his face of nonchalance and willful stupidity briefly faded.

"What do you mean?" he asked.

"How does whether I'm sleeping with her or not have anything to do with my ability to run the company well or not?"

He looked at me incredulously.

"She's a member of the board?"

"So? She doesn't know her own mind? She doesn't have a brain?"

"She has emotions, and she's a woman?"

I stared at him.

"Meaning?"

He didn't speak, and I folded my arms around my chest.

"Meaning?" I asked.

"You know exactly what I mean. Of course, she's going to side with the person she's sleeping with. It's already happening."

To me, talking to him truly was a waste of time, and I couldn't believe that I was somehow being dragged into this.

"I don't want to have any more conversations with you, and I do not appreciate you coming over to my home. Our business stays in the office and nowhere else. And I sure as hell don't want you alluding to my personal life in any way or making wild claims that you have no evidence of."

“So, you aren't sleeping with her?”

"Did you catch us in any act of the sort?”

He smiled.

"You two are cut from the same cloth."

"What are you talking about?"

“She insinuated the same thing," he said, and I was slightly taken aback. But then I realized that it was a very valid argument he was making.

"Stop making wild claims, otherwise I'm going to sue you for libel and stop running away from your battles. You picked this fight, and I'm going to engage in it till the very end. And there are only two solutions. You lose, or I have mercy on you and decide to let it go. And let me assure you, the latter most definitely is not going to happen. So, you better get ready to shell out what little money you have left to cover the bills that are about to start incurring against you fast. I'm hoping to drag this out for the next two years. You were supposed to be working at the company until your equity vested anyway, so let's see how you navigate this.”

With this, I shut the door in his face and returned inside my apartment.

22

Lena

I really didn't want to be bothered about everything that had happened thus far in the day. It had been an eventful Sunday morning indeed, but now that I was rested and could think a bit more clearly, I couldn't help but wonder about how things had gone between Dylan and Kane.

I had been so thrown off by seeing him that it hadn't even occurred to me to question if those kind of visits to Kane were normal because if they were, then something was seriously off.

Whether personal issues were kept aside or not, the fact of the matter remained that they weren't on good terms. And even if it was all for show, there was no way that this kind of visit to his apartment was normal. Or perhaps he had specifically come to see him for something else? The lawsuit, for instance. Throughout the week, that had been the topic of discussion everywhere. I was even surprised that it had somehow leaked, given the fact that it was supposed to be an internal affair. But I had been too busy creating my expansion plan to worry about any of this.

But now that it was the weekend and the hours had slowed down, I really wanted to know what was happening. I had his phone number, but it wasn't for contacting him at leisure for information. It was strictly for business. But then, this was business, wasn't it? And I had already crossed quite a number of lines, hadn't I?

It was hard to ignore this attention as I had a multitude of work to handle for my scents business in LA. Currently, a photoshoot had been commissioned for a new scent I had spent the last eight months on. It would most probably be the last one I would be launching in LA.

I felt a wave of sadness come over me, or perhaps it was simply nostalgia setting in. Regardless of what it was, I returned to approving the photos and then placed calls to the needed workers to arrange the dismantling of the current office.

However, just before I did, I couldn't help but be skeptical. The proposal hadn't been approved by the board at all, yet I was already fixated on moving my entire life and business. The thing was, after spending the week here in New York, I realized that it was the exact change I needed, the next step that made sense. So, I truly didn't want to go back anymore.

But I didn't have to completely get rid of the staff and office in LA either. I could simply downsize if it was needed, but I really didn't have to tamper with a system that I had spent years trying to get to work absolutely seamlessly for me. So, I let go of that for the meantime and got up.

This hotel suite had a balcony that offered surreal views, so after making myself another cup of tea, I headed out to take in the night view. It was slightly chilly, but a cardigan thrown across my shoulders resolved this issue.

I thought about the very current shaky state of my life, and then I thought about him. Reaching out was the last thing I wanted to do, but once again, I gave in. He answered immediately, as though his phone had been close at hand, and it startled me slightly because I hadn't actually expected him to answer.

"Hello?" he asked, and I responded in kind.

"Hello?"

"I, uh..." I began, but then couldn't recall if he even knew who was talking or not. Perhaps he didn't have my phone number.

"This is Lena," I said.

"I know," he replied. "What is it?"

"Oh, I, uh..." I decided to just go straight to the point. "My brother," I said. "Did you see him? I met him in your lobby on my way out."

"I did," he replied. "He came up."

"Did he demand something?" I asked. "Or is it usual for him to visit you?"

"I was as shocked as you were," he said calmly.

"Oh," I said.

I wanted him to respond to my earlier question of whether my brother had demanded something, but I really didn't want to repeat it, so I waited. Pretty soon, the silence got awkward.

"Alright," I said. "Goodnight."

"Goodnight," he said and ended the call. I was left

staring at the phone, almost speechless. But what else did I expect? In fact, it was preferred. But as I returned to my room, I couldn't help but feel unhappy.

I wondered if we would ever be somewhat friendly to each other. Not that I wanted to, but it just truly made me wonder. Beyond the electric, physical attraction we have for each other, there was really no other rapport I felt with him. Or maybe it was because I had been closed off to it from the beginning. Maybe because he had been closed off to it from the start. He wasn't exactly my favorite person in the world, but could we be civil, somewhat?

I considered this over and over again until I eventually decided that for both of us to come out of it unscathed, things were perhaps better left the way they currently are.

The next Monday morning at the office, all was abuzz. I could feel it as I came in and ran into some of the employees. It was hard to miss the suddenly lowered tones of speaking, the whispered conversations, and the stares. I was sure it had to do with the ongoing wrongful termination suit filed by Dylan against Kane, and of course, the board meeting that would be taking place just before lunch. I didn't even know how they had gotten wind of this, as it had been an internal request sent by Kane.

I was sure then that the leak came from the assistants and secretaries, but there were four of them, so you couldn't exactly pinpoint anyone. I didn't care as I continued on with preparing my project expansion with my team since it was sure to be discussed at the meeting.

About half an hour before, however, there was a knock on my door. Usually, it would be my secretary handling these, but he had been drafted to assist the team, so I was seated alone, going through the compiled data. We still needed a bit more time to put things together, but I had been researching this possibility for years on my own, so there was very little I missed or wasn't informed about.

"Come in," I answered, and a few seconds later, the door was pushed open. I held my breath without even realizing it, and only when the visitor came fully into view and I saw that it was my brother, did I release my breath.

Such a disappointment, I had secretly hoped it was Kane. My heart was beating ever so slightly faster, and my stomach became warm and fuzzy, especially with the sharp reminders of how Kane and I had been in that shower stall just a day earlier. After our first encounter together, I was able to convince myself that I could get it out of my mind, that I could get him out of my mind. But as the night wore on and I found myself so aroused that I could barely sleep, I realized that it would not be so easy to forget after all.

And now, it was Monday, and I had skipped breakfast. Yet, what I realized I had a craving for was him. Even just a sight, I couldn't quite describe what it was, but I wanted to see him looking into my eyes. I wanted to see if I could read anything into it, if there would be a change in the way we interacted with each other. I didn't really want this to happen, but I was so curious that it was beginning to physically hurt.

"What is it?" I asked as I returned my attention to my work, and he made a sound.

"Well, good morning to you too, Sis," he said as he pulled the chair out before my desk and took his seat. I lifted my gaze then and stared at him.

When he still didn't speak and instead maintained that silly smile on his face, I grew impatient.

"What do you want?" I asked, and he shook his head and straightened.

"I thought you'd call me," he said. "After our run-in on Sunday."

"Why would I call you?" I asked, and he genuinely seemed surprised.

"You're really not concerned that I saw you at Kane's place?"

I leaned back in my chair.

"I'm sorry, is it off-limits to be at Kane's place? What does that have to do with you?"

"Your staff is worried that rumors are going to spread," he said, and I smiled.

"What rumors? That I'm sleeping with Kane? Well, if I hear something that ridiculous, I'll know exactly who it came from, won't I?"

I picked up my pen again while he stayed silent.

"Back me in today's meeting," he said, and I sighed in relief because finally, it was clear why he was here.

"On what grounds?" I asked, and his smile was dry.

"The fact that I'm your brother should be enough grounds, but since that clearly doesn't mean anything to you, then on the grounds that Kane firing me should be unacceptable."

"Why?" I asked as I worked. "He's the CEO, he has the power to fire or hire anyone he wants."

"So, you're not going to back me?" he asked, and I gave him a direct answer.

"No, I'm going to back whoever has the best ideas."

"So... does that mean your project has been approved then? You won't need approval by the board?"

I lifted my head then to look at him.

"Is that why you're here?" I asked. "To get me to back you by promising to back me?"

"It's a fair trade, Sis, isn't it?" he asked, and I replied,

"Dylan, I really have no interest in internal politics. And I have nothing against you, nor will I sway towards Kane's side for any personal reason. Whatever is said at the meeting, I'll take it into consideration, and then I'll make an informed decision as needed."

He stared at me.

"I'm asking that your decision be swayed in my favor," he said. "Because I'm your brother."

I looked at him, however, I didn't have anything I wanted to say at the time, so I returned my attention to my work.

"Do we have an agreement?" he asked.

However, I still didn't respond.

"We don't know yet what matters will be discussed first," he said. "So, saying anything now will not work in either of our favors."

I decided upon my response then.

"I'm not swaying anything in anyone's favor. I'll hear all the facts presented and make my decision as appropriate."

He looked at me, gave a wry smile, and rose to his feet.

I couldn't help but note how out of place the chair was as he left, and how he had almost slammed the door on his way out if not for the fact that it was quite heavy.

I knew what he was asking me, and I truly had no intention of being involved in this thing that was brewing between him and Kane. This was a business that we were in charge of running, and the more I thought about it, the more I thought about how difficult it must have been all these years for both Kane and our fathers to build the company to where it was. It annoyed me that we were the ones now taking it lightly, especially Dylan. So, truly, I had no shred of sympathy for him.

Kane was obviously trying to punish him. He wasn't going to lose his equity but rather playtime. And maybe afterwards when he was reinstated, he'd learn some responsibility.

23

Kane

This time around, everyone appeared on time. My sister, who had been on some sort of leave, was finally present, and so was Dylan and his lawyer. The only person who ran a few seconds late was Lena, but this was easy to ignore when she appeared nearly out of breath. It was obvious that she had probably lost her way on her way here or been held back by something or the other. I didn't mind. I almost couldn't take my eyes off her as she settled down. Unfortunately for me, Dylan saw this as his opportunity to bring it up.

"I guess she doesn't get to be fired because she was late to the meeting, does she?" he shared a smile with his lawyer as my attention turned to her.

"No external parties can attend this meeting," I said.

"Harold is my lawyer."

"And I don't give a fuck," I cursed harshly, and the room went silent.

"It's against the rules," I said. "And I know you don't

know this because you haven't read the bylaws of this company, but-"

"Actually," the idiot lawyer interrupted me. "An external party can be privy when an invitation is extended by a member of the board."

I turned towards the idiot.

"Just extended?" I asked, and he stared at me. I dared him to repeat that lie.

He lowered his head; however, I wasn't going to let him go.

"Just extended," I asked again, and probably not one to run from a fight, he responded.

"Extended and agreed upon by the other members," he added, and I gave him a straight look. He got up then, but before he could take his leave, Dylan stopped him.

"I guess this is it then," he said. "We can have the first official vote of the meeting."

The room went silent while I set my pen down. I was fuming as this level of stupidity felt like nothing but wasted precious time to me. Still, I couldn't outrightly reject his request, so I allowed it. Plus, I knew what he was doing. I had thought it over and over, and now that he had come up with such a brilliant solution, I was almost impressed. By taking a vote against something so inconsequential and seeing which side his sister would sway to. He was trying to see just what she would do, and in all honesty, so did I before the stakes became much higher.

My sister was the first to raise her hand. I nearly rolled my eyes then, but instead, I stared directly at her, and she did the same to me.

"I think he should stay," she said. "After all, he's here to protect Dylan's interests, which are currently being severely threatened by you."

Of course.

Sighing, I turned to the next person, but Dylan interjected.

"I think I should stay out of this one," he said since I'm the subject of the vote. "This way there's no tie.".

I looked at him, and then I moved over to Lena.

She was sitting just off to my side, a few seats away. However, for the first few seconds, I forgot whatever the hell I had wanted to say.

I knew she was beautiful; it was an established fact in my brain already. However, there was something about the way she looked this morning that literally stopped me dead in my tracks. I had seen her when she'd come in, but I had barely given her a once-over. But now, as I stared directly at her and her steely green eyes held my gaze, my thoughts went, "Shit".

She had her hair tied behind her today and wore deep red lipstick. There was almost no makeup on her face, which made the color of her lips even more striking against her pale skin and dark hair. She wore a soft blue blouse, which, though low on her shoulders, had quite puffy sleeves. The exposed skin of her shoulders was all that was needed to toss the entire meeting out of my mind and instead take my focus back to our time in my shower stall. I hadn't been able to keep it out of my mind throughout the weekend, and every time I walked back into that stall for whatever reason, the memory hit hard like a train.

"I, um..." she began, and then she turned to look at her brother. She stared at him for a while and sighed.

I knew what she was going to say then, so I turned away and opened the folder on my desk.

"If he truly feels that the lawyer being present will benefit him, then I see no problem with it," she said. "He's bound by attorney-client privilege anyway, so I don't think we have much to worry about."

"You don't have anything to worry about," the man said from across the room. However, she ignored him and opened her file as well.

I knew it was what she was going to say, but it didn't make the fact that she did say it any less annoying. It took a little while to regain my bearings, but I didn't even have to bother about carrying on with the meeting because Kate soon addressed her.

"We haven't officially ever met, have we?" she asked, but Lena didn't respond. Not until her name was called and she was addressed properly.

"Miss Mercer?"

She lifted her gaze then.

"No, we haven't," she said. And that was it. I began with the agenda for the day.

"As you're all aware by now, Lena proposed an expansion project. The offer on the table before this was for us to buy her company in order to free her up to be able to engage in the operations of this one since she is a majority shareholder. However, she came up with what I personally think is a better idea and will be of greater benefit to Standard Rock in the long run."

"To keep things short, I'm sure you all have read over the proposal which was sent last week. I told her to put on a brief presentation, which will enable us to better understand her plans for the project and her vision, and that way we can make a better decision."

After this, she started to rise to her feet, but Dylan interrupted rudely, as always.

"Since she has to give an entire presentation, then why not discuss the issue of my reinstatement first?"

I sighed, but before I could respond, Lena did.

"Sure, we can do that," she said and sat back down. I was about to counter this, but I knew that he would cry foul otherwise, so I gave in.

"Sure," I said. "Go ahead."

His lawyer addressed me.

'We've been trying to get you to agree to a settlement. As these are internal matters, we don't see how it can benefit either Standard Rock or you all individually if this matter proceeds the way it is going and eventually makes it to court. It will be an arduous battle and will deplete plenty of resources that can be better utilized elsewhere.'"

I stared at the stubby man.

"So, you're here to plead on his behalf?"

"I'm not pleading," Dylan said, and I gave him a look that visibly showed my annoyance. To say it was unsatisfactory was an understatement.

"Not to plead," he said and brought out a folder, which my assistant behind got up and brought over to me.

"These are our terms, and we think that they are mighty favorable."

I received the folder and began to look through the document.

"Publicly dispelling any rumors that he was fired in the first place with an internal memo issued out to all employees?"

"Yes," his lawyer replied. "This will help to repair Mr. Mercer's tarnished reputation."

"Tarnished?" I raised a brow as I kept reading.

"Yes," the lawyer said, and I shook my head.

"In exchange for this, we're willing to drop the damages claim so that all things can become amicable once again, and we can proceed with business as usual."

I continued to look through it, almost amused, and then I pushed it aside.

"I hear you," I said. "But what's in it for me?"

The room went silent until Kate let out a low laugh.

"Kane, let it go. He didn't embezzle any money or start a fire. He was late for one meeting. I wasn't here either."

At her words, I went silent, knowing that I was about to lose control of my temper.

Eventually, I was able to regain control, so I looked around the room and initiated the voting.

"All in favor of restoring Dylan Mercer," I called, and my sister put up her hand, much to Dylan's wide-grinned glee. Soon enough, however, that smile began to falter. I turned and saw that Lena had kept her hand down and was staring straight at him, completely unapologetic.

"Are you serious?" he called, but she didn't respond.

"Lena!" He raised his voice, and I turned to face him.

"Currently, you're not eligible to be reinstated in this company for a year. I've replaced you with appropriate staff, so your contributions and interruptions are no longer needed."

"What?" He interrupted me, but I kept going.

"Any more of these antics from you, and it will be extended by an additional month."

At this point, I wanted to end the meeting outright, but

Lena's proposal was too important, and the decision to make was one that would allow us to move forward. Dylan's lawyer took his leave, while Dylan remained, and Lena began her presentation. She briefly went through the materials she had prepared, proposed budget, and first products. It took all of fifteen minutes, and by the time she was done, I was convinced that it was indeed a viable proposal. I had been looking for a way to expand in this way, but this hadn't come to mind with fragrance, so I was incredibly intrigued.

At the end, however, she rose to her feet, and I looked at the other two board members present. This was going to be difficult since I didn't kiss Dylan's ass, but after what I had just heard from Lena, I was more than willing to give it a go.

"The offer to buy her company is off the table, and in return, we get her experience and contribution in this field. All not in favor of her joining, please raise your hand."

The results were expected. Kate had thrown questions at her throughout the entire presentation, but Lena had kept her cool and eloquently explained how this would benefit us. However, Kate's hand went up as well as Dylan's, and the answer was clear. I was somewhat amused.

"She's not allowed to vote, right? Just like Dylan wasn't allowed."

"Majority wins," I said and folded the file. Then, without any further word, I rose to my feet, grabbed my files, and left the room.

24

Lena

I understood now what he had been dealing with and why he hadn't even hesitated for even a little bit in firing Dylan. Having to do serious business with these kinds of people sure had to be a great waste of time and energy, and it made me truly wonder what our fathers had been thinking by leaving each of us an equal share of the company.

Without a word, I got up as well, surprised that Dylan hadn't brought up meeting me at Kane's apartment. Somehow, though, I knew it was going to come back to bite me in the ass, so I began to exit the room. But then he stopped me with a call from across.

"You really couldn't back me up?" he asked, and I turned around to see both him and Kate staring at me.

"You didn't need my vote," I told him. "With the both of you, wasn't the outcome already decided?"

He gave me a dark look, but I ignored it and walked away.

I was already stressed and exhausted from all the work I'd put in, but I didn't quite let myself feel anything until I had returned to my office. When I got there, I took my seat and looked around. If the project hadn't been approved, then was there any need to be here?

I felt quite lost, and it was the exact feeling that I had wanted to get away from in Los Angeles. But now that it was coming to this and my back was being pushed against the wall, I didn't even know if I wanted to fight. I looked across all the files on my desk and couldn't help but recall all the work put into bringing it together. It was aggravating that those two had shut it down like that, but it was to be expected.

Yet, despite knowing all week long that things could happen like this, I had still gone on anyway and refused to stop. That was because I enjoyed every bit of what we were discovering and what we were trying to put together. The project was massive, but now I was no longer intimidated by what it was but excited by what it could be. With this thought in mind and my excitement somewhat coming to life again, I rose to my feet and headed over to Kane's office.

This project wasn't dead. I suspected he felt the same way, but I needed his confirmation. So, even though I really didn't want to deal with any board members for the day, I started to rise to my feet. However, just before I could walk around the desk, there was a knock on my door. I had many speculations as to who it was. It could truly be any number of people, but as my secretary came in to inform me, I realized that at this moment, and even though I was reluctant to admit it, there was only one person I wished was at the door.

"Miss Mercer?" he greeted, and I found myself holding my breath.

"Mrs. Lloyd is here to see you." I was a bit stumped by the name, wondering who this was, but he soon explained when he saw my confusion.

"Kate Lazarus," he said. "She's the CEO's sister."

I had never cared to notice this before, but now I had to take a double look at her to see if she in any way resembled Kane. I found a few minutes later that they absolutely did not, especially since the sterling reviews about him had never quite extended to her, both managerially and otherwise. Still, she was here, and although I didn't expect her intentions to be anywhere near positive or even civil at worst, I admonished myself to be as accommodating as possible so that this mental maze of a day for me could hurry towards its finish line.

"Lena," she called as soon as she came in with her heels. She was also tall like Kane, and so one couldn't help but feel dominated when in her presence, but not me.

"Have a seat," I ignored her casual call of my name when I was certain that I had never exchanged two words with her or even seen her in person before now. Maybe from across a room during one of our family gatherings, but definitely not this up close and personal.

"I brought a gift," she said, and my gaze lowered to the pretty blue and white mug in her hand.

"You didn't have to," I said dryly as I stared at it, and she responded.

"Yes, I did. I should have welcomed you about a week ago, but as you well know, I had to take a leave of absence." I watched her, still incredibly suspicious as to what this visit and her gift actually entailed.

She took her seat and then she smiled after pushing the box towards me.

"The presentation you shared today was brilliant," she said. "Anyone with even half a brain would approve it. It's the best expansion plan for anything since the home division was established."

"So, my question for you is, why wouldn't you just support your brother's reinstatement so that you could do whatever you want? You've turned down a buyout deal, and your project is being rejected. What was so heavy about lifting your hand?"

I smiled at her words.

"What you're seeing right now, and what Kane is fighting about, is insubordination and not his employment. You should know this since you ran the company longer with him," I said.

She stared at me.

"So, you're open to letting Kane control you?"

"He's the CEO!" I almost yelled at her. "There's a reason why there is a CEO, despite the fact that we all have an equal stake."

With a smile, she leaned back in her chair, continuing to watch me.

"What will it take?" she asked me. "What will it take for you to back your brother so that we can put this whole thing to rest? As a result, of course, you get your expansion and everyone's happy."

I sighed as I stared at her.

"Why are you discussing this with me and not Kane?"

I was surprised by her question.

"What do you mean?"

"What do you mean by 'what do I mean'?" She watched me, then smiled.

"Are you sleeping with him, by any chance?"

I was so stunned by this question that my blood froze over. Yet, I didn't react. I pleaded with myself not to react until I could completely regain my senses and composure.

"That, Kate, is a very rude question to ask."

"You're right," she said. "It does cross the line, but I see no other explanation."

I didn't respond.

"Please leave," I told her. "You've definitely crossed my line today."

"Sure," she said and rose to her feet.

"I'm guessing you've also heard about the dividends proposal that we put forward and was rejected. To be honest, at first, I thought he was trying to bring you in to vote so that someone could be on his side, but I didn't exactly expect you to jump to it the moment you arrived."

"Are his objections bad?" I asked. "He's trying to run the company, and you two are standing in his way. The dividend increases that you're oh so interested in are a result of his efforts-"

"I'm not here to hear you kiss his ass," she said. "I'm just here to let you know that we can all serve each other's interests. We don't necessarily need to clash heads. I know... if you ended up sleeping with him, you might think that having him on your side is all you need, but it's nothing. It's 50-50, and so no one moves forward. I know you're a smart woman. I've heard of your business efforts back in LA. I did think the offer made to buy your company was a bit much but seeing you actually coming up with a way to expand Standard Rock here is more acceptable. But you have to root for the right team."

She watched me, and then she smiled.

"Enjoy your gift," she said, and there she went on her way.

I remained seated for the longest time after she left. I expected this much. She had come to upset and rile me up, or maybe she had just come to speak her mind. But whatever it was, I couldn't lose my cool. However, I did want to speak to Kane because suddenly being here and amidst these vipers was no longer a transition that seemed appealing.

25

Kane

I had expected her to come to the office sooner or later. I just didn't know exactly what topic of complaint she would be coming in for. There were many, and I had pushed them out of my mind in the meantime so that I could focus on the other pressing matters. But eventually, when her visit was announced, I was more than ready to give her my attention. I pushed my files aside as she entered and took a seat before me. It was a first, I realized, her sitting down in my office, ready to have a conversation, and I couldn't quite recall the last time I had paid rapt attention to someone who stopped by. Usually, I would be impatient, giving them the least attention possible so that they could be prompt with whatever they had come for and be on their way.

But not this time.

"Ready to head back to LA?" I asked, and she gave me a peculiar look.

"I'm to head back now?" she asked. "Because the proposal was rejected."

"No, I'm asking if you'd want to head back now after seeing all the bullshit that's going on."

She smiled.

"To be honest, it's a bit aggravating and truly a bitter pill to have to swallow when I think of it, but I really didn't expect anything less. Anyway, that's part of the reason I'm here... Is the project really dead because it wasn't received well, or is this just a roadblock?"

"It's a nuisance," I replied. "But we'll go ahead regardless. Nothing either of them can do to stop it beyond a lawsuit."

"What if they vote you out?"

"Well, that's the only way they're going to take control out of my hands. So as long as voting doesn't come to a tie or three against one, then I should be fine."

Her gaze lowered slightly, and I could almost predict exactly what she was going to ask.

"You're not worried that I'm not going to vote in your favor when the time comes?" she asked.

I'm amused.

“I'm not a moron. Up until now, I've chosen to ignore a lot of things because I understood I was walking a slippery slope, so I didn't allow conversations that could lead to stripping me of my position to come up."

"And now you do because I’m here?"

I stared at her.

"I can't say I'm as cautious."

"Hmm," she replied, her gaze lowering in contemplation.

"What if I side with them?"

"Then you side with them," I said, and she smiled.

"I'm curious as to why?"

"What is it?" I asked, and she replied,

"They all think I'm colluding with you and that whatever comes up, I'll always take your side."

"That's not true," I said. "For example, what happened this morning."

"Doesn't matter what they think," I said. "The only way I think we can solve all this animosity and anonymity is for us to actually work on our personal relationships with each other. I mean, how did it get so bad?"

"Kate's husband used to work here," I told her. For a moment, I hesitated in going any further, but I decided to mention it so that she could get a bit of understanding about where we were all coming from, in case she wasn't already aware.

"He joined the company after they got married, and then I joined. Since he was significantly older than me, they expected my father to focus more on him, giving him responsibilities and moving him up the ranks. But as time went on, it became clear that he wasn't performing well. So, Kate decided to join the company herself. However, even then, my father didn't acknowledge them much."

"For a while, I was bothered by this because, despite not being the best of friends, she is still my sister, and I couldn't help but be concerned about her. I confronted my father and warned him that he was creating a rift between us. His response was that he didn't care because he wasn't doing it because she was his daughter or because her husband wasn't his kin. He claimed it was because they were mediocre and didn't know how to operate the business without clear instructions from me, and that was his criteria for choosing who to acknowledge."

"Did she believe you?" Lena asked.

"Of course not," I replied. "Well, I didn't try to clarify things after she confronted me and refused to listen. But during our gatherings, it became a huge problem, and my father made it clear."

"That's how our relationship deteriorated. Today, I'm closer to most of the employees than her."

Lena then asked about Kate's husband, and I informed her that he quit and found another job that required him to travel extensively, so he's rarely here.

She nodded in response, and I watched her. I didn't expect her to share her own side of the story about her relationship with her father, but I waited a few seconds to give her the opportunity. When she didn't, I was ready to return to work.

"Did you want something in particular?" I asked, and she lifted her gaze to meet mine.

I expected her to say no and continue on her way, but instead, she observed me for a moment and then nodded.

"Yeah, I want to find out what my next step will be. Do I still have a job offer, or should I completely back off in the meantime until everything is resolved?"

"Of course, you should stay," I replied. "Keep working as needed. Their approval only releases funding, and I'll guarantee that happens in the end. It doesn't stop us now from making all the preliminary preparations."

She stared at me, and I could tell something was seriously gnawing at her.

"What is it?" I asked, and I could see her hesitate to speak. Eventually, though, she did, and I empathized with her concern.

"Are you really sure about my expansion plan for this project, regardless of their approval or not?" she asked.

"I wouldn't be wasting either your time or mine if I weren't," I replied. "It's something I've always considered but could never quite find the time or talent to handle. But now that you're here, I am more than delighted to hand it over to you."

She looked as though she didn't believe me, but then, without me having to ask, she rose to her feet and prepared to leave.

"I'll keep all this in mind," she said, and I nodded in agreement.

I watched her leave, and as she did, something came to mind—an invitation I had received to an engagement party that I usually would have had no business attending. But as I looked at her curves and felt the desire to see her beyond this stiff and tense work atmosphere, I understood that I wanted nothing more than that.

'If I just asked her outright, she might never have responded, but perhaps through an invitation, she would consider it,' I thought.

"What are you doing Thursday evening?" I asked Lena. "Do you have any plans?"

She turned around to look at me, surprised by the sudden question.

"I don't know yet," she replied. "Why? Is there something happening here?"

I noticed her emphasis on the word "here," indicating her desire to keep things strictly business between us.

"I'd like to introduce you to the city a bit more, specifically the social scene. I rarely go out, but once in a while, I receive rare invitations like tonight or on Thursday. A friend of mine is getting engaged, and I agreed to attend. Want to come along?"

"Come along or come with you?" she asked, and once again the distinction she wanted made was very clear.

"Whichever suits you," I replied. Without even waiting for a response this time, I went straight back to work.

26

Lena

"So... are you going to attend?" Diana asked.

"He said, 'Whichever suits me best.' And neither of them suits me."

"So, you're not going to attend?"

"Nope, I'm going apartment hunting, and I imagine I'll be famished at the end."

"Oh," Diana said. "Alright. Valid-ish excuse, even though I know you being tired is a stretch."

I didn't respond to this. Instead, I silently sorted out my laundry to hand over to the hotel services.

"So, are you two on friendly terms now?" Diana asked, and I found myself stopping immediately.

At first, I was appalled by the question, but her extended explanation made me thoroughly think about it.

"You two seem to be on the same side, as opposed to your brother and his sister," she continued.

"Hmm," I said. "We kind of are, and we kind of aren't."

"What does that mean?"

"We're quite professional and astute when it comes to business and logical interaction, but then anything personal, and both of our defenses come up."

"You mean the walls come up," she said, and once again, I had to admit that she was right.

"Exactly."

"Why do you think this is?" she asked.

"I don't know," I replied as I pondered on the question. "The thing is, I don't want any sort of relationship with him, especially since my memory of him back then remains intact and aggravating. That sealed the fate for any future we could have together."

"But so far? Is he a dick?" she asked.

I was amused.

"Let's just say he's a logical dick."

"As opposed to?"

"An unreasonable one. Dylan's an unreasonable dick. Definitely can't be attracted to that."

"Also, he's your brother, but that's irrelevant, of course," she added. I smiled.

"I'm going to visit you during one of the upcoming weekends as soon as your place is ready, so keep that in mind. I'll be your first guest. Well, of course, that's if Mr. CEO doesn't christen the place before I get there."

"I'm having so much trouble keeping my head screwed on straight because of you," I told her.

"What?" She sounded appalled. "How?"

"Your comments keep putting the worst of ideas in my head, and they don't leave."

"Well, despite all your inner torment, it seems as though you're having a blast-"

"I'm hanging up," I told her, and before she could say

anything else, I ended the call.

Today felt like a Friday evening, though it was a Thursday, and it almost made me want to take the following day off so that I could truly begin to settle down in the city. From what I heard, finding an apartment here was going to be quite a struggle, and if I was to stay for long, then I had to settle in and start putting down some sort of roots.

I thought of my phone call with Diana, and as usual, all she had said about Kane occupied my mind as I went around the hotel suite, arranging the pile of scattered clothes and toiletries I had thrown about and ignored for the better part of the last four days while trying to get to work on time.

Was I really not going to accept his invitation and completely ignore him? This was sure to send a clear message, and that was the fact that I didn't exactly want to be fraternizing with him. I was reluctant, but it was probably for the best.

My alternative plan to order in some pizza, wash it down with some wine, and watch a movie sounded pretty good. So, after taking a long and invigorating bath, I wrapped myself up in a robe, ordered my pizza, and started searching for a movie. It came much quicker than I expected, which was a welcome relief from trying to find one thing to watch from the hundred available.

My hair was clumped together and damp, forcing me to pull the towel wrapped around it away as I hurried over. I was naked underneath my robe, but a quick tightening of the lapels, and I was decent enough.

"Thank you," I said happily as I pulled the door open, ready to swipe with my card. What I soon found, however, was that there was no pizza and no delivery boy. Standing there was a dangerously looking Kane with his bowtie loosened around his collar and his expression far from happy. My heart skipped several beats.

I instantly became self-conscious, pulling the already closed robe even tighter together, especially as his gaze ran down my body.

"W-what are you doing here?" I asked.

"I extended an invitation to you," he said, and I felt somewhat sheepish.

"Well, I didn't accept it," I said. "It was just an invitation." I met his gaze and internally felt sorry in case he had truly expected me, but that was as much politeness as I was going to expend for the evening.

"I'm expecting someone," I said and tried to work up a smile. "Goodnight." I tried to close the door, but his hand shot out to stop it.

"Who are you expecting?" he asked, coming even closer, and it was then I smelled the slight hint of alcohol on his breath.

"You've been drinking?" I asked, even though he seemed immensely coherent, and his gaze was clear.

"It was a party," he replied and somehow found his way in. I had no choice but to shut the door and turned around to try and get him out.

"You shouldn't be here," I said, and he turned around to face me.

"Why?" he asked, and annoyingly, it took me quite a while to come up with a response.

"Because it's my personal space, and I need to rest."

He stared at me, and I stared back.

"Good enough reason for you?" I asked, and he sent a devilish smirk before beginning to approach me.

I fully noticed then just how attractive he looked tonight. He always looked so polished and put together, and the same was the case tonight, but with a twist. The loose collar and dangling tie and the suede of his tuxedo presented him in such a devastatingly and sexually suggestive manner that I understood then that I was in trouble. The night could easily go a very different way from what I had planned, and unless there was some sort of interruption or the other to smack me in the head enough to refuse, I knew that my robe was going to come undone, most probably by my own doing.

I stared at him.

"You need to leave."

"Why?" he asked. "You don't want me here?"

"I don't," I replied.

"Why?" he asked, and I was a bit taken aback by this line of questioning.

He was different from how he usually was. He was usually curt and somewhat abrasive, but tonight it seemed like he had all the time in the world. Maybe he did, and had invited me out as a result, and yet I had turned him down. My emotions were a mix between satisfaction and a slight guilt.

Shaking off this mental distraction, I thought of what I had intended to say.

"Well, I have food coming and I have to pick a movie," I told him. "So... that's quite the amount of work."

He smiled softly.

"It is indeed." And then he stopped and looked towards my bed, and to my surprise, he nodded and then headed over to sit on it.

"Sounds like a great plan. Much better than the party I was at."

"You seem to have enjoyed yourself," I pointed out, and he smiled again. Then he took off his jacket and flung it across the room. To my surprise, it landed on the couch by the window, and I couldn't help but be impressed.

"That's a solid throw," I said, and he nodded. He began to sift through the shows, and suddenly I was curious as to what he would select. In short, I was genuinely curious about his current mood. He almost seemed like a different person.

Eventually, he settled on a sitcom, and even though I internally struggled with the choice, I had the time it took to answer the knock at my door announcing that my pizza had arrived. I paid for it, brought it in and set it on the table.

"I like this, but you should have confirmed with me when I wanted to watch it."

"It was a recommendation," he said, and to my surprise, he got up once again and began to strip. I wasn't exactly sure what was happening as I stared at him.

"You're staying?"

"Food just came, didn't it?" he asked as he headed into the bathroom, and I was left staring after him, lost.

"There was no food at the engagement party?" I asked, and he didn't respond. A few seconds later, he came out with all the buttons of his shirt undone and a huge towel in hand. I was still standing in the middle of the room as I watched him lay the huge fabric across the bed, and then he lay down across it.

"Bring the pizza box over," he said and tapped on the bed. I still wasn't sure what was happening, so all I could do was stare until eventually I did as I was asked. Afterwards, I brought over some paper towels and plastic plates I found, and then I laid them on the towel.

"Are we settled on the sitcom?" he asked as he pulled it open, and I found the remote.

"No, let's watch something else."

We went to Netflix, and I knew the exact show I had in mind. It was one that I had been eyeing for a little while now and was finally released, yet I hadn't had the time to watch it. It was raunchy but in a peculiar scenario, and it just felt like it would be suitable.

There was nothing I could put on that would make me comfortable and accepting of his presence here, so I might as well try to ignore it and do what I wanted anyway. Except eat recklessly. That part of being alone I was going to miss, but not if I kicked him out first.

27

Kane

"Let's make a deal," she suddenly said as I reached for a plate and a slice of the meaty pizza. I wasn't one for junk food of this sort, but I wasn't one for suddenly coming over to women's hotel rooms either and then doing nothing but watching movies. I had come here simply to fuck her brains out and her, out of her mind. I had been furious and restless when she had been absent from the dinner party, and although I wasn't surprised, it didn't change the fact that I had been annoyed.

Thus, the reason for my coming over, despite every attempt to talk myself out of stepping out of line, she was the one who did so every single time she came in contact with me. It had been nearly a week now, and it had taken every bit of strength and self-control I had to keep my hands away from her. But I saw the way she looked at me at the office, as though I was a stranger and as though I didn't know how she tasted, and it aggravated me to no end. And then there were the moments when I caught her looking, and those were quite jarring even to me because the longing in her eyes was unmistakable. Her expression would soften, and all of her walls would seemingly come down. It was a precious moment that I would relish until she noticed and looked away, and it had become something of a joy to watch her become flustered afterward.

ANYWAY, and to my surprise, she had truly kept away, and it hadn't been easy at all for me to put her out of my mind. I was starting to realize she was the best lay I had ever had, and this was the only explanation that I could give for why I constantly found myself thinking back to all the intimate things we'd done with each other so far and how much more there was to do, over and over again. And so, I had made my way here, wanting her no matter what.

BUT THEN SHE looked so homey and relaxed as she opened the door, and I didn't want to leave. I suddenly didn't even want to fuck her anymore, at least not immediately, but in this moment, the silence and warm ambiance of the room, coupled with the dark but massive and brightly lit view from outside, was more than enough to make me want to stay.

. . .

AND THEN, of course, there was the woman herself. Flushed and clean and so relaxed... I wanted to feel that way. Seeing her made me realize that it had been a long time since I had felt that way, and I wanted it to change. At least for the night, so here I was, eating pizza with her and feeling quite comfortable.

"WHAT DEAL?" I asked.

"YOU EAT one slice of pizza, watch twenty minutes of this show with me, and then you leave."

I looked up, perplexed.

"WHY DO I HAVE TO LEAVE?"

SHE LOOKED at me as though she didn't understand why she had to explain this, and then she sighed.

"YOU'RE USED to women usually just giving you whatever you want, aren't you?"

She asked, and I smiled because there was very little lie in her statement. It didn't mean that I was going to admit it. She wasn't currently going to react to me being pompous or arrogant.

. . .

I REALLY JUST WANTED TO STAY, AND the way things were going, I didn't even mind if we didn't fuck. It would be better much later in the night anyway, and from the look of things, it was almost as though it was going to rain, which would be just so bloody fantastic.

I FINISHED another slice of pizza; however, just as I reached for another, she caught my hand and looked into my eyes.

"I'M SERIOUS," she said, and I couldn't help but smile. This was quite entertaining and so domestic that I truly couldn't stop the warmth I felt. It had to have been at least a decade since I fought for a slice of anything with anyone.

"DO WE HAVE A DEAL?" she asked. And I didn't bother taking my hand away because I loved the feeling of her touch on me. It was already causing a lot of reaction from my libido, but it was ignorable.

"NO DEAL," I replied. "The bed's big enough, and you should be able to ignore one other person."

“YOU’RE MY BOSS,” she said.

"AND THIS IS NOT THE OFFICE," I countered, and I turned my attention to the TV.

. . .

"So basically, I'm not kicking you out?" she asked.

"No one kicks me out of anything, Lena," I replied. "I leave when I want to."

At this, I visibly heard her groan aloud and was amused.

"You're so..." she gritted her teeth.

"Infuriating?" I supplied, and she immediately agreed.

"Yes, infuriating."

I let go of her wrist and reached for another slice of pizza. This time around, she didn't stop me.

"You're really going to stay?" she asked, and I nodded.

"For a little while. Change of pace and environment."

. . .

"So basically, you don't care that I didn't come for the party."

I heard her question loud and clear, but it took me quite a while to decide on how I wanted to respond.

"I was irritated that you didn't come, but not anymore."

"Why were you irritated that I didn't come?" she asked, and I turned my gaze away from the television, but when I did, the sight of the male character turning the female around and pressing her against the wall caught my eyes. I returned my gaze to the television, my brows slightly lifted as I watched him ravish her against the wall.

"Probably not appropriate for the current circumstances," Lena said in a low tone. "I'll change it."

"Leave it," I said and continued to watch.

"That was why I was irritated," I replied and turned to meet her gaze. "Because that was supposed to be us at some point tonight, wasn't it?"

She smiled, and then she picked up a slice of pizza.

. . .

"As I've said - presumptuous."

"No, realistic," I corrected.

"So, it's a given to you that I'll have sex with you?" Lena asked.

"For now, yes. There was music and a packed crowd, and the possibility of you being there was the only reason why I had considered it. Being pressed up against you in more ways than one in such a public setting was bound to be interesting," I replied.

The room soon filled with the sound of the girl moaning and her body hitting against the wall. And then they were done.

"Well... that was quick," Lena said, and I reached for what I told myself would be the last slice. However, she was far from pleased at this.

"When are you really?" she asked. "Truly."

. . .

I KEPT my attention on the television, not at all bothered by the fact that she kept insisting that I depart. I continued to watch the movie, and then a few minutes later, I had a response for her.

"AFTER THIS MOVIE," I said. "We're going to watch it all, and then you're going to pick an exact scene you want us to replicate. We'll do that, and then I'll leave."

I EXPECTED her to reject this, but when she remained silent and instead focused her attention on the television screen, I knew that I had broken through her walls.

WE CONTINUED to watch and eat, with anticipation building as we went through several scenes. Surprisingly, we didn't talk much with each other, but it didn't take long for me to see what the scenes were doing to us. The room was incredibly quiet, but we could both have heard a pin drop.

THERE WAS nothing impressive about watching, instead our awareness of each other continued to rise. Suddenly, the room became too warm, and my eyes strayed over and over to her. Her hair was dried now, and it had quite the curl pattern that I had never noticed before. The robe slipping off her shoulder, however, was something that I couldn't ignore. The swell of her breast jutted against the material, as well as the hardened peaks of her nipples. I was hard and wanted her on top of me, riding my cock with abandon.

However, I also sort of enjoyed the slow burn of this moment.

It started to rain then, and only the sharp strike of thunder alerted me to this fact. Otherwise, I was fully lost in her presence. I turned to look at the window and watched rain droplets as they rolled down the glass. I couldn't help but appreciate just how cozy the world seemed.

I turned then and caught her gaze. At first, it had been on the window, just like mine, but now it was on me. She looked away, and as I stared at her, I would have given anything to know what she was thinking.

"Enjoying the movie?" I asked, and I could hear her smile.

"What's it about?" she replied. I was incredibly amused.

"The storyline's not interesting?" I asked, and she turned to me.

"Is it to you?"

I stared, and her expression soured.

. . .

"Please don't tell me you have bad taste in movies. There's already enough to dislike about you."

I was taken aback by this.

"You dislike me?"

She hesitated, but at the end of the day, she responded. However, she could no longer hold my gaze when she said this.

"It's no secret that you're not my favorite person. I'm not your favorite person either."

"Sure," I replied. "But dislike is a strong word."

"Yes, it is," she said.

"This has(have) anything to do with that day in the study?" I asked, and I couldn't help but scootch a little bit farther up, then I began to unbuckle my belt. She ignored the crinkling sound as she continued to watch, but she didn't respond.

"Of course it does," she said.

. . .

"THAT WAS THE START."

"AND NOW?"

"IT'S EVEN WORSE."

SHE DIDN'T SEEM like she meant this at all, which served to amuse me even more. I pulled my pants off, and this time around, she couldn't claim to not notice, so she turned to look at me.

"WHAT ARE YOU DOING?"

"Getting comfortable," I said and returned my gaze to the couple who were now in the bathroom at a family party.

SHE DROPPED to her knees and took his cock in her mouth, and my hand went into my briefs to pull my dick out.

IT DIDN'T TAKE LONG for me to begin creaming at the tip, and despite how much she tried to ignore this, it couldn't be forever.

. . .

"This is what I mean right now," she said. "You're being a dick."

"I have a dick," I told her calmly as I watched the scene.

"You might be able to tolerate your reaction to this, but I don't want to."

My eyes went to the tip of my cock, and at the slight leak of precum, coupled with the fact that she was outrightly watching, my heartbeat picked up its pace.

"Don't mind me," I said. "You can keep on watching this boring show."

"What?" Her mouth fell open as she maintained her gaze on the screen.

"It's not boring."

"It is because there is no basis for the story. The man is obsessed with his son's fiancée and then—"

. . .

"Oh my God!" she suddenly exclaimed, and even I had to stop.

The room was quiet for a few seconds as we processed what had just happened. And then I burst into laughter. She turned to me astounded.

"That's your response?"

"Finally, some action."

"His son just dropped to his death seven stories up. His head is splattered on the ground."

I smiled as my pace on my cock quickened, my eyes fluttering closed as pleasure began to burn through my veins. I loved the fact that she was watching and was more than eager to put on a much more interesting performance for her.

"For fuck's sake, Kane," she said, and I let out a moan as I stroked my thumb against my head.

And then I heard her move. My gaze snapped open just in time to catch her head over on her knees, her robe now so loose that it was barely hanging on her body. One of her breasts was exposed, and she didn't bother covering it up as she sauntered up to me.

"I SO HATE that you're getting your way... again," she said, and I stared into her eyes as she positioned herself astride me.

"THAT'S one way to look at it," I said as she came closer until our chests were almost touching.

"IS THERE another way to look at it?" she asked, and I nodded.

"OF COURSE. You could see it as me getting you out of your own way."

"OF COURSE, you'd see it that way," she said as she held my face in her hands.

HER GAZE LINGERED on my eyes before it went down to my lips, and then she slanted her head to kiss me. My eyes fluttered shut to relish the contact, and it was a few minutes later before I was able to think clearly again. Maybe it was because of the fact that I was already aroused, but I enjoyed this kiss more than any I could remember in recent times.

. . .

THERE WAS JUST something about it, so much so that neither of us wanted to pull away from the other. Maybe it was because of the hourlong mental foreplay that had been involved, but suddenly, the more I watched her, I felt my heart begin to swell in my chest.

THERE WAS something very special about this woman, and even I had to admit it.

SHE PULLED the sleeves of her robe down in no time. The material was soft and bunched around her waist. Her breasts were fully exposed then, and as I held them in my hands, I couldn't look away.

"THERE ARE a lot of things I want," she said. "I just didn't know where to start."

I LEANED FORWARD and took one of her breasts into my mouth, keeping my attention focused on the mound until it was time to move on to the next. She writhed against me, and I couldn't resist reaching down for her clit. My hand felt her so wet that it was drenched, making my mouth water.

"SO, YOU DID LIKE THE MOVIE," I said, and she smiled before kissing me again.

. . .

"I LIKED it just as much as you did," she said, gasping into my mouth as my fingers slid into her.

However, it wasn't enough. I wanted to devour her, so I moved, lowering us down on the bed in the opposite direction. In no time, I had untangled myself from her, and I kissed every inch of her skin as I descended to her sex.

SHE LIFTED her leg and spread wide open, her hands in my hair as she tried to contain the excitement coursing through her and just savored the feel of my touch.

I LOVED EVEN MORE the taste of her soaked cunt as my tongue took its first swipe. She was tender and sweet, and I couldn't get enough. I loved her scent, her heat and most of all, the sweet, tortured sounds she made as my fingers and mouth worked in tandem to push her to the edge of ecstasy. She moaned, cursed, and writhed, and even when she started to pull away, whimpering and crying, I tightened my hold on her until she came in my mouth. I took my time with her now more than ever before, and I realized that my earlier plan to leave at some point wouldn't be the case. We had all night, and I was going to fuck her over and over until both of us collapsed in complete exhaustion.

28

Lena

I WAS SOMEWHAT HANGING off the side of the bed as I tried to catch my breath. I had almost fallen off, and I couldn't even find the strength to right myself as all the blood rushed to my head.

I COULD FEEL the harsh rise and fall of my chest and the shivers that ran through my body as he kissed my neck and every inch of my skin. I wished he would let me recover, but he seemed to have no interest in allowing that to happen, and truthfully, I had very little complaint.

. . .

I WANTED to find the strength to bring myself back up so I could have him in my arms again. However, he grabbed my legs and pulled me into position. I welcomed the feel of his body against mine, warm, strong, and heated. It was shaping up to be an unbelievable night, much more exhilarating than I could have ever anticipated.

BUT MORE THAN ANYTHING, I wanted to ride him. So even though the last thing I wanted was to move from underneath him, I managed to do just that and positioned myself astride him.

THERE WAS AN ADDED bonus as he squeezed my breasts in his hands and sucked intensely on my nipples. The sensation pulsed all the way to my sex, and I couldn't contain myself.

ONCE HE WAS POSITIONED against the headboard, I grabbed his cock and began to stroke it. It was the thickest cock I had ever seen, and I loved every bit of it. The sight of it in his big hands was something that would never leave my mind, quickly becoming one of my favorite things to think about. The way he handled it and smiled at it made me so hungry for him, but my clit couldn't wait. It was throbbing with eagerness, so I couldn't help but stroke his length against it.

I rode him, the wetness and heat of his skin providing more stimulation than I could have imagined possible. I especially loved the slight arching of his back as I increased my pace, and once again, I began to release.

. . .

I CRIED out in sweet ecstasy, but the last thing I wanted was to disengage from him. So, I lifted myself up and shut my eyes, relishing the feel of his thick cock as he slid into me. Everything felt rushed because every moment seemed unreal. Shocks and sparks of pleasure coursed through my body as he stretched me wide open, and then he was completely sheathed inside me. I leaned forward, holding him in my arms, wanting to savor this moment as I breathed him in. He kissed my hair, my cheeks, and my lips, whispering into my ear.

"BET THOSE TWO idiots could take several lessons from us," he said, and I laughed more than what was needed but it had very little to do with what he had said. I just felt completely undone and unwound and free from everything that was holding me down or back, no reservations, no concerns. I let everything go and solely allowed myself to be in this moment.

HE HELD my hips caressing my skin and ass as I clenched and unclenched my walls around him.

"FUCK," he whispered into my ears, and I couldn't resist kissing him then.

. . .

And then he began to move me. He lifted my ass while I held onto his neck and my head fell back as I slid down back onto his dick. Over and over again until we could no longer go any slower. With my knees solidly positioned by his sides I rode him in every single way that I could.

Thrusting up and down until his dick popped out of me nearly blowing my mind, but having to grab him, milk him and then slide him back in was the sweetest compensation. Over and over, I fucked him until I had him grabbing me so tightly that I couldn't move. I loved what I was doing to him... loved the effect I could have on such a powerful and assertive man, and I didn't hold back. I knew that there was little more between us than this but the way he held me kissed me and buried his face in my neck told me a different story. It was so easy to fall in love with him at this moment. After all I had already surrendered my body to him in a way that I never had with anyone else.

And this was why when we came together one last time and tears filled my eyes at the sheer intensity of it, I wasn't even the least bit surprised. Maybe it was the weather or maybe it was the fact that we both needed the release or maybe it was because we were so physically compatible that it seemed unreal but, in that moment, I was lost to the world and him.

Nothing else mattered as my frame tightened and shook at the mind-numbing orgasms. I could hear his groans in my ears and his body as it clenched and hardened against mine at his release. We held desperately onto each other as I savored the warm sweet mess. Eventually and even after we came down to earth, he still didn't let me go. I had no qualms about this and preferred it even but then my head began to come in to remind me of the fact that this was now beyond fucking. It was too intimate, and I felt too exposed and so before he could be the one to tell me to get off, I did it myself but he held on and refused to let go.

"KANE," I smiled, amused as he lowered with me on the bed and then fitted my frame against his.

"KANE."

"REST. AREN'T YOU EXHAUSTED?" he asked, and I didn't have to respond to this. I could feel all of him begging me and how my body fit oh so perfectly to the crevices of his.

I COULD HEAR the rain pattering against the window and truly all I could feel was the magic of the moment.

I WAS surprised by the heat and dare I say a connection so warm that it might have been love. It most definitely wasn't because of how it felt so damn good, I couldn't help but think about how the real thing... perhaps with him ... could feel like.

29

Kane

Things moved fast in the business world, which is why in no time the office space assigned to Lena was ready. I looked over the report and completed the design, nodding in approval.

"Should I send it over to her office, Sir?" my secretary asked. I was tempted to decline because what I truly wanted was to walk her over there myself. It was a significant milestone and an opportunity to see her, which seemed rare these days. Since that night, I had a strong suspicion that she had been avoiding me. Either that or our offices had magically grown in size, making it nearly impossible to run into her. Perhaps she wasn't even coming into the office anymore, but I couldn't be certain as I had also refrained from seeking her out.

I knew what we were both running from, and it was that night. I had initially convinced myself that it was the ambiance, but when I reminisced about how we made love again in the middle of the night, it became even harder to deny the connection that had formed between us. Perhaps the distance between us was an unconscious or perhaps even a conscious attempt to suppress the tenderness that had emerged. And it seemed to be working. Because as much as I desired to see her now, my thoughts and anticipation were driven by the explicit memories of being inside her, and I longed to experience it again.

Soon... before I lost my mind.

Self-control had never been my strong suit, and in this case, I couldn't quite discern my own motives. Was I struggling to stay away, or was I simply hooked and unwilling to admit it just yet? I had no clue, but these questions and many more were reason enough for me to take the folders with me and personally head over to her office.

Her secretary seemed surprised to see me since I hadn't sent any messages indicating my interest in seeing her. He immediately called her, and as his gaze lingered on mine, I wondered if she would instruct him to turn me away. He appeared nervous and struggled to speak, but eventually, he set the phone down and looked at me with relief.

"Please go in, Sir," he said, and I gave him a pitiful look.

A few seconds later, I pushed open the door to her office and entered. I realized, with a quickened heartbeat, that my heart had recognized her presence before I did. She stood at the windows, positioned against the backdrop of the city, exuding sophistication, determination, and beauty. As I took in her attire for the day, a pink tweed jacket and skirt, I couldn't help but stare at her until she cocked her head, wondering why I was still standing there. I wondered the same as I came to my senses, shook my head, and took a step forward.

"I came bearing gifts," I said, and she took her seat just as I did mine.

I handed the folder over and watched her expression as she began to peruse it, and then her eyes widened.

"It's ready?" she exclaimed.

"We can head there right now?" She blinked severely, and it was quite amusing.

"This was put together quickly... much more quickly than I thought was possible. Wait, I thought moving forward with this at all was on hold, given the vote from the others."

"It was," I replied. "But then I realized that there was no reason truly for it to be."

"What do you mean?" she asked.

"They didn't reject it because they didn't agree with the proposal, but because of diplomacy. It's thoroughly aggravating that I have to deal with these kinds of pettiness, but I guess it comes with the management territory and truly I wouldn't have it any other way."

She cocked her brow and then narrowed her eyes at me.

"You wouldn't have it any other way?"

I was amused as I knew exactly what she was implying.

"Dealing with foolishness is part of the job and I happen to enjoy the job so in order to keep my temper from constantly rising I've decided to change my perspective on things. I get to manage those idiots... and they don't manage me or this company hence why I'm the one who ultimately decides whether to keep the wheels rolling on this or not."

"Well, this is obviously a decision that I have absolutely no problems with," she said, and I nodded in agreement.

"Want to head over to take a look?" I asked and she hesitated just as I had anticipated.

30

Lena

His smile caught me off guard. Almost as much as his presence here, as well as his invitation that we go check out the new offices together. All of these, I could very easily say no to. However, without exposing the fact that I had gone out of my way to avoid him, then there was no other explanation for doing so.

However, I didn't want to fall under my own trap once again of telling myself that I could handle this. He watched me, and then he rose from his seat and started to leave. I watched him, and then before he could exit the room, I stood up as well.

"Sure," I said, and thankfully, he didn't point this out as he turned to watch me. His eyes... those were what I had been avoiding the most, because somehow, they seemed to absolutely strip me bare. And I couldn't say that it was currently among the least of my favorite things.

He held the door for me and waited, and I accepted it just as I would do if he was just any other male colleague.

This was what I told myself, that all I needed to do was treat him like every other male colleague, and nothing we did in the way we interacted with each other within these walls would be out of place.

Soon, we headed out quietly, side by side. As he accepted greetings, I got a feel of what it meant to be by his side. This was probably the closest we would ever get, and it was enough for me. But from what I could tell, he was deeply respected, maybe even a little bit feared. And as we got to the elevator, I couldn't help but glance briefly at his face.

He didn't have that somewhat softened demeanor that I realized he had when talking to me. His guard hadn't been up earlier, I realized. And it made me once again turn to him. He met my gaze, and I noted this again. And it was the absolutely wrong thing to notice. It was the last thing that I wanted to notice, because then my heart once again would start misbehaving and entertain thoughts that it truly had no business entertaining.

I had tried to push away so many things about us and that night out of my mind, but yet here I was failing once again. I had made progress, though, and that in itself had been torture. But then I had immense help in the form of the distraction of picking out a suitable apartment in New York City. It was quite a struggle, but the realtor had repeatedly espoused concerning the annoyances that I'd had to deal with. It was all together a smooth process for me because I had the money and prestige. Apparently, the rest of the world had to deal with much, much worse.

But now it was done and almost completely decorated, so I couldn't help but feel nervous once again. I had thrown myself into it, so it was more than easy to put a great many things out of my busy mind. Not anymore, though. But then again, he was launching this project now, and so I couldn't help but feel relieved.

Soon enough, we arrived at the designated offices, and I found that there were already many others on this floor. However, a wing had been assigned to us with multiple rooms and the most striking view of the city, and I loved every possible bit of it. He took me from one room to the other alone, and I was amazed by just how spacious the division seemed.

"You have your own reception," he said. "Well, more like an entry, but I plan to have them install a sign on the wall that bears your division's name."

"It has a name?" I asked, and he smiled.

"It should, shouldn't it? To make things official?"

At first, I didn't catch on to anything else he might have been insinuating since I was so lost in the moment. But eventually, it hit me like a ton of bricks. But then, as I looked at him and laughed, his piercing eyes looking at me once again, I couldn't help but consider that perhaps it wasn't all in my head.

However, it didn't matter since that wasn't currently why we were here, so I returned my attention to what was important at hand.

"You can start officially assembling your staff, conducting interviews. That can be quite stressful, so my condolences in advance."

I was amused.

"You know I have staff back in LA, right?"

"Yeah," was all he said, and when I turned to glance at him, I saw that he was lost in thought and probably hadn't heard what I had said. Shaking my head, I returned my attention to the rooms and could imagine all the plans we had coming to life.

He came up to me then, and I could smell his familiar scent before I even heard him coming.

"Budget allowance," he handed the file over to me, and I was reluctant to take it because, of course, I had already seen it. However, doing so forced me to look into his eyes, and just as he had probably intended, my heart stopped.

"You can begin purchasing the needed equipment to start your tests for the laboratory. I'm especially excited to see how that part will turn out."

"Yeah," I said, but he didn't let go of the paper. And neither did I pull it out of his hands.

"Have you found an apartment?" he asked.

In the quiet of the space, where I considered whether to respond or not, we were going into personal territory. Even though we were alone, I didn't see it as something I was interested in doing because I now knew that going down that rabbit hole spelled nothing but trouble for me.

31

Kane

I DIDN'T KNOW why I had asked this question. I had stared at her for too long, I guess, and just as I had expected, I wanted to know anything I could about her. I could easily have asked her assistant, as he was technically under my employ, yet I had held myself back from doing this.

To PROVE what I had now confirmed to myself, which was the fact that I was both struggling to keep away and hooked, but I didn't want to admit it yet. The fact that I even thought that these were separate questions at first showed just how much trouble I was in. But as she stared at me, wondering whether to respond or not, I realized that we just might be in the same boat.

It was somewhat amusing to watch, especially as I noted the time that passed and understood that it was way too much time to take in considering the answer to such a simple question.

"Um..." she said. "I, uh... yeah. Actually, yes. My friend is coming in soon from LA."

She stopped suddenly, then abruptly, which made me understand that she wasn't certain as to why she had done that.

I waited, and soon she smiled and started to turn away. I wanted to stop her, but I caught myself just in time. But just before she reached the door, I spoke.

"Why is she coming in?" I asked.

She stopped and then turned around to face me.

"I found an apartment, and I've been somewhat busy setting it up. It's not done, but it's hospitable, and I wanted to share it with her."

. . .

"Oh," I said. "You don't have any friends in New York? Just with her?"

"I have acquaintances," she replied. "Just not friends close enough that I'd want them at the opening. It's a little private affair. Just the two of us. I mean... casual."

"Okay, am I invited?"

She looked at me, and I knew then that I had solely asked the question just to see the myriad of emotions that would pass across her face. She stared at me, and I waited until eventually her gaze narrowed, and I knew that she had caught on to me.

"You're enticing me, aren't you?" she asked, and I smiled.

"Why would I do that?"

She paused as though to ponder my words but was eventually convinced that she was right.

"I'd prefer it if it was just the two of us," she said, giving me a harsh look, and then she continued on her way.

. . .

I LET it go after all. I had a meeting with my sister that I was most definitely not looking forward to.

As THE VICE President of Marketing, she had so far allowed her assistants and management to bring products to her that all she had to do was approve. It was the arrangement of her being that one kid in a group assignment that never showed up to class or contributed, and yet had no shame about it, and it was pretty fine. Except now she was informing me that she was personally spearheading the second quarter's marketing campaign, and I had no clue why. I suspected, though, that it was an attempt to aggravate me for the afternoon. However, unexpectedly, this brief time with Lena had put me in a great mood. Nothing remarkable had happened but being with her in such a quiet space had given me the dose of excitement needed to neutralize the impending threat.

"ALRIGHT," I said and started to walk away. However, she didn't move and just continued to stare at me until I reached her, and by the time I arrived, she didn't seem as though she planned to actually leave either.

I PAUSED as I stared into her eyes, waiting for her to speak, and eventually, she did.

. . .

"Do you..." she shut her eyes, and I almost smiled. "Would you want to come over tonight? We can have dinner and discuss a bit more about my plans for this space."

My brows lifted as I considered this, and then she shut her eyes again and released a sigh.

"Please don't let me regret this."

I was amused as I knew then what had happened. We both felt it, and there was no mistaking the fact that we had both come to some sort of consensus.

"I'd love to," I said.

My gaze lowered to her lips, and I had the urge to lean forward to kiss her, but I knew that it would be too soon. Whatever this consensus between us was, it was so fragile that neither of us could admit it out loud, so this time around, I truly decided not to taint it.

"Do you want me to bring food over or wine? I don't expect you to have the strength to whip something up after work."

. . .

SHE GAVE IT SOME THOUGHT, and then she replied,

"I'M NOT SURE YET. I'll ponder on it as the day goes by. I'll have a response for you soon."

"ALRIGHT," I said and continued on my way.

32

Lena

"What are you doing?" I stared at the door as I asked myself the question over and over again. However, when I held it open just to watch him and his gorgeous ass walk away, it made sense to the dampness between my thighs.

"Of course, I wasn't thinking with my brain." There was nothing to contest about this fact, and no woman, I was sure, would think reasonably if they were blessed with this sight.

Broad shoulders, a haircut that I found fucking beautiful for reasons that were inexplainable, and of course, that tight ass that I had missed digging my hands into with all my heart. I had done my very best to stay away, but now, truly I needed my bed christened, and it had to be no one but him. Soon, he was out of sight, and I promised myself that I wouldn't involve Diana in this. But on my way, and in order to avoid the many greetings and stares that were coming my way, I pulled my phone out of my pocket.

"Hey," she called, and I felt relief at her tone. And then I tensed up because I was well aware that I was about to be severely mocked.

"Hey," I replied but kept silent.

“Hello... why are you calling? Are you okay?”

"Yeah," I said, and she paused.

"Hmm hm... sure. This is about Kane, isn't it? I haven't heard about him in a while, and I wonder what's going on between you two."

I didn't respond.

"Should I tell you what my suspicion is about this matter?"

I sighed.

"What is your suspicion?"

"You were trying to avoid talking with him or speaking with him, although I have absolutely no idea why this would be the case. Wait, actually, I have ideas, I'm just hoping they weren't detrimental to your work."

"You're thinking a lot about us," I said, and she laughed.

"You know my heart is tied down with that gremlin, so I can only experience the escapades of the dating streets through you."

I smiled at her term, just a step before the elevator opened, and our eyes connected with an employee who nodded to me and then turned around. I had to be careful with the way I spoke then, but I didn't want to end the call so abruptly either since I was still yet to tell her about what I was planning for later on.

"Actually, I've been busy with my apartment," I said.

"Yeah, I know," she said. "I'm just teasing you. Thank God you called because I was going to call later with an idea. It's hospitable now, so what do you say I come over this weekend or next for a housewarming?"

I smiled at her suggestion.

"That was one of the reasons I called you," I told her. The elevator doors opened then, and I exited on my way to my office.

"So, I am actually hoping that you can come out next weekend for a housewarming."

"Oh, this is just perfect," she said. "I was ready to do so this week if you asked, but next week is even better because Matthew will be out of town, and I needed somewhere to go to celebrate my momentary freedom."

"Momentary freedom? I'll be sure to mention to him the next time we see each other that this is how you view his absence."

"Go ahead," she said. "I tell him all the time that I'm sick of his presence."

"But you actually aren't, right?" I asked.

"Of course not. In short, I think I'm in love with him. And I think he's going to propose soon. It's been two years, and because of our rough patch earlier in the year, I was sure we weren't going to make it, but now... things are good... really good."

"Wait, what? You had a rough patch earlier this year?" I asked.

"Yeah."

"How come I don't know about it?"

"Well, it wasn't exactly the easiest of times for you, was it?" she said, and I nodded.

"Yeah... hell."

"Which is why I'm so glad that you're truly getting back on your feet and even perhaps getting ready to fly again, and

I couldn't be more excited for you. I'm also glad that Mr. Insane CEO is bringing you out of your shell."

I arrived at my office then and decided that it was time to speak.

"And that is the final reason I called you," I said.

"What do you mean?" she asked.

"Well... I want to... I invited him over to have some dinner with me... at the new apartment."

She went silent for a while, and I shook my head at myself.

"Oh," she said. "Okay."

I smiled.

"What I want to hear from you is that it's a bad idea and that I should cancel immediately."

"You know I won't say that" she said, and I frowned as I plopped into my chair.

"Why?"

"Because he just might be good for you," she said, and I couldn't believe her words.

"After all I've told you about him."

"So, what if he was an edgy youth? So far, he's been nothing but pleasant to you, and I'm his fan for that, so... I am more than interested in hearing so much more about where you two are taking this."

At her words, I went silent, more than grateful that I wasn't the one who broached this topic.

"Why are you quiet?" she asked.

"Well... being busy with the apartment is not the only reason why I've been more or less MIA."

"Uh oh," she said. "What happened?"

I sighed and gave the simplest answer.

"The sex was phenomenal."

"And now you two want this to be a thing?" she asked.

"Not a thing," I replied as I turned around to look at the striking skyline view of the city I was beginning to envelop affection for.

"Just... it's not completely nothing anymore."

"Wow," she said. "I expected this to happen, but much, much later."

"Yeah," I said. "I prayed that it wouldn't happen at all."

"Tough luck," she said, and I had to nod to that.

"So... just dinner?" she asked, and I was immensely amused.

"What, you want me to give you explicit details?"

"I won't complain," she said, and I shook my head.

"Freak. Anyway... I'm hoping it just stops there, but with the way it all happened, I'm doubting it will. I'm just worried because this seems like an incredibly dumb move on my part. But unless I completely stick my head in the sand now and don't even bother coming up for air, I have no idea how this will be resolved."

"Right," she said.

"Well, it's time to come up for air, if I do say so myself, and I am here for it. What do you have planned?"

33

Kane

It had truly been a while since I had been this excited. I tried my best not to show it, but it was truly difficult, especially as I arrived at her building and realized that it was within running distance of mine. Granted, most of the high-end apartments were close together, but this was a fact that especially lightened up my mood. I was already cleared with the concierge as I was expected, so the moment I announced my name, I was led to the appropriate elevator and guided up. She was on one of the higher floors, but the elevator was fast, so I arrived in no time, although it didn't feel like it.

Apartment 8306 was what she had informed me it was, and I loosened the knot of my tie as I arrived. I realized I was exhausted, but with the hope of ending the day on an especially good note, I had pushed this to the back of my head, so by the time she was opening the door, I was covering up a yawn.

"Hey," she said, immediately noticing it. I watched as she

smiled in response, and maybe it was the warmth of the lights all around, but her eyes sparkled, and I couldn't look away.

"You're exhausted?" she asked, and I nodded quietly, not yet ready to speak.

"Come in," she said, and I did. It had a foyer very similar to mine, though much smaller in size. Still, it was striking.

What mine didn't have, especially, was the huge vase of calla lilies in the midst of it, which seemed to distribute its smell around the entire apartment. It was gorgeous and so similar to my style that I had to turn and ask.

"Did you copy my home's interior?"

At first, she was taken aback by this and was about to become defensive, but she finally noted the lightness in my tone and beamed.

"Absolutely not. This is my style. I don't like brighter or sharp colors, so beige and white and warmth is what I went for. It calms me down. Plus, yours has a lot of black. Black is very limited here, if even."

"True," I replied, and she led me past the spacious living room and towards the kitchen.

"Have a seat, please," she pointed to the island counter, and I did so. It was polished glistening marble, and as I watched her walk ahead to a wine rack by the corner, I couldn't help but notice just how attractive the silk gown she had on was. It was paper-thin and had sleeves that went down her arms, but the material clung to her body in all the right places, and this drew my attention like nothing else. She turned around then, with two bottles in hand, and my gaze lowered to the drawstring underneath, which pushed her full breasts even closer together and revealed the most gorgeous cleavage known to man.

Her hair was down and flowing all the way to her back, as opposed to being tied back away from her face earlier in the day. Her makeup was always minimal, and I couldn't tell if she was wearing any now, but all I could feel was that she looked even more stunning than I thought was possible. Just like a breath of fresh air or a dream rolled into one.

"Wine or something stronger?" she asked, and my attention went to the two bottle selections she had in hand.

"There are other options," she said, and I nodded.

"Any dry wine will do," I replied. I have my preferences, of course, but at this moment, I just wanted her to be done with whatever she was doing and to be here by my side. Savoring those breasts was a more urgent demand, but before that, I just wanted her to sit down beside me. I was itching for a good time tonight, which I realized included a good, long conversation, and I couldn't wait for all of this awkwardness to pass so that we could get started.

She brought a bottle over, as well as a wine opener. I tried to take it from her, but she refused.

"No," she smiled. "I can handle it."

I smiled and let her proceed for a while, but the more I stared at her, the more I decided that I truly couldn't wait another moment to have her. So, I got down from the stool and went behind her, my hands going to her hips. They were wide, soft, and so shapely that I couldn't help but run my arms down them. She let me, especially when I leaned into the space between her neck and shoulders to breathe in her scent.

She allowed it, and then she looked sideways at me. I held her gaze, and for a moment, we were lost in each other.

"So... no dinner?" she asked, and I gave her a look.

"Of course there is." I moved away from her then and

took my seat back at the counter. I had been tempted to do all that I could possibly think of to her, but now, as I looked around at her gorgeous apartment, I realized that I truly just wanted to spend time here and be with her. For the meantime.

I pushed the stem of my glass forward, took the bottle from her, and this time around, she allowed me to uncork it. Afterwards, I poured the dark red contents into both our glasses, and then she picked it up, and the glasses connected.

She took a sip, and I watched as the wine went down her throat. To my surprise and amusement, she nearly completely drained the entire glass.

"That stressful a day?" I asked as she set it down, and she blushed, her skin flushing a slight hint of red.

"It's always a stressful day, but I haven't truly had wine in a little while either, and that tasted good."

"It did taste good," I said as I took a healthy drink of mine and then set it down on the counter as well.

"I'll warm up dinner," she said and started to leave, but I held onto her hand and stopped her.

"Let's do what I actually came here for," I took her. "I'd like a tour of the place."

"Really?" she asked, and I nodded.

"Alright," she said, and we got started.

It was a big apartment with three bedrooms. One she had as an office, and the other was actually a guest bedroom, but the shape of the house was such that except for going through a hallway overlooking a skylit garden, you didn't really see much else of the apartment.

And so, the tour took a little while, and although I didn't have much commentary to give on it, I had to appreciate just how suited the place was to her. It was oh so calming and warm, which made me want to stay here with her. Soon, we arrived at the main living room and back to the kitchen, and we both turned to appreciate the space—the white walls and beige accents, the dark wood and greenery.

"There's still a lot of work to do," she said. "But it's livable."

This amused me as I headed back to the island counter stool.

"My interior designer told me my place was ready two months after I considered it ready."

"What do you mean?" she said as she headed over to some foil plates by the counter and began to pop them into the microwave.

"I mean when I saw it, I was sure it was done, but it was only two months later that she agreed with me enough to let me move in. I knew she wanted to keep making changes, and I didn't want to constantly have her come in, so I just told her to tell me exactly when it would be done, and only then would I bother moving in."

At my words, she stopped with a spoon in hand, and then she turned around to face me, her eyes narrowed.

"What?" I asked.

She watched me as though in disbelief about something, and then she shook her head and returned her attention to the pan she retrieved and placed on top of the stove.

"I find it hard to believe that you didn't know the real reason why she was dragging on with completing the house and insisting that you move in, even though she would have to keep working on it for a bit more."

This was a mouthful, but I managed to get the gist of what she was saying.

"You're saying she did it to find a way to spend some time with me."

"I didn't invite you to dinner because I could cook," she said, and I laughed, but then something crucial occurred to me.

"Wait, you don't know how to cook?" I asked as I watched her put a cut of steak in the pan.

"Not really," she said, and I shut my eyes.

"Am I in danger of food poisoning?"

"Maybe," she said as she glanced back so gorgeously at me. "But given the evening in exchange, wouldn't it be worth it?"

"Nothing is worth food poisoning," I replied, and she laughed even harder.

I watched her as she cooked, and then I moved over to the corner because I found that I wanted to be close to her, even though I would just be standing there... watching, since I sure as hell couldn't cook.

I watched as she seared the steak in butter, and pretty soon, the scent was surrounding the entire kitchen.

"You plan to stay in New York for a long time?" I asked as I watched what she was doing, and then I lifted my gaze to watch her.

"Who knows?" she said. "Given this apartment, though, I think I can say that I'm down for staying a little while."

I nodded in response, and this, I had to admit, was certainly pleasing.

"What about you?" she asked. "Do you plan to stay in New York forever?"

This, I realized, was not a subject that I had ever given much consideration to. However, since she was asking, I went over to the counter to grab her glass and mine, and then handed it over to her.

"Yeah," I replied. "I think so. I love the city. It has its severe flaws, but because of my wealth, I can rise above it. And I travel all the time. I've been to so many countries, but not once did I ever think that I wanted to leave. I always wanted to return."

She nods in response.

"I understand. The only country I've ever felt that way about was England, the city of London specifically, but that was when I visited many years earlier. I got a job there after college, and against my dad's wishes, I headed over. But then, in three months, I was lonely. Turns out, it can be quite difficult for me to make friends, plus my fascination with the city got old. So, I went back to LA."

"Were you close to your father?" I asked, and she shook her head.

"No, we clashed all the time about everything. That's why I went to college in LA. Yet, I called him all the time. Our relationship was best from a distance. What about you?" she asked, and I leaned against the counter as I thought about my own father.

"Our relationship has always been strained. More than anything, it was always based on performance, and that wasn't good for anybody. But when I left college and joined the company, and I was able to perform well, we never ran out of things to talk about concerning the business, at least. And naturally, this extended to other personal topics from time to time, but nothing too deep."

My thoughts drifted away to the man that I had revered and was incredibly fond of, and for the first time in a long while, as I thought of him, I felt something of warmth come into my heart. I really did miss him, but I had never been able to take his loss as anything but tragic. He hadn't suffered for too long with his illness, but in my selfishness to have him here, I had always wished he had, if it meant that he could remain longer. But now... I was beginning to truly live in a world where he wasn't around, and as I stared at the gorgeous woman before me, who was also lost in thought about her own father, I suspected, I could trace one of the reasons why.

"Do you ever think that our fathers wanted to pit us against each other by giving us all equal equity of the company?" she asked suddenly. It wasn't a strange question to me at all, but the fact that it was coming from her felt particularly funny to me, so I couldn't help but laugh.

"What is it?" she asked as she handed me a plate.

"It's something that I've thought about," I said. "But in a different light."

"How so?" she asked as she handed over another plate and began to cook a second steak.

I watched her, wondering if I could reveal this bit to her. She was a competitor, I was certain, but I didn't think she was antagonistic enough to always want to be in the spotlight, or else she would have been gunning for my position in one form or another from day one.

"I know he gave us all an equal share to level out the playing field for sure. What I'm just not sure of is how many people he wants remaining."

At this, she stopped and turned to stare at me.

"Oh shit," she said, and I smiled.

"Yeah. This is some kind of game."

"Yes," she replied.

"At first, I was somewhat upset about it, but not

anymore. Playing favorites would have definitely caused even more strife than we are currently dealing with."

"You're right," she said in a contemplative tone. "I wonder, though, if they did this long before either of them even thought about dying or with some hint of it in mind."

"What do you mean?" I asked, almost certain of what she was getting at but still not completely sure.

She met my gaze.

"Do you think they were going to step back beforehand and enjoy watching us fight to the death for it?"

I smiled.

"I considered this at one point, but now I know that it wasn't the case at all."

"Really?"

"Yeah, I think they just did it to give us all a chance, including you."

"Including me?" She stopped briefly to look at me.

"Sure. He knew you had your own thing going and that you probably had no interest in the future to join Standard Rock, but there was always a possibility that you would. He used to talk to me about it from time to time."

Her eyes widened as she heard this.

"He did?"

"But he mentioned it so casually that it was easy to miss. But now that you're here, and in retrospect, a lot of things seem much clearer."

"Yeah," she said, growing silent. I returned to the counter and took one of the filled plates with me.

"Was he sure I was going to join the company?" she asked without looking back.

"From what I know, no," I replied. "He just mentioned it from time to time. The things you were doing with your company and the divisions he would have loved for you to take over and handle in this company."

She returned her attention to what she was doing, while I pulled out my phone to check the last batch of emails for the day.

34

Lena

I truly hoped that the meal was edible. I had gone over dinner options with Maria, and we had decided on steak. It was the one thing I could do fairly well and couldn't exactly order in. She insisted that ordering anything else would be a better option, but in the end, I decided on the steak, and now I knew why.

I wanted something more personal with him. In the moment, it didn't feel like we could have anything else that was personal. I was open to discussing it, but I couldn't even fathom it. However, sharing a meal together in this manner before indulging in whatever else the evening had in store for us felt quite apt.

And it had worked. As I glanced back to see his deep concentration on his work, I had to admit that he was no longer the distant and vexatious stranger that I wanted nothing to do with. I hadn't expected our conversations to delve into the areas of our fathers, but it made me realize how much we shared in common.

I took my plate over to join him, poured us another glass of wine, and dug in. I didn't want to admit it, but I cared about how it tasted to him. I had been hoping that the awkwardness between us would drive me to concentrate, but somewhere along the line, I had gotten distracted, and I hadn't been wowed by what I had tasted.

I had told myself that I wouldn't care or watch as he dug in after me. However, when I was barely chewing my steak and sensed, without looking directly at him, that he was enjoying it, it became undeniable that I gave a damn.

"Pretty good," he said, and something in the pit of my stomach fluttered. At first, I didn't believe him, but then, as I took another bite and the grilled lean cut melted in my mouth, I realized it wasn't half bad at all.

I turned to him, licking my lips, ready to agree, but stopped when I met his intense gaze. He was watching me closely.

"Tastes good, doesn't it?" he asked, and I decided to tease him a bit.

"The steak or my lips?" I inquired, and his gaze lifted to meet mine. At first, his expression was completely blank, but then slowly, the corners of his lips curved, and that was all I was getting. Before I could look away, his huge hand slid gently yet powerfully around the side of my neck.

I closed my eyes, not caring to question what he wanted to do. When all I sensed was his scent but not the warm, sweet taste of his lips, I opened my eyes once again. I couldn't quite tell what I was hoping for, or perhaps I just didn't want to admit it. Admit that there was something more here, because if I did, I would be tormented for not pursuing it. All my life up until this moment, there was nothing I had ever wanted yet not actively gone after, so I didn't know how to deal with the fact that this just might be the first.

He leaned forward then to kiss me, but it wasn't deep. I sensed the affection in his gaze and in the way he held me so delicately, but I knew that by wrapping his hand around me the way he had, his intention had truly not been to place a simple kiss on my lips.

"Thank you for the food," he said, and I had to keep myself from rolling my eyes. He wasn't being honest... with himself or me, because we were both aware, I was certain, that there was more. The question now remained as to which of us would have the courage to admit it.

We kept eating in silence, but I could no longer quite taste the food, which was a shame because I was already aware that it was good. There was something there, just like our relationship.

"Ready?" he asked, and I turned to look at him, a bit sour about the question.

"Ready for what?"

He watched me as though trying to figure out if I was just acting or not until eventually, I forced a smile on my face and responded.

"Oh, for that, of course," trying not to sound unimpressed.

"You don't seem like you're in the mood, though," he said, and I looked at him, wondering if he was in any way catching on to my dissatisfaction and would be able to put into words the things I couldn't outrightly say.

A long silence passed, and I quickly accepted that this was a pipe dream, but I couldn't wait until I was always in the mood either. Perhaps it was best to go at it when I had no interest, so maybe if I convinced myself hard enough that

I didn't care to continue this with him, I would actually, in the end, believe it.

"I'm not," I replied truthfully, "but if it's something we can make quick work of, then I'm open."

His brows slightly raised.

"Quick work?" he asked, and I felt a little alarm blaring through me. Was I crossing a line? Was I being insensitive or dismissive?

"Yeah," I replied, giving a little smirk, and then he rose to his feet.

"You must be exhausted," he said, and my heart began to race. "So, I think I'll give you the evening off to rest. We've just hit a busy time ahead in the office."

At his words, my eyes welled up with tears because there was no doubt that I had offended him. However, I didn't know how to apologize. I didn't even know if I wanted to apologize.

I watched as he took his plate with him and dumped it in the sink, the loud clanging against the metal startling me. He gave me a nod and began heading towards the front door. It took a little while, but when I realized that I might actually be getting what I wanted and about to lose him, panic set a fire underneath my feet. I didn't have time, I had to catch up with him quickly in the foyer as he was pulling the door open.

"Wait," I said, but he didn't stop.

"Kane!" I called, and just as he was about to leave, my hand held his down on the handle.

He turned to me, his face completely expressionless, though I knew it reflected nothing of his true demeanor. I looked into his beautiful and stern eyes, trying to find a way to resolve this. The only way I saw it happening was if I told him the truth, but I couldn't accept anything else except that. How was I going to tell him to his face that I was beginning to long for more, yet it was the one thing I couldn't accept? I looked at him, wondering if it was time to end this. However, I couldn't bring myself to do it, so I took the opposite route, which in essence was half-truth, yet not.

"I think..." I hesitated, concerned. "I've been concerned that I'm becoming quite attached to you."

At my words, his eyes somewhat narrowed, and I felt even worse. Still, I fought to continue, or there would be no way to resolve this.

"I wanted to see if I could say no to you, at least once. I'm sorry if it came off as disrespectful. I was just... I had to find a way to lie to myself so that I could believe it."

He looked at me and nodded.

"I understand," he said, making to leave again. But knowing the man I knew, I realized that if he left without this being somewhat resolved, I would immensely regret it. It would truly be the end I dreaded, and for the first time, I had to confront the fact that perhaps I was more invested in this than he was. But that didn't mean it would always be this way, and for a moment longer, I just wanted to hold on.

So, I held his wrist and pulled him in. Though reluctant, he went along with me. I took him all the way to the kitchen, and when we arrived at the counter, I stared at him, wishing I could read his mind. However, he was completely unreadable, so I focused on the fact that he was here with me. But I definitely couldn't be with him on the bed in my bedroom, as we had been before. However, what I did want, what I had been unable to stop thinking about, was kissing him. The fact that I had been able to resist it for so long while yearning for it almost every moment was indeed a miracle.

But it was to be rectified now, and I wasn't going to hold back. However, I couldn't expose any more of myself, even though as I looked at him, I was almost certain that he could read me, that he understood. And so, as I slanted my head and leaned towards him, I truly wished that he would save me from myself, from the both of us, and push me away.

Instead... he remained still and received all that I was giving. The kiss was sweet, much sweeter than I could remember, and it swept away any remaining willpower I had. His tongue danced in and out of my mouth, slow and deliberate, causing my body to weaken in response. He held me close, his hand sliding up the side of my waist and resting on my neck. He pulled away briefly to look into my eyes. I tried to conjure up a smile to smooth over the tension from the last few minutes, but it had no effect on him. Without hesitation, he leaned in for another kiss, this time with more intensity. It left a slight bruise, but strangely, it was exactly what I needed. The kiss was filled with a desperate longing and an unspoken need that couldn't be put into words.

I realized then and without a shadow of a doubt that he was in control and this I realized was exactly what I wanted. I wanted to feel and not think and so I completely surrendered to all that he wanted.

He sucked on my lips, pressed intense kisses down my neck and I felt all the barrage of emotions in the pit of my stomach. He kissed me like he cared... like he knew, and I allowed myself to pretend just for this moment that it was alright. And so, I wrapped my arms around him and held on even more tightly. And then it turned heated. His hands moved, tracing the curves of my body and then he grabbed my ass, and a gasp escaped me. I loved every bit of the force, intensity and unpredictability and so when he lifted me up and placed me on the counter. I was more than ready for all that he wanted to happened between us.

Spreading my legs apart I pulled him in and kissed him even more deeply and then I was pulling my shirt over my head. My bra came off next, but I couldn't tell if I had taken it off myself or if he had been the one to do this.

In didn't matter anyway because in the next moment his mouth was on my breasts and my head fell back. I especially loved the way he plumped them with his hands and how he took his time. He was careful yet the pull on my clit was immense. I writhed and moaned into his mouth nearly unable to contain all of the excitement that was setting my blood on fire from the inside out.

I loved the way he touched me. His hands seemed to be everywhere, and they glided across my body like it was a treasure that he couldn't get enough of.

He kissed me again and as he went even deeper, I realized then just how turned on I was.

I needed to get fucked in the hardest, roughest way possible. I held onto him and whispered in his ear.

"I can't wait anymore," I told him, and he kissed me as though to shut me up.

I had no complaints, especially when he grabbed my thighs and then lifted me off the counter once again. He took me over to the nearest wall surface and I almost couldn't breathe from the excitement and anticipation. He tried to pull my thong down but when the process took a bit longer than I saw he had the patience for he ripped the edge of my panties, and I was exposed before him.

The sharp sting was something beautiful, the pain shooting straight to my core and when he pulled out his beautiful cock and stroked the head across my soaked sex, I was left out of breath.

He stared into my eyes as he slipped into me, and I wanted to close mine. I wanted to look away so he wouldn't see what I was aware he wanted to yet couldn't exactly put into words. Maybe it was the extent of my vulnerability or just how taken I was with him but neither of these could I show to him, at least nothing more than what had already been exposed and so I simply shut my eyes as I leaned against his shoulder and savored the magical feeling of him entering me.

I relished the feel of his length as he stretched my walls and how I pulsed around him. It filled me with a deep hunger that was being quenched but still insatiable. I closed my eyes and rocked my hips, milking him as he sunk into the depths all the way to the hilt, and I could barely contain the pleasure that boiled in my veins. Connecting with him in this way and so intimately had come to be one of my absolutely favorite things and it awed me now more than anything else just how against it I had been from the very beginning.

But not anymore. Now I knew I couldn't get enough of him and when he began to slam into me, I didn't hold back my moans. I let it out just so that he could understand what he was doing to me. Just so that he could see that I had meant every word I had said to him, that this truly was becoming much more than I could take.

He was more silent than usual, but I could feel his intensity from the way he fucked me and from the way he held me. His chest heaved and his body became warmer and warmer and yet he didn't stop. He kissed me over and over again and then towards the end he just buried his face in the crook of my shoulder and pounded me as hard and as fast as I wanted. He didn't stop, not until I was yelling out my release and he was doing the same with me. I could feel our juices flowing between us and the harsh sounds of our breathing filling the air. It was a quiet space, yet it felt like I was in a bubble. A bubble that I never wanted to leave and yet was terrified that I could burst at any moment.

It took a while for us to come back to earth; however, this time he let go much sooner than I would have liked, much sooner than our usual encounters. I understood. Perhaps he was trying to salvage this... save us. That was the purpose of our agreement from the start. Fucking in the most emotionless and harsh way possible, so that neither of us would be worse off in the end.

I agreed with it, longing to feel that same level of detachment with him again. When he departed from me and left me to find my footing alone, I had no complaints. I did, however, have to lean on his arms, my eyes fixed on the skirt bunched around my waist. He didn't even have the patience to take it off.

It was exactly what I wanted. I had no complaints whatsoever. When he looked into my eyes, I could already sense the lingering animosity from earlier. I welcomed it, yet at the same time, it made my heart sink. Regardless, it didn't matter, because the euphoria from our encounter was still strong enough for me to feel emotions I probably had no business feeling.

I couldn't help but think that if I hadn't said a word, he probably would have stayed the night. I wanted him to stay, but his withdrawal was something I had to accept. So, I nodded as he finally let me go and composed himself.

"Congrats on your new place," he said, and I listened to

his words. He remained confident and unaffected, yet I could see a flush on his cheeks and a sparkle in his eyes. It made me smile.

I nodded, and he turned around to leave. I watched him go, but this time I didn't follow him to the foyer, which brought immense relief. However, as he opened and closed the door behind him, I felt overwhelmed by silence and sadness. I made my way over to the half-filled bottle we had shared, and it somehow soothed me. I took a seat on his stool and started to drink straight from the bottle, but then I changed my mind and used his glass instead. I was certain I could still taste him, so I savored every sip until I was finally satisfied enough to head to bed.

35

Kane

I had to make a decision, or else things would continue to drift apart between us, and there was nothing that could be done about it. From being people with a casual relationship, we would eventually become people without any relationship, simply coworkers. This was supposed to be the plan... it had always been the plan. However, I was no longer satisfied with it.

I couldn't let this passively fade away like it had been doing, yet I was still uncertain about what decision to make. It had been a week since I last left her apartment with the intention of it being the last time. We were both extremely busy individuals in charge of major departments, so it wasn't difficult for us to avoid running into each other. However, I still receive reports about her department daily, about how she managed and excelled with her staff, even making adjustments to the design by removing colors that were too bright.

I enjoyed observing her from a distance, but during

times like these when things became too distant, and all I wanted was to be near her, I was forced to rethink my decision. Currently, I was staring at a photo of her reviewing equipment for the laboratory she was setting up. Though there was nothing explicitly sexual about the image, the coat and glasses she wore couldn't hide the elegance and beauty she possessed. She was sophisticated and focused, and the more I watched her in this way, the more I realized that she might have been what I had been searching for but never truly believed existed.

When I was with her, things seemed too good to be true, but now... I wanted them to be this way. However, it would take me a little while longer to gather my thoughts and eventually present this to her because, with her, there was no turning back. On one hand, I loved that it was this way with her, but on the other, I truly wished it wasn't the case because I didn't know if I was ready. But as life had taught me so far, I might never be ready.

Suddenly, there was a knock on my door, pulling me out of my thoughts. I had been losing focus of my surroundings, getting lost in thoughts of how to resolve this situation.

"Sir, Mr. Mercer wants to see you," my secretary said, and I frowned at the announcement. He was the last person I wanted to be dealing with at the moment. I checked my watch.

"It's almost eleven. Do I have a scheduled meeting then?" I asked.

"You do, Sir," he replied. "A meeting with the marketing manager."

"When it's time, come right in and insist on it," I told him. "This could run longer than it's supposed to."

"Yes, Sir," he replied and left the room. A few minutes

later, Dylan entered the office. Of course, his face was stern and guarded, but I had no interest in wasting any more of my precious time catering to him.

"I come bearing gifts," he said, and I sighed.

"What do you want?"

He went silent for a little while, then took a seat across from my desk. I was forced to look up at him.

"I want out," he said to me. "You were right, and I don't want to be managing this company. But that doesn't mean I have to lose my inheritance, does it?"

Upon hearing his words, I looked up and pondered the response to give.

"Actually, it does mean that you lose it. That was the point of your father stipulating that you have to work for two years—emphasis on the word 'work'—before any of it is vested to you."

"Well, I'm the kind to eat my cake and have it too, and it's difficult to change."

His words reminded me of why this conversation was a waste of time, so I ignored him and tried to refocus on my work.

"I'm serious, Lazarus," he said. "Having me out will make things easier for you."

"So, what do you suggest I do?" I asked, and he sighed.

"Drop the lawsuit and, in exchange, just buy me out. Or reach a settlement with me equivalent to my equity, so when it vests, it's all yours."

I frowned as I tried to process what he was saying.

"So, pay you now and keep your equity?"

"Well, not all of it," he said, and I couldn't help but smile.

"I'll keep about 20 percent of it... you know, for sentimental reasons."

"20 percent for sentimental reasons?" I repeated.

I shook my head and went back to work.

"I'm serious," he continued. "I'm coming to you now because of this bullshit lawsuit between us. And it's a chance for you to gain power over the rest of the stake-holders because, in case you haven't noticed, we're all sort of equal in this, which cannot be interesting for you."

I sighed again and looked up at him.

"Actually, it is," I said.

"Really?"

I shut my document.

"Have you ever thought that the challenge you're facing now and the reasons you want to leave are why your father stipulated those terms in the first place? Sure, you're a pain in the butt, and I want to let you go more than anything else, but wouldn't it be disrespectful to his intentions for me to agree?"

Furious, he rose to his feet sharply, almost startling me.

"You know what, Kane," he said. "You have the most to lose if you don't accept this, so I thought it'd make sense to come to you to quickly resolve this as soon as possible. But I should have known that all you'd have an interest in is making life as fucking difficult for me as possible."

He wasn't completely wrong there, so I didn't bother arguing.

"I'll take it somewhere else," he said, and I shook my head.

"That doesn't dissolve our lawsuit. Wherever you take it, you better be sure you have the money because it'll be coming back to me once again once we win."

With that, he glared angrily at me, exited the office, and I had to admit that he had given me something to worry about. The next person he could and would probably take this to was my sister, and if she ended up having more stake over us, she could make things incredibly difficult. Maybe not now, but in the future, and that was the last thing I wanted to deal with. And if he took it to Lena..."

I tried hard to think but realized that I wasn't certain at all about what she would do and how she would react to this. I wasn't sure if she would have the money to buy him out immediately, and I knew that was the real reason he had come to me. But if it went to my sister, I suspected that even if she didn't have the funds now to buy him out, she would most definitely be able to come up with something. Actually, her husband has the funds to buy him out.

Sighing, I picked up the phone and called our legal counsel, and a few minutes later, he was in my office.

"Well, technically he can do this," he said. "He can get paid, have his rights transferred, but of course, whoever he transfers it to can't exactly participate in the company in any capacity for the first two years. But they don't have to, at least not directly. All they have to do is claim it's Dylan's stance because, of course, they bought him out, and that's automatically two votes against you. He doesn't have to be present, and he can sign his rights to be assigned to someone to relay on his behalf if, for any reason, he has to be absent. This is a reasonable clause that was included in the will."

I listened to his words and then I asked.

"So, what is the best course of action?"

"Anything that will ensure that your sister isn't the one who gets his rights, because if she does, then she's automatically higher than the rest of you and she'll be making the decisions."

I nodded at his words and began to ponder what to do.

36

Lena

"This wasn't approved by the board."

At these words, I didn't have to look up to know whom they were coming from. I was quite familiar with the voice and had been since we were kids, though now he did feel more like a stranger than anything else.

"What are you going to do?" I replied as I went around setting up equipment in the laboratory, marking off what was settled and what wasn't.

"Well, I could make trouble for starters," he says, and I am almost amused.

"It wouldn't be the first time."

"Exactly." he said, and we both went silent until eventually, I turned around to meet his gaze.

"What are you doing here?"

He stared at me for longer than was necessary, and I wondered why. And then it made me concerned because for once he had his somber look on, which told me that he wasn't here to taint me or be dismissive or play games.

Whatever he was here to say was immensely serious and required all my attention.

"Are you alright?" I asked him, and he nodded.

"I'm perfect. So perfect in fact that I've come to you with an offer that you shouldn't dare reject. Unlike your dimwitted boyfriend."

I was immediately offended and ready to block out the rest of what he had to say for several reasons, but I decided in the end to just hear him out so I could return to my work.

I turned around and saw that he indeed had his serious face on.

"If this is about the lawsuit, I really don't know that I can make any difference to what's happening now."

"Wow," he said, "You're already defending him before I even got started. Is it that serious between you two?"

"There's nothing happening between us," I said, and he smiled.

"Honestly, for the first time, I hope there is."

"What do you mean?"

"I went to him and told him to buy me out because, despite how hard it is for me to admit this, the fact of the matter is that he is right, and I really don't belong here. I'm not cut out for this, and playing dress-up is enough. I want out."

I stared at him.

"You know that's not possible."

"It is," he replied. "I consulted with my lawyer, and he says that it is, technically. There's a clause that allows decisions to be made on my behalf if I'm mentally incapable."

"By your lawyer?"

"Could be but can also be by any upstanding individual of my choosing, so this is how I'm going to go out."

I had to admit that even though we weren't particularly close, I was sort of hoping that our proximity to each other would somehow rectify things, that he had truly found a way to leave, but now it was not at all pleasant for me despite what he believed.

I put down my document and focused my attention on him.

"I'm not happy to see you leave," I told him. "I thought... I know there's no point in saying this, but a part of me had hoped that working closely together would give us a chance to... become a family again."

He stared at me, and I waited for whatever smartass comeback he had to deliver, but it didn't come.

"We don't have to remain estranged," he said. "We don't even have to be in proximity to each other to be best friends. Picking up the phone helps and being polite enough and supportive of each other can go a long way as well."

His sarcasm was as heavy as anything could be, and I couldn't help but smile.

"Alright," I said. "Tell me what you need."

"I went to Kane to buy me out," he said, and I sighed.

"Yet he rejected me, and truly I am surprised because I was sure he'd jump at the chance to finally get rid of me, but apparently not."

At my silence, he paused briefly and then explained.

"I would have come to you first, but I am actually in need of the money, and it is not a small payment. Plus, to pay me, you'd probably have to sell some of Dad's assets, and I don't know if you're willing or even ready to do that right now."

There was sense and consideration in his words, so I nodded.

"Anyway, he turned me down, so now I have no choice but to go to his sister."

This wasn't a pleasant option, and he didn't need me to react to know this. But I was curious as to why Kane would turn him down.

"I know what you're thinking," he said and explained. "You're wondering why he would turn this down. Well, turns out he can be a moron as well."

I gave him a look, and he explained.

"He said something about wanting to honor Dad's wishes of making me actually work here for two years."

I considered his words and was touched.

"Yeah, I can see him thinking that."

"But it could also be because of his pride, and all that could have been, was bullshit," my brother said, and I smiled.

"And how exactly would his pride come into play here?" I asked, and he shrugged.

"Who the fuck knows. Anyway, my point is that I'm coming to you now to ask you to buy me out, if you can. And I need to have your decision immediately or at the very least in a few hours."

I gave him a look and then shook my head.

"I think you should make him see reason in taking the equity," I said.

"Having the power over the both of them might not look every good."

"To whom?" He was annoyed by my comment. "To him?"

I didn't respond and he sighed.

"Fine, whatever. Talk this over with him. It has nothing to do with me, and I'd rather cut off my own arm than go back to be spit at."

"I could transfer this thing at any time, so if you call to take me up on it and it's too late, then sorry in advance, but don't be late."

He turned around to speak to David, but I had one more question for him.

"Where are you going?" I asked.

"What do you mean?"

"I mean when you leave here, what exactly are your plans? What do you need this money so urgently for?"

He looked at me and then responded.

"Romania," he said, and I was immensely surprised.

"And Vegas, actually, but mainly Romania for now. I want to go into business with some acquaintances, and we want to invest in a couple of ventures. Casinos, nightclubs, vodka, and the like. I enjoy this thing more than selling thread count sheets and being a real estate agent, so I want to try my hand at it to see."

I was extremely happy to hear his words, yet at the same time, I was also sad because I deeply suspected that he was going to love all of these things and perhaps never come back.

"Thank you, Lena," he replied.

I nodded, either way, and wished him the best from the depths of my heart.

"I wish you the best as well, Lena," he said. "And good luck on your new division. It's coming along nicely."

I watched him leave and tried to get back to work, but as all the possibilities of how things could go, both good and bad, sank in, I let the offer linger briefly and headed up to his office.

37

Kane

So far, and as usual, she'd been avoiding my office at all costs, so I couldn't say that it wasn't a surprise when my secretary announced that she was requesting to see me. However, given the machinations her brother was busy with, it made sense that she would come here. However, I just couldn't make out why.

"Hey," I greeted, and she smiled in response as she headed in and, to my surprise, took a seat.

"You seem relaxed," I said, and she smiled again.

"I'm usually not when I come here, am I?" she asked.

"No, you're not," I replied. "You're usually with a loaded gun or two."

"You're right," she said as she nodded.

"You're here peacefully, so go ahead."

"It's about my brother," she said, and I nodded.

Though I was disappointed because I had expected it would be about something personal or the other between us, but it wasn't.

Usually, I would continue with whatever work I had to get through, even when she or anyone else, for that matter, was present, but this time around, I didn't want to. She was seated... and I dropped everything else and gave her my full attention. She watched me, and I couldn't help but notice just how softened she looked. It had very little to do with what she was wearing and instead concerned more about her demeanor before me, and it surprised me. Yet, I found out that I wasn't on guard. I just simply and truly enjoyed that she was seated before me.

"Is my brother's offer something that you're considering, or have you truly completely rejected it?"

At her words, I thought of the right response to give. Then I decided to just tell her the truth.

"You want me to take it?" I asked, and she nodded.

"Of course," she said. "I don't know why you didn't. I mean, he's just going to take it somewhere else that I'm pretty sure neither of us wants it to go. No offense."

I smiled at her words.

"None taken," I responded, unsure of how much of this I wanted to share with her. Before I could speak, however, she rose to her feet.

"I'll tell you," I said, and she stopped.

"I'd like that," she replied. "I just didn't want to force your hand in case you didn't want to."

"Well, I want to," I said and rose to my feet. I rounded the desk and went one step closer to her. I didn't go too close, but it was just close enough that I could smell her and see her.

"I guess... at first, I was just angry that he was trying to shirk his responsibilities and run off again, which I was immediately reminded shouldn't have been any of my concern, so I was sure that wasn't the main reason. But then, after he left, I thought a bit more. And I guess that I was just angry. I didn't pay much attention to this, but even though your father did a great job building this company, it grew more than 300% after I came in. I was so desperate to protect myself that I worked harder than anyone else here, and in a lot of ways, I contributed significantly to what this company has become."

Her gaze softened even more.

"You care," she said.

"Immensely. And with the way things have been going, it felt as though everyone was taking it for a joke. A place they could waltz in and take whatever they wanted... something they weren't entitled to. I didn't even see the equity gift to him as his, so when he came in asking me to buy it, I snapped. Because it was mine in the first place, or at least I believed it was mine. And he came here acting like he was about to sell something that he owned. All of this is from the emotional perspective rather than the logical one, but I was trying to make sense of my actions as well because him going to my sister rather than me wasn't a sound move. I was just quite rash, and... anyway I'll find a way to fix it."

She stared at me, and then she nodded.

"I understand, and I know you know exactly what to do. But he's not just trying to sell to get the money and blow it up. He truly has no interest in the operations here, and I don't think he's wrong for not wanting to spend the next two years of his life proving otherwise."

"I understand," I said. "I've spoken to my lawyer, and I'll find a way to resolve it, but..."

"But what?" she asked.

"I want you to take control of the equity from him."

At my words, she went silent.

"You do?"

"Yeah," I replied. "Our fathers were partners, and I thought it befitting that 50% of the company belonged to both of them. So rather than hand it over to me, I'd rather leave it to you. I can navigate my own way with Kate."

She started to speak, but I stopped her.

“Mull it over. I know you have your father's assets and ways to make the sale and transfer, but in case you don't want to go that route, then I'm willing to support you whatever way you need, okay?”

After this, I turned and returned to my desk. However, to my surprise, she didn't move.

'Why would you want to support me that way?' she asked.

At first, I was unclear about her question or what she even meant by it.

'What do you mean?'

'This is not a small company,' I said. “And this is not a small sale. Are you just in the habit of giving money, and millions, and millions of it, I might add, to just anyone?”

I understood then where she was coming from, and I sighed as I leaned into my chair and watched her.

“You're asking if this is purely professional?”

“Yes,” she replied, and I was sure it would be easier for me just to admit that this is the case, the more impossible it became for the words to form.

“No, it's not"' I replied.

For the first time, I couldn't read her expression at all. This was where the shrewd part of her came out, and I could do nothing but watch it.

"Why isn't it purely professional?" she asked, and I sighed.

"You know why."

"'You want me to assume why?" she asked.

"No, I don't." I wanted to get closer to her, but I stayed right where I was.

"Lena... I know this is not appropriate to say, but I want to say it. I don't want you to assume."

"Go ahead," she said.

"I think... things stopped being professional between us a while ago. I also think that they stopped being casual with us as well. I know it wasn't the plan, but... I'd like us to stop for a moment and acknowledge it."

She nodded, and I could see then that this wasn't all in my head. I had suspected at least that she felt the same way, but now I was immensely glad that I had spoken up.

"Is it possible?" I asked, and she finally met my gaze.

"Is what possible?" she asked.

"That we take a shot at this for real. That we see where it could go?"

She stared at me for so long that I was sure she was going to reject me. But then, to my almost disbelief and relief, she nodded. However, before I could say a single word more, she turned around to leave.

"Think about resolving the issue with my brother as quickly as you can," she said. "He did give us a heads up, but he's quite impatient, and at the snap of a finger, he can take this to your sister instead. Maybe he'll get pissed off at something or the other, and that's it."

"Alright," I replied, and she exited the office.

I couldn't take my eyes off her as she left, at the gentle sway of her hips and her calm movements. Her hair was flowing down her back today, and she had on white tailored pants and a jacket. She looked wonderful, and when it dawned on me that soon enough, we could be together for real, I didn't know how to contain the excitement that I felt. It had been a while since I felt this way, and suddenly it made all the looming problems that I had to deal with seem like they were a million miles away.

38

Lena

I hated airports. Generally, anything that had to do with me traveling was not the best of experiences, but the outcome was usually worth all the pain. Like, for instance, today I was welcoming my best friend in the whole world to New York, and I was so excited that I arrived early. Another reason why I found myself walking around the airport and being restless was because I felt quite weak. I was sure it was the fatigue from focusing on setting up the new department, and staying cooped up in the office was making me clouded.

There was also the reason that I was avoiding one person in particular, and this time it made absolutely no sense to however, I couldn't help it. I was surprised by what he had said to me in his office just earlier that morning; however, I was also happy. So happy that it had contributed to my restlessness and mental fog. In essence, I felt too much from the day and needed the relief from her... the change in perspective. The moment she came out from the arrival gate, I was more than ready to give her a hug.

"Oh my God, why are you here?" she asked in surprise.

"I could have just taken a cab; I know how busy you are."

"It's fine," I told her. "I needed the time away."

She gave me a look like she wasn't sure that that was the whole story, but the excitement at reconnecting again soon trumped all of that, and soon we headed back to the car.

"First, food," she told me. I was rushing so for this flight that I had absolutely no time for lunch." I obliged her request, and we soon got into the back of the car that had driven me over.

"Company perks," she said, and I nodded.

"I approve. Your company in LA could have never afforded this luxury."

I laughed at this, but as the sun set, I couldn't bear the air conditioning anymore, so the windows were rolled down for much-needed fresh air. I shut my eyes to take it all in, as well as the city, and she soon tugged on my sleeve for my attention.

"You're alright?" she asked, and I nodded.

"I am... just a little tired from the day."

"Want us to go to the apartment just to rest?" she asked, and I lifted my brows.

"If we do, I'm not coming back out."

"Can we order in?"

"Pizza?" she asked, and I made a face.

"Let's go out. There is this fascinating gourmet pizza place that has just opened up with incredibly unique toppings, and I really want to try it out."

"Alright then," she said, and we were on our way.

We had a reservation, so the waiting time was very little

before we were seated at our table. The room was warm, with the smell of dough, cheese, and meat filling the air, along with light conversation. And pretty soon, I was able to forget my exhaustion.

"So," she said after taking a sip of the sweet wine we had just ordered.

"So what?" I asked as I noticed the interest in her eyes.

"You haven't said a word all evening about Mr. CEO."

"Do we have to talk about him?" I groaned, and she gave me a look.

"No, but I haven't heard you mention him at all in the past week. You've literally gone out of your way to not discuss anything about him on the phone, so that's why I'm here."

"My mouth slightly fell open.

“You came all the way to New York to hear gossip about my love life?”

“"I plan to share as well," she told me. "Matthew is proposing some weird stuff in the bedroom, and I have no clue how to respond."

This conversation immediately captivated me, and as a result, we soon delved into the dark and exciting world of toys. Our tones did reduce, though, when the waiter came over, so that we would spare him overhearing just how badly things had gone for her when he had taken the remote control of the anal beads too far.

"My boss thought I was having a stroke," she said, and I couldn't contain my amazement.

Afterwards, a square-shaped gourmet goat cheese and shrimp pizza was delivered, along with four more slices of gourmet options, and I was more than ready to dig in. Due to the enlightened atmosphere, I was ravenous, and so the plate was empty in no time.

Eventually, though, my exhaustion and slight body aches came back, and I had to go to the bathroom. We went together, and it was lucky for me because out of nowhere, as we were washing our hands, a powerful dose of nausea hit.

She was talking about a dress she had bought that had the most gorgeous beading of a filigree she had ever seen, and then my face changed. Before she could say another word, I rushed into the bathroom, and once again, collapsed to my knees in front of the toilet bowl. I emptied my guts into it, and when I lifted my head once again to gaze at her, her eyes were wide.

"You really don't like seafood, do you?" she asked, and I almost laughed.

"Yeah, or I mean no... maybe I ate too much."

"You did, but that's not a reason to throw up that way." She came over to help me get up and held my hand in support.

"You alright?" she asked, and I nodded as she escorted me over to the sink. After rinsing my mouth, we exited the bathroom, and soon we were on our way home.

I didn't want to speak about Kane in the car, given that our driver was company staff, but the moment we got back home, and I was seated on the sofa, I couldn't hold back any longer.

"Kane asked me to make things official today," I said, and she stopped what she was doing.

She turned around to stare at me from the cinnamon tea she was making for us in the kitchen, and I nodded to confirm that she hadn't misheard me.

"What?" she asked.

"Yeah."

After putting the kettle on, she hurried over to me and sat on the couch. She stared at me, and I stared back, yet I was reluctant to speak. I wasn't sure exactly why, though perhaps it was because I wasn't feeling too well and was just generally exhausted. But she wasn't going to let the admission go, and I didn't want her to anyway because somehow, I needed to make sense of it.

"You don't want to say anymore?" she asked, and I nodded.

"I do, I just don't know what to say or how to feel. I haven't even responded to him yet, and I should have, right? I mean, I should have been excited by the very prospect and relieved, but I just felt foggy. A lot happened today. Dylan is trying to leave, or he's left, and he's transferring equity, and all of it was just a lot to take in."

She nodded and I could see immense relief in her eyes.

"I could tell from earlier," she said, "that you were extremely exhausted."

"Yeah?" I asked, and I nodded.

"So, we won't talk about any of it tonight any longer. Maybe after a good night's sleep, things will be clearer. Plus, I'm here until Sunday, so there's no rush."

"Yeah," I said. "Thank you. I'm glad to have you here, though, just the perfect distraction."

She got up then to return to the kitchen, while my gaze returned to the TV, but I couldn't register anything that was playing. It was all just moving pictures and sound as I felt more and more nauseous.

"I found a tuna sandwich in here," she suddenly called

out. "I'm gonna warm up a bit for myself. Those pizza slices were not filling. Do you want some?"

I started to picture them, feeling a bit hungry myself, and just like that, the nausea hit, and this time much harder than before. I was sprinting from the living room like I was on fire and retching like I was about to spill out my guts. Thankfully, it was dry, but then the moment I got to the bowl, it was as though my body registered that I could let loose, and for the second time that evening, I was spilling my guts into the toilet.

It seemed to take forever, and when I was done, I could barely hold myself up. Diana ran into the bathroom then, and upon seeing my dejected face, hers turned white.

"Okay," she said. "It's either you're really sick or..."

She stopped and I knew what she was about to say... what I had suspected all along but refused to even give a single thought to. I didn't deny it either way or put words or a voice to it, so I ignored her and spat one more time into the toilet bowl and then flushed.

"I'm fine," I said and tried to get up on my own to prove just that, but she refused, insisting on helping me.

I accepted her help so as not to make a big deal about things, plus I truly believed I needed it anyway.

We walked back to the living room together, and after helping me get back onto the couch, she sat back down beside me.

We were silent for a while, and then she asked.

"Does the smell bother you?"

"No," I replied. "I don't think it was the smell."

After this, she was silent again, and it truly began to bother me, so I turned to her and gave her a look.

"I'm not going to argue with you," she said, and I sighed.

I didn't want to argue as well, so I kept silent as well.

"Maybe it's just the flu," she said, and I agreed.

"It's just the flu."

"You used protection?" she asked, and I went silent.

She turned to me then, her eyes wide open.

"You didn't?"

"I'm on birth control."

"And you were consistent?"

"Of course I am," I said, but I didn't actually believe myself one bit.

"We weren't... it wasn't a regular thing between us. We would do it when we couldn't hold back, and then we'd stay away from each other for a while."

.

"So, you weren't consistent with the pills?"

"I was, but you know, sometimes you're in a rush and you forget."

She started to scold me again but then stopped and sighed.

"Maybe this is not a bad thing."

"We don't know anything yet," I said, and she gave me a look.

"I'll go buy a test."

"No," I told her. "I just want to rest today. It might be absolutely nothing at all. I've been eating out recently, so food poisoning's on the list."

"Well, it better be," she said. "Especially after all the alcohol you drank this evening."

"Jeesh, you sure know how to rub salt into someone's wounds," I said, and she laughed.

"You're not wounded. You just might be pregnant with your boss's baby."

I let out an aggravated groan at her words, but despite her complaint, I was glad she was here. Otherwise, having to deal with this alone... the suspicion and fear... alone. It would have been a hundred times more difficult. She got up a few minutes later to retrieve our sweet cinnamon tea, and it was just what I needed.

A few sips later, I was completely refreshed, while she was scrolling through the channels on TV. And then she sighed quietly.

"What will happen if our suspicion turns out to be true?"

"I have no clue," I replied reluctantly. "But it won't be. I'm fine. It's not that."

She turned to look at me.

"And if it is? Is he absolutely horrible?"

I thought of the man in question and how our relationship had changed over the time I'd been here.

"He's not the same, Diana," I said, and she turned to me.

"In what way?"

"Back then, he was cocky... confrontational... I hated his guts. But now..."

"You have feelings for him?" she asked, and I nodded.

"Maybe," I said, "but he has earned it."

"So why exactly are you so worried?"

"Everything," I replied. "Just a few weeks ago, I would have preferred the guy not exist, and now... My point is, wanting to make things official is great. It's a wonderful thing, but... I want time. And if this is... I'm afraid," I looked down at my stomach, "if this is what is happening, then that takes time away. From both of us."

She went silent again, and then she turned to me.

"Beyond your need for time..." she said, and I knew where she was going.

"Nothing is beyond time."

She looked at me and didn't push it, but in my mind, it was already a question that I had been ruminating over.

"If I didn't have time," I replied, "it would be a no-brainer. But I've been in business too long... been logical too long to just go with my gut."

She cocked her head.

"I remember saying your gut is the key."

At this, I laughed.

"Right, but I had experienced that it worked for business matters. For relationships... it's trash."

"I think you're confusing your gut with your heart."

I laughed again, knowing she was right.

"If there was a way for me to clearly differentiate, we wouldn't be having this conversation."

At this, we smiled, and then she squeezed my shoulder and got up.

I kept my gaze on the television and listened to her comments until eventually, I couldn't take it anymore. I got up and went to my room to pick up my jacket, and then I grabbed my wallet and started to head out.

"I'll be right back, Dee," I said, and she finally noticed me.

"Where are you going?" She came after me with a tiny teaspoon in hand.

"Pharmacy," I replied, and she gave me an encouraging look.

"Don't take it there," she said. "Come up here. I won't ask if you don't want me to, but it's cleaner here."

I was amazed that she was saying this, and her eyes narrowed in response.

"You were planning on taking it there, weren't you?"

"Maybe, but if I was going to hide it from you either way, I wouldn't have said I was going to the pharmacy."

"Semantics," she said. "Just get back here soon so that I know you're safe."

"Alright," I replied and headed out.

The pharmacy was very close to the apartment, but I decided to take an even longer route and head to the 7-Eleven instead. I was sure they would have the kits I needed, so I headed over.

Soon, I arrived and walked in, and quickly found the kit I was looking for.

I truly considered asking about their staff bathroom and just taking it there. It seemed as though the walk back home would take several hours otherwise, but as I saw the state of their bathrooms, I turned and went on my way.

The moment I arrived; Diana was thankfully not in sight. I had a spare bedroom which was now hers for the duration of her stay, so I was sure she was enjoying a snack. Without a word, I headed straight to my own bedroom and closed the door to the bathroom.

I tried not to make a big deal about it because I already felt better, and chances were that it was just the flu. But eventually, I couldn't stand not knowing anymore. I opened the stick and waited, stopping myself from opening my eyes.

These kinds of things I preferred to do alone, so eventually, I opened my eyes to look at the results I found...

39

Kane

When I walked into the conference room the very next morning and saw only my sister seated and waiting, I didn't know what to say.

."Where's Lena?" Matthias asked by my side, and my sister shrugged.

"That's not important. We have a decision to make and a lot of work to do," she replied. I ignored her, and just as I was about to send my secretary to her office to find out why she wasn't present, my secretary came in.

"She called in sick, Sir," he said, his phone in hand. She thought she would be able to make it, but she couldn't. She apologized.

At his words, I was immediately concerned, but I couldn't show it. After he exited, I looked at Kate and her lawyer and decided that there was no point in proceeding with this meeting when only half of the partners were currently present.

"Let's postpone this meeting," I told her. "We have very

crucial matters to decide upon, and I think it's best that we do these when she's also present."

"No," my sister replied. "She could have called in way ahead of time if she wanted to make it. No one gets sick ten minutes before a meeting."

"We can't have this meeting without her, and Dylan isn't here."

"This is exactly why this meeting is necessary."

I stared at her. There was a lot to process, but I knew her well enough to understand her demeanor when she is certain that she has won a war.

"You called for this meeting," I told her. " I'm assuming the reason is related to Dylan's equity."

"How sharp," she replied. "Yes, it is, among other things, but I do believe that it's the most important, so I'd like to officially announce it and immediately exercise my right."

"What right?" I asked, and she smiled.

"Starting from today, you are automatically suspended from being CEO."

My brows raised at her words, while Matthias turned to her in surprise.

"On what grounds?" I asked.

"You can't do that without any grounds."

"Oh, I'm prepared," she said, "And I think mine are pretty valid."

"What are they?" I asked, and she smiled and continued.

"During the last meeting we had, the agreement we came to was that the expansion of the science division wouldn't be pushed forward. However, you blatantly went ahead with it to appease her, and this cannot be accepted."

At her words, I sighed and fully turned to address her.

"Kate, rejecting that expansion had nothing to do with the merits of it being beneficial to the company."

"Doesn't matter," she said. "You suspended her brother for being late to a meeting, which, the last time I checked, doesn't directly benefit the company in any way. So, when the same is about to be applied to your suggestion, I think it makes no sense."

"Unacceptable."

I stared at her, and she went on.

"I'll take over the operations of the company from this morning. My assistant will be in your office before we get there so that you can hand over all the related files."

Shaking my head, I started to leave, sure that this nonsense could be resolved at a later date.

Given her current state of mind and the changes she wanted to make, I had no response to give in return. Thus, rather than stay here and make things worse, I turned around and headed straight for my office. When I got to my office, I gathered documents that I needed from my desk but after giving it further thought I dropped them, grabbed my jacket and headed out. My secretary saw all this and came in in a panic.

"Sir, I'm sorry to say this, but you can't do that. You have meetings scheduled for today and-"

"Give them all to Kate."

"Sir..."

I could see the panic on his face, and it made me understand that this was exactly what needed to be done.

"Don't argue with me. Just hand them all to Kate."

I could feel the tears and frustration in his eyes, but I wasn't in the mood to care. In short, the more I thought about this as I headed out, the more relieved I felt. Since I had joined the company over ten years earlier, I had taken on as much as my shoulders could bear and then some.

But now, especially given my relationship with Lena, it was time to step down and see things from a different perspective. Things would fall apart, but I would be able to bring them back up if needed. That was the skill that never taking a break for this long had given me.

"Sir, a lawsuit is coming," she reminded me. "About the copyright infringement with the packaging design for the light bulbs for-"

"Give it all to Kate," I said and headed out with a wave.

It was amusing, truly, but none of it surprised me. I was upset, but I knew I would be fine after a morning scotch, something that had never happened before. However, first of all, there was somewhere I needed to be. My driver was waiting outside to drive me, but before that, Matthias met me at reception.

"I'll have a way to overturn this by the end of the day," he said, and I didn't respond. But then, just as I reached the door, I stopped and turned to him.

“Don’t do anything.”

"You're sure about that?" he asked, and I could see the element of amusement in the corner of his lips.

"Yes, but if not, perhaps it's time to move on anyway."

"I'll keep in touch," he said and turned around to return.

The moment I got into the back of the car, I looked outside the window at the skyscraper, and then I gave him the needed instructions.

"Lena's apartment.” I said, and he nodded in response.

40

Lena

This was the third time I had gone back to bed within the space of an hour, and it was frustrating me to no end. I wanted to sleep, but every time I did, I would wake up again, fraught with fear and worry, unable to find rest. And then I would feel hungry, but whenever I tried to eat something, I would lose my appetite.

Eventually, and for the last time, I emerged from my bedroom. This time, I found Diana at the counter with sleepy eyes, pouring herself a cup of black coffee. She stared at me, and for a moment, I wondered if she truly saw me.

"Do you have your contacts in?" I asked, and she frowned.

"It's 10 am."

"So?"

"Well, no, obviously, but that doesn't mean that I'm blind."

I smiled as I pulled the fridge open to grab the oats that I had been wanting to eat all morning.

"I heard you moving around constantly, but I thought you'd be at work by now."

"I'm taking the day off," I said, and she paused when I came over to join her. I caught her watching me.

"I need it," I said, and she nodded.

"I know."

"Anything I can do to help?"

"No," I replied. "There's a farmers market though; I've been meaning to visit. They're usually only open on Saturdays, but today is Friday, so maybe we might find something. Maybe we'll run into a flea market on the way."

"That sounds fantastic," she said. "I was actually going to go to a cafe for breakfast and have it outside, just like in Paris."

"This is not Paris," I said, and she nodded.

"Trust me, I know. But since you're not going to work, would you like to join me?"

"Of course," I said, and she nodded. "Though don't eat all of that, or you won't have any space for the café."

I was about to agree to this, but then I remembered that yes, indeed, I might not have the space for more, but I would most definitely need it. I sighed and put the jar away.

She picked up her cup to head over to the stool on the opposite side, but just as she set it down, there was a knock on the door.

"Oh?" she said as she looked behind. "Are you expecting someone?"

"No," I replied as I stared at it, but I couldn't help my nerves. "Maybe it's the building maintenance but they would have called first," I said calmly as I finished the rest of my oats. She gave me a peculiar look, and then she headed over to the door.

I wanted to head over to my room because I truly wasn't ready for whatever the day had in store for me. In fact, I wanted to hide. But I waited, at least to see what the day had for me because it truly might not end up being too bad.

She looked through the peephole, and then she pulled away. She looked through it again, and this time, as she turned around to look at me, her eyes were wide.

"What?" I asked.

"Were you expecting Kane?" she asked, and my heart dropped into my stomach.

"Expecting who?"

"You know who," she said, and the knock came again. This time, however, it was brief.

I immediately turned around and began to head to my room.

"Lena," she called, and I stopped in my tracks. Then I turned around and nodded.

After giving me a look, she opened the door, and there he was. The man I hadn't been able to get out of my mind for even a single second since last night. He looked at my friend and then looked at me before looking at her once again.

"Is this a bad time?" he asked, and I shook my head.

"No, it's not."

Diana looked back at me, and then she smiled as she got out of the way and invited him in.

"Would you like something to drink?" she asked. I'm Diana, by the way."

There was, however, no recognition in his eyes since I hadn't ever mentioned her. I hadn't ever mentioned anyone because we'd never really sat down to talk about our personal lives beyond the connection that we held with our fathers. And that was the whole point of my dilemma and hesitation with him. However, as I stared at him—how handsome he was and how strong I knew his character was —and how I felt, it was so difficult for me to lament the fact that I was now aware that I was pregnant with his child. He was a perfect specimen of a man, and I knew my heart was already taken with him. We just had to remove the mental and emotional roadblocks we had both put in our own way so that we could become completely open to each other. If we were ever able to do this, I could imagine how it all would be. I could breathe, and for the first time, we could give each other permission to feel what we already felt for each other. At least, what I knew I already felt for him.

I stepped forward for the first time and introduced her.

"This is my best friend... from LA."

He looked at her and then at me, and then he nodded. He smiled and held out his hand once again, and she took it excitedly.

"Hello, Diana. I'm Kane. It's a pleasure to meet you."

"Same here," she giggled, with something that sounded akin to the sound of a little girl. I almost rolled my eyes, but instead, I sighed, and she soon turned away and went into her room while I faced him.

Seeing him so impeccably dressed, I was suddenly self-conscious. I was in oversized pajama pants and a huge T-shirt from last night. I hadn't exactly considered what I would wear to bed. I had simply been exhausted and panicked, and then somehow, halfway through the night, sleep had come to me.

"Come in, please," I said and headed back to the kitchen.

"Would you like something to drink?" I asked as he came over to the counter.

I looked around my house, wondering how he saw it through his own eyes until I recalled that he had been here himself not too long ago. In short, he had taken me against the wall I was now staring at, and even though I didn't think that was the time exactly I had found myself in my current mess, it was something to think about.

"I already had coffee at the office," he said and took his seat on the stool across from me.

"Alright," I said and then turned to stare at him from across the counter. "Something to eat then... fruits... pancakes?"

"You're not surprised to see me here?" he asked, and I smiled.

"I am, but I know whatever reason you're here, it must be serious. And I also know that given the time, you most definitely haven't eaten, so it wouldn't be bad to talk as you eat."

He smiled at this, and then his gaze softened on me.

"Are you alright? The message was that you skipped the meeting because you aren't feeling well?"

"Yeah," I replied. "I felt a bit... nauseous and just feverish. I think I had food poisoning or something. Plus, things have become quite hectic with the department and all and I really needed the day off."

His gaze went to the closed door by the side.

"Sure it has nothing to do with the fact that your friend is in town?" he asked, and I smiled.

"'Maybe."

"It has absolutely nothing to do with what we talked about yesterday?" he asked, and I was somewhat taken aback.

"I hadn't even thought about it."

"Oh," I said and frowned. "Is that why you're here? You're here to take it back."

He smiled, and I felt a bit more comfortable enough to joke with him about it.

"It better not be the case."

"It isn't," he said, and I nodded. Then he watched me again.

"You don't want me to take it back?"

"Absolutely not."

"So, you're going to accept?"

"Of course I am," I said, and despite the apprehension I saw on his face, mine was accompanied by a sinking feeling because there was no way now that he was going to accept that I was not just agreeing to this because of the baby. I wished more than anything that I had told him just how glad I was by what he was proposing yesterday that I had accepted it on the spot.

I sighed then and pushed my worries away. There was truly no point in having them because they weren't going to solve anything. I wanted to go even closer to him, but I hesitated.

"Is that why you came over?" I asked. "You were worried that I'd say no."

"No," he said, and my heart deflated again. Maybe I was getting too ahead of myself.

"I came over because I got fired today."

The moment the words left his mouth, my entire senses screeched to a halt.

"What?"

"Yeah."

"Apparently, your brother got impatient or maybe not.

Either way, he transferred his rights, or rather guardianship over his rights, to my sister this morning." I was flabbergasted.

"And her first order of business was to kick you out?"

He shrugged.

"Apparently."

"And you just let her?"

He nodded, and I was so confused.

"What's happening?" I asked. "How is it possible that you just let her?"

"Because I think I need a break," he said. "From all of the nonsense."

"Sure, I could have fought it. There's probably a way to have it backfire, but I think this is not the right move to make right now. Plus, I could really use a break. I mean... I looked around and you weren't there, and..."

My heart began to race in my chest.

"I don't know. I have no qualms about resting, just as you are."

I was a bit torn stricken as I listened to him, yet I was amused at the same time.

"My break was for a brief period. Just today... the weekend. I would have come back on Monday."

"Well, you don't have to go back," he said. "Plus, I suspect that another thing she'll be doing is shutting down your project."

I was even more horrified, alarmed, and annoyed. I found myself going closer to him then.

"What? And you're not... I mean... why are you so calm about this?"

He smiled.

"That is a billion-dollar company," he replied. "You can't develop the skills to run it overnight."

"So, you think she'll come crawling to you?"

"There are a lot of fires I put out on a daily basis that I don't really report about. That alone is going to overwhelm her in the next day or two. Then there is a huge lawsuit in progress that, again, she is not aware of. If she can handle all of these pressures and resolve them within the next day or two, then I'll gladly step down."

"So, you've already stepped down now?"

"I have, but I'm sure she won't make it official. After she sees what she's just fought for, she'll struggle a bit, and then perhaps she'll reach out to me."

"And if she doesn't?"

He shrugged again.

"I really don't want to think about any of that right now. Like I said, if this hadn't happened, I don't think I would have willingly taken a vacation. And I need one. With you, preferably."

I finally listened to what he was saying.

"Are you inviting me to take one with you?"

"Why not?" he asked, and for the umpteenth time within the span of two days, I was stunned. I stared at him, and he stared back, glancing at the door to the side to see if Diana was somehow overhearing this.

"You're serious?" I ask, and he nods.

"Yeah. That's if you're really considering what we talked about yesterday. I mean, our only options right now are to either fight for the next two weeks or leave the country."

He said it so calmly, but something about the words just made me want to laugh. In relief, in amusement, in agreement.

"Can we really do that?"

He rose to his feet, his gaze on me, and then he came over to me. And with each step he took, I could feel my heart about to burst out of my chest.

Still, I managed to hold my ground, and eventually, he was before me.

I could smell his sweet, familiar scent of musk and vanilla bean, and it caused a whiff of intoxication, even though I knew he didn't smoke. And it was all intoxicating. My gaze fluttered down to his lips, and I knew exactly what they could do to me, to every inch of my body, and all over again, I wanted him so much that it felt like I was going to lose my mind.

His gaze slightly went to the door Diana had disappeared into, and when he came even closer to where our chests were touching, I knew what he wanted to do, and I had no qualms whatsoever about it. He held onto my arm, and I could feel goosebumps breaking out across my skin.

"I must look a mess," I had to admit then because he was now incredibly close, and I could feel my hair sticking out everywhere.

"You do," he said, and I laughed again. But then his arm slid slowly around the side of my neck, and then he pulled me in even further to kiss me.

It was slow, elevating, electrifying, and in no time, I was melting into his arms. He sucked softly on my lips, slid his tongue in, and we both completely lost ourselves.

Suddenly, however, there was a noise coming from Diana's room, something sudden and loud as though she had knocked something over, and as a result, we were forced to come to a stop. I didn't want to, however. I couldn't have cared less if she walked in on us, but he did, especially because they were just meeting for the first time.

"Where would you like to go?" he asked, brushing the hair from my face.

41

Kane

Turkey was definitely not my destination of choice, but as I looked into her beautiful eyes and felt the excitement in them, there was nothing else I could say but yes. Plus, I didn't have any better ideas. However, as I picked her up from her apartment later that evening and we were driven to the private tarmac, it quickly became clear to me that if I agreed with every request she had, we wouldn't have much to talk about or anything to argue about, for that matter. Still, I found it quite peculiar that she was so calm.

As soon as we arrived, we were rushed up to the private plane, and there we took our seats, though they were across the aisle from each other. There was a sofa just up ahead that we could have shared, but neither of us seemed familiar enough with each other to do so, and so we remained in our own seats. I was extremely tempted to check for news from the office, but I refrained from doing so to the best of my ability. After shutting off my phone, I put it away, and that's when I faced the second problem of what the hell I was supposed to do with myself if I wasn't fully occupied with work.

I glanced at her from time to time and noticed that she was continually typing messages on her phone, which made me wonder if I was the only one who had completely let go of the reins.

"Are you in touch with Standard Rock?" I asked, and she looked up.

"No," she replied. "We got a new graphics designer back in LA. I'm just reviewing some of the newsletter designs he created to see if he's a good fit."

"So, no contact with Standard Rock at all?" I asked, and she shook her head.

"I'm scared to have any contact with them after what you told me. I instructed the guy at the front desk that any attempts to contact me should not be allowed."

I nodded and turned away, and eventually, I noticed that she put her phone away and turned to face me.

"You're really not going to do any work?" she asked, and I nodded.

"Yeah."

"How does it feel?"

"How do you think it feels?" I asked, shutting my eyes. Although I wanted to look at her and engage, I also wanted to settle, so I chose to approach things a bit more casually.

"A quiet storm," she said, and I smiled.

"Is a storm ever quiet? You just choose to ignore it."

"You're not going to actually enjoy this vacation, are you?" she asked, and I turned to stare at her.

"Are you?"

Her smile was much brighter than I had ever imagined.

"I'll make sure we do."

"How?" I asked, and she started by pulling something out of her purse that looked like a wooden case, and then a bag that she lifted to her ears and noisily shook for my benefit. But for the life of me, I couldn't picture what was in there.

"What is that?" I asked, and she came over to my table. She took the seat opposite mine, and the game she soon revealed on the table was none other than Scrabble.

I gave the game a look, then glanced at her, not quite knowing how to react.

"We're playing Scrabble?" I asked, and she nodded, although her smile faltered.

"You don't like it?"

"It's a boring game," I said, and almost regretted it when I saw her face fall. And then her eyes.

"Okay, so what kind of game would you prefer?"

I hadn't played any games in so long that I couldn't even remember what that was like, but I thought hard, and a few that I had enjoyed in the past came to mind.

"Monopoly is good," I said, but her expression didn't change. "I especially like chess," I added.

"You're a snob," she said and leaned back in her seat, and I couldn't help but be amused.

"And why is that?" I asked.

"Look at the two games you just stated as your preferences. One is about money, and the other is about control."

"Maybe, but they're both mostly about winning."

"All from a guy who just got fired, I don't think you're doing much of that lately."

She said this under her breath, which was so shocking that all I could do was stare at her.

"Too soon?" she asked, and I shook my head, truly amused.

"Oh, maybe you want to play these games because you want to win at them, right? I mean, Scrabble is mainly just intellectually stimulating, but you—"

"Waste of time," I said, and she frowned.

"We're on vacation. The point is to waste time."

"Just playing games is not very appealing," I said. "Let's put wagers on the table... incentives to ensure that winning is encouraged."

"Winning is encouraged?" she repeated.

"Oh," she got up then and came over to my table. "You're on."

I watched as she took her jacket off, revealing a fitted dark waistcoat that did very little to hide her cleavage, and from this one move, I was pretty certain that I was already losing. My eyes lingered, and at the same time, she had the most sheepish smile on her face.

"Distracted?" she asked, and I shook my head. Then I called the air hostess over and requested my chessboard.

"You have a chessboard here?" Her eyes widened, and I nodded.

"Of course I do," I replied. "I've earned millions off it."

"Wait, what? Millions? By taking other people's money?"

"Through winning," I said, and she still looked shocked, then lowered her head.

"I've stepped into deep shit, haven't I?"

"Very, very deep," I replied, and she gave me the naughtiest of smiles.

The board was brought over and set up before us, and through it all, I couldn't take my eyes off her.

"Should I assume that you're not taking this very seriously because we don't have a wager?" she asked as she made her quite excellent moves across the board.

I smiled.

"Who says I'm not taking this seriously?"

"Well, going off the millions you've claimed to have made, my guess is that you took those games seriously by actually putting in an effort to win."

"I am putting in the effort to win," I said, and she shook her head.

"I don't think that's the case at all."

I chuckled quietly.

"Why would you think that?"

"Because we're more or less the same now. I thought you'd be so far ahead, or the game would be over by now."

"Is it because there's no wager?" she asked.

"I'm putting in my best," I assured her until I lifted my gaze to hers. Her expression was dry and unpleased, and I knew then that I had to admit that I was going soft on her.

"You don't feel well," I said. "And this plane is quite small. The last thing I want to have to deal with is a sore loser."

Her mouth fell open at this jibe, and all I wanted to do was kiss her senseless.

"That's not true," she said. "Up till now, you didn't even remember that I wasn't feeling well. You're just trying to find an excuse because you've been so distracted."

"By what?"

Without a word, she started to pull off her jacket, and to say that I was surprised was an understatement.

She flung it away to the couch, and all I could see was the most petite frame and a rack of breasts I knew exactly what they tasted like and was hungry for.

"What?" I asked, and she moved her knight.

"Feeling hot," she said, and then straightened to look at me.

"I know money might be tight for you now, given that you just lost your job—"

"Suspended," I corrected, but she kept going.

"However you want to spin it. My point is that there has to be a reward for there to be apt motivation. So, let's make a wager now."

I looked at her and wondered what she wanted as well as what could make this immensely interesting as well. However, she brought up her ideas first.

"How about ten thousand dollars?" she asked, and I smiled.

"That's not enough incentive to make you feel like shit today, Miss Mercer."

Her expression narrowed darkly at my words.

"Then what is?" she asked, and I shrugged.

"Nothing comes to mind right now. But when it does, I will sure as hell let you know."

"No," she leaned back into her chair. "Decide on something now, or I'm going to take a nap."

"What do you want?" I asked, and as mischief came into her face, I knew that I was going to hate it.

"I want you to sing me a song."

42

Lena

I might not be a hundred percent certain what I felt for him, but as I watched the blood leave his face completely white as it drained out, I was convinced that it was the closest to love I had ever felt for someone.

From powerful and impenetrable, he became uncertain, terrified, and even annoyed, and the range of expressions nearly brought me to tears with amusement.

"Not funny," he said, and only when I could catch my breath was I able to respond.

"Actually, it is," I replied. "It's fucking immensely funny."

He sighed then, and I shook my head.

"Never happening."

I knew that I could push it, but I didn't want to over wield my newfound power over him, so I thought of what else I could want. And then it came to me.

"I want to ask ten very personal questions about you, and you have to respond without lying whatsoever."

"Ten questions?" he asked. "Who has ten personal things about them?"

"It includes history, fears, wishes, all of that, and you have to be honest. It will be the foundation of our relationship."

He watched me for a while, and then he nodded.

"You have to be honest," I reiterated again. "They'll be vulnerable questions, and I need you to be able to share these parts of yourself with me."

"I might not be able to share all now," he said. "That takes time."

"I know," I replied, my gaze lowering.

I felt sad all over again because the need for time once again reared its ugly head. Of course I knew it took time but how was I to tell him that I didn't have any time? That both of us no longer had any time?

"Okay," he said, and my head snapped up.

"Okay," I understand you, and even though I can't reveal all... at least I can't promise that I will be able to... maybe I will. I do promise that I will be completely honest with you."

I stared at him, and he stared back.

"Lena," he called. "I don't think I've ever had a relationship that has gone beyond two months, and even those, I don't think have ever been more than two."

"Really?" I asked, and he nodded.

At first, I found it strange, but as I began to think about my own story, I realized that I wasn't any better, and this immensely amused me.

"What?" he asked, and at first, I hesitated in telling him, but eventually, I decided that it was for the best. That I had to succumb to my own desire as well and tell him what he needed to know.

"I'm the same. Actually, I've only had one serious relationship ever, and it lasted a mere seven months. And for most of that time, it was long-distance."

At my words, his eyebrows shot up, and then he nodded.

"By the end of all of this, we might have much more in common than we ever realized."

He played a move, and then I thought of something more interesting.

"Rather than waiting for the end... for either of us to move, why don't we do something else?"

"What do you have in mind?" I asked and watched as he took off his glasses.

Finally, we were both becoming completely comfortable with each other, and I absolutely loved it.

"With every move we make, let's ask each other questions. And then at the end, money is the wager."

He narrowed his eyes as he contemplated this, and then he nodded.

"But to make me as engaged as possible, let's take the wager to fifty thousand dollars."

"Hey!" I complained. "I'm out of a fucking job too."

He smiled, and I loved that relaxed sound he made, as though he owned the whole world and absolutely nothing could touch him.

"You can make up for it in other ways," he said, and I knew whatever he was going to say was going to be the best for me.

"What ways?" I asked, and he briefly glanced out of the window in thought.

Then he turned back to me.

"I want you to suck me off," he said, and my heart

stopped. And then it resumed once again because I didn't understand why this would be too special.

"I was going to do it at some point during this flight," I said, and he smiled.

"I know, but the more you do it, the farther the date for payment is postponed."

"Oh," I said, and he smiled.

"Yes."

"How much after for each?"

"Two weeks," he said, and I immediately countered this.

"A month."

"Three weeks," he said, and I smiled.

"Standard negotiation tactics."

He shrugged.

I gave this a thought, or rather, I pretended to because I could see absolutely no downside to this whatsoever. My mouth was already watering, and butterflies were swarming in the pit of my stomach at the mere thought of it.

"Okay," I said, and the wager was on.

I made the next move, and then I thought about the question that I was going to ask him first.

I thought hard, and he watched me, but eventually, it came to mind. It was a little weird, but it was something that I had always been curious about.

"What was your first perception of me?" I asked. "I'm just curious."

He smiled, and I listened attentively.

"My perception of you the first time I saw you or the first time you noticed that I saw you?" he asked.

"You mean in the library or the latter?" I asked, and he nodded.

"The first time you actually saw me and then that time."

"Oh, two questions in one."

"We're allowed to do that," I said, "as far as the major topic of discussion is related."

He smiled and then nodded.

"Maybe you should have been a lawyer."

"I would have been," I said. "But I fell in love with scents more."

"What are you wearing right now?" he asked. "I was meaning to ask, it smells divine."

"It's our Enchanted Collection," I replied. "This one is made of dogwood blossoms."

He nodded.

"Would you want me to make one specially for you?" I asked, and he met my gaze with those beautiful eyes of his. If I was to go through this, I couldn't help thinking... if I was to truly have his baby, I wondered what color of eyes they would have, my hazel eyes or his piercing gray stare?

"I would," he replied. "You'll choose the scents specifically?"

"Yes," I replied and straightened up with interest.

"They'd represent me?"

"Yes," I replied again.

"Hm, so what would you choose?"

I smiled and thought about this.

"Sandalwood for... a note of sophistication ... strength ... bergamot for freshness, maybe a little lime, and most definitely vanilla bean for allure."

"Hm, sounds wonderful," he said, and I nodded, now suddenly so excited to make his scent.

The one that would remind me of him at every turn.

"It will be," I promised, and we got back on track.

43

Kane

"The first time I can recall seeing you was at a bar," I said. She seemed surprised, but I was certain that my recollection was accurate.

"I think we were at some family function or the other, and you were a kid for sure because that was what stood out to me."

"A kid at a bar?"

"Yup," I replied. "Caught my attention instantly. You weren't allowed to drink, of course, but you had something else more... mature about you. Despite your age, you just sat there, drinking and watching everyone. What was funny to me back then was that it seemed as though you were trying to avoid mingling with the other kids, but you didn't just go hide in a corner. You sat where everyone could see you and I noted the difference."

"Oh my God," she said. "I can assure you that that most definitely was not my intention. I probably just liked the drinks or something."

"I think so as well," I agreed. "But it was just so interesting to me. Plus, you were gorgeous, and I remember thinking you'd be so dangerous when you grew up. When you came to the study that time and walked in on me... actually, I had seen you before that during that event, and I was struck. You'd grown... my gaze went down to your hips and breasts, and I didn't miss your blush."

"You sound like a predator," she said and was amused.

"Maybe," I said. "At that time, I was in my early twenties, I think, and was having a very difficult time carving out a path for myself. Especially since my father was insisting that I join the company. So, in many ways, I think I was lashing out and allowing myself to be distracted with the recent discovery that I could make a woman cum so loudly that she nearly screamed my ear off."

She smiled at this, and then she lowered her gaze and continued playing.

"Why did you invite me to join, though?" she asked. "I mean, you could have done the decent thing and told me to leave...or look away."

I smiled.

"I wanted to, but then your gaze lingered, and you looked so fascinated. Plus, I had always had you on my radar, and I was in the throes of a very um... exciting event. I couldn't resist wanting to take it as far as possible."

She shook her head at my words, and then we kept playing.

"Did you really detest me, though?" I asked, lifting my gaze to meet hers.

"Who said I did?"

"Well, you acted like you did at every single turn."

This made her laugh, and more than anything, I just enjoyed the free way in which we communicated.

"I didn't. I thought you were a cocky bastard, but now... I think maybe you're just... confident."

I laughed.

"Apt. Being confident is the ultimate excuse for every cocky bastard."

"You are right," she said.

"Anyway, that incident was a particular sore spot in my mind, and I think it was because I was just shocked at your audacity and how unapologetic you were. I mean, most people would have been shocked and horrified, but you fucking invited me to join. So maybe, in a way, it made me envious."

"Of the woman?"

"Hell no," she reacted. "I mean, of course, I was, but I'm not ever going to outrightly admit that to you or anyone else or myself for that matter. Let's just go back," she said, and I nodded.

"Anyway, now that I think of it, your audacity must have given me a backbone. I mean, it just stuck in my head that there were people in this world who did whatever the fuck they wanted and were unapologetic about it, and it just made me want to go after the things I wanted. And that was very difficult for me at the time because I didn't have much courage."

"Sure didn't look like it," I said, and she nodded.

"Yeah."

"But can I ask, though, how were you able to resolve the dilemma you had with your father concerning all the angst you were feeling at the time, I mean?" she asked.

I understood the questions she was asking me exactly and had no qualms about responding.

"Well, I think the issue is actually that me and my father were quite similar. We each wanted to have our own world, but he wanted to have everyone else just be a side character within his, and that wasn't going to fly with me. I was just as arrogant as I can ever imagine being, and at every point in time, he could never hold back from reminding me that I was nothing without him. But it was true, which just made me angrier, and so I was determined to follow my own path."

"So what made you change your mind?" she asked, and I nodded as I thought back to the time, realizing though that we were now so engrossed in this conversation that we had all but forgotten the chess game.

I was enjoying revealing myself in this way, though, so I continued. I didn't think I had ever done it before.

"Respect," I replied. "He most definitely didn't give it to me for no reason, but for the first time in my life, I could see him kind of humble himself to ask for something that he wanted. He could see that I had a choice, and... in a way, I was sure he also saw that I really held the interest of becoming an entrepreneur as well and working with him. His attitude was going to drive me away. For the first time ever, he approached me quite softly, and I was stunned by it, so I decided to give it a chance."

"Hm," she smiled, and it was so sweet that I felt a fluttering in my chest.

"Why?" I asked and nodded.

"I didn't know you could be so humble?"

"Respectful," I corrected her. "Plus, I also have a brain, just like what's happening now. Being constantly hard is not the answer to anything. You need to know when to show your strength and when to lay it down, when to advance and retreat."

As I said the words, I watched her eyes lower and then slightly widen.

"Oh my God," she said, and I understood exactly why. "My dad used to say that."

"Yeah," I replied. "He did."

Her smile widened, then I watched it fade as well.

"Sometimes I forget that you worked so closely with him. I really wish I had as well."

I didn't know what to say to this, so I made my move on the chessboard, and unfortunately, this claimed her bishop, getting her attention.

"Hey!" she complained, and I was relieved that I had gotten her attention again and pulled her away from the sour memories.

I was incredibly happy, though, that I could speak to her this way. More than anything, it felt as though I was speaking to a family member and given that she was also my lover and perhaps girlfriend, it was truly the cherry on top of the cake. I continued playing with her, my heart filling and swelling as this impromptu vacation was turning out to be an incredible decision.

44

Lena

Turkey was one of my favorite places to vacation. Back when I was in college, just before our finals, I and my group of friends at the time had taken an impromptu trip, and it was so far one of the most memorable vacations of my life. We had all chosen the cheapest hotels and accepted anything free that we could find, but the ambiance and experiences had cost little to nothing. It was a distraught time for me internally, I can remember, because back then, I was fighting the battle of what I wanted to do. My interest was in scents and starting my own business, but my father thought it was all nonsense and pointless. After all, if this was my interest, then why didn't I come to work for him?

"Our stories are quite similar," I said as I got into the gorgeous suite room overlooking the Bosphorus Strait.

"What do you mean?" Kane asked as he tipped the porter and shut the door behind him.

"Remember when I came here with my friends and

made the decision that I was going to start my own business myself? Actually, I was going to get a job eventually, but I started anyway before my final year because I was scared that I wouldn't make it, and my dad would be right."

He laughed softly.

"You're right, we are indeed similar."

"I recall speaking to him from the beach over there," I said. "We had a campfire, or rather we joined a campfire, so I had to walk away to respond to him."

"That was such a mentally tumultuous time," I said. "I felt his presence behind me and ached to lean on his strength. However, although there was nothing that technically needed to stop me, I was still reluctant because it was so easy to depend on him, to want him, almost need him even."

"If you'd joined the company then we would have met much earlier," he said, and I almost gave in then.

I was amused as I wondered about it, and then his arms came around me.

"Yeah," I said. "Do you think we would have..."

I stopped myself because truly I didn't know how to phrase this question.

However, he understood exactly what I was trying to say, and in a way that made my chest hurt so much that it felt like it was going to burst.

"We definitely would," he said. "It might have taken some time, though, seeing that we would have been much, much younger. Our pride would have most definitely held us back from each other."

I turned around to face him.

"So you're saying that the glue that's holding us together right now is the fact that we don't have much pride?"

He was beaming with amusement as I turned around to stare at him.

"Am I wrong?" he asked.

"I don't want to think too much about the question because then I won't rest until I find the appropriate answer."

"Alright," he succumbed and held me even tighter, and this time around, I held no qualms whatsoever about completely going into him.

The views were gorgeous, the company immaculate, and for this moment, I allowed myself to completely dream. That there were no concerns about anything, that we weren't fired or kicked out of the company. It all just seemed far away or at least so small as I took in the vast and expansive horizon.

"I think it's our maturity," he said, and I was brought back to earth to listen to him. His answer made me smile.

"Really? You think so?"

"Don't you?" he asked, and I beamed.

"I don't think I can completely vouch for myself being mature. I mean, sometimes I am, and sometimes I most definitely am not."

"Again, I agree with you," he said with a sigh, and I laughed out loud again. Then I turned around to face him.

"Agreeing with me seems to come awfully easy these days."

"Right," he said.

"Sure, it's not because our relationship is new, and the butterflies are running rampant?"

"We've never really disagreed before," he pointed out. "It's just that both of us have very strong personalities, like predators sizing each other in the wild. Turns out when the defenses are somewhat down, we can coexist. Intimately."

I held onto him, resting against his strength. However, as always, my desire to completely give in to him was blocked. This was the time that I needed to be with him, to see clearly and to get to know each other without any deadlines. But as I thought of the little one growing within me with every second that passed, my heart grew heavier.

45

Lena

Dinner was at Ulus 29, situated atop a hill, offering an incredibly stunning view of the Bosphorus Strait and the two bridges connecting the European and Asian shorelines. At first, it had been almost difficult to get a table on the terrace, but after a massive tip paid in advance, we eventually found one. It was in a secluded corner, away from the bustle of the center, which was very much appreciated, and thus we were able to focus even more on each other. Not that it would have been difficult, given that his attention on me was unparalleled. I was so impressed by his attentiveness that at some point, I had to wonder whether he knew about the fact that I was pregnant.

"Are you really okay with being away from the company?" I asked, just as our bottle of wine was delivered. He took a long sip before answering me, and then his attention shifted to his phone.

"I would probably not be if I had brought my actual phone," he said, and I looked at him in surprise.

"Really?"

However, I couldn't help but panic.

"What if something goes really wrong?"

"Then Matthias knows how to reach me, but only in extreme cases of emergency, like a fire or complete annihilation."

I smiled.

"He's the only one that has it, right?"

"Yeah," he replied, and I noticed that he quickly added my number to his phone.

A few seconds later, his call began to come in, and I smiled. I picked it up, wondering what to save his number as, but in the end, I couldn't make up my mind since he was in close proximity with me and would be for a little while longer. So, I just used his name and shut the phone.

Our dinner was served course after course, and I took my time with each, relishing how it felt to just eat without any looming deadlines or schedules. It truly felt like I had never been on a vacation before, and I had to attribute it to being with him. Seeing him so relaxed made me feel as though everything was handled, and I was able to fully dive in.

There were a lot of first-time dishes for me, mostly because he recommended them, and it was a thoroughly enjoyable experience. I avoided the wine as subtly as possible and stuck to water and thankfully he didn't seem to notice. We had dishes like Rockefeller oysters, grilled lamb, liver, crispy duck spring roll, ricotta ravioli del plin, beef fillet tartare, and the list went on. And by the end of it, the reasonable option to cap off the evening was to go for a walk.

We went down to the beach, and although we didn't hold each other's hands, our sides brushed so closely against each other that we were practically bumping into each other time and again.

However, we didn't stop and pull away, and the silence we basked in as we took in the rolling waves and horizon was wonderful. I spotted a few campfires along the way and reminisced about my younger days with him, and then we stopped at a bar. After ordering cocktails with me going for a non-alcoholic option, we took our seats on the stools as he told me a bit more about his family, especially what it was like growing up with a sister that was quite a bit older than him.

As we talked, someone came over excitedly and passed us a flyer, and as I perused it, I realized it was an invitation to a club. Instantly, I started to suggest walking away, but to my surprise, he stopped me.

"You're down for this?" I asked, and he looked over the flyer and then shrugged, though it was impossible to miss the flickering of excitement in his eyes.

"I probably haven't been to a club since I joined the company. I mean, I've had business meetings in lounges, but actually going to a club, I can't remember exactly what that feels like," I told him, expressing my dissatisfaction with my lack of recent club experiences.

His eyes widened at my words, and I nodded in agreement. We discussed the idea for a while, but as it started to get chilly outside, I halted and gave him a meaningful look.

"What's on your mind?" he asked, and I nodded in response.

"Let's try out the club. We'll both probably never be out

of jobs like this again in the near future, so let's give it a whirl. Who knows, it might be a much better experience, especially with company," I suggested.

Upon my suggestion, he nodded, this time grabbing my hand, and we set off on our way.

46

Kane

She was absolutely right that going to the club seemed like a dreadful and unpleasant idea. However, ever since I held her hand on the beach and hadn't let go, I had little to complain about. She clung onto my hand even tighter as we weaved through the crowds until we eventually reached the lounge area on the second floor.

The moment we arrived at the less crowded and more private bar, she burst into laughter, and I couldn't help but wonder why. Although I was curious, I didn't ask immediately; instead, I found myself fixated on her.

Noticing the way I was looking at her, she quickly assumed that I was wondering about her laughter and explained.

"You said you wanted to go to the club, but this is a private lounge. The club is down there."

I glanced down at the bustling dance floor, with people swaying and grinding to the deafening music. The thought of immersing myself in a sea of sweat and jostling elbows held no appeal to me. Just then, our drinks arrived, and I took a long sip.

"I think I'm too old for that scene," I remarked.

She leaned closer, her body pressing against mine, and her hand gently curved around the back of my neck. I couldn't quite discern whether her newfound audacity stemmed from her tipsiness or her desire to be affectionate and even provocative. Nevertheless, I had no objections as I willingly surrendered, and before long, her tongue was entwined with mine.

Setting the glass down, I fully engaged in the kiss, and by the time she pulled away, I was left breathless.

I kissed her repeatedly, convinced that the best way to revel in this night and its indulgences wasn't by retreating to a private lounge.

"Want to dance a bit?" I asked, breaking the kiss once again, and her eyes widened in response.

"Really?" she exclaimed, taken aback by the suggestion.

"Yeah," I replied, "and not on the balcony like those pretentious pricks. Let's act like college students for a while."

She stared at me, her teeth lightly sinking into her bottom lip as she scanned the dance floor.

“A little boost to help you decide," I said, offering her my drink, but she declined.

Instead, she grasped my hand, and we ventured into the crowd. It felt a bit awkward as we made our way through without a clear purpose, but eventually, we found a spot that seemed just right, and we simply observed.

"I feel old," she sighed, and in response, I pulled her closer against me, whispering in her ear.

"How about now?"

"I absolutely no longer feel old," she replied, pressing against my hardness. I wrapped my arms around her waist and kissed her neck. It didn't take long before we were swaying to the music, free from hesitation, concern, or awareness of our surroundings. It was just the music and us.

As I closed my eyes, her scent and body filled my senses, the heat between us intoxicating, and the taste of her skin even sweeter than I remembered.

"I've always wanted to... you know, fuck on a dance floor," she suddenly said, and I processed her words before smiling.

"You don't mean that," I teased, and she smiled back.

"No, I don't. But I've heard people talk about it, and I can only imagine how exciting it might be."

"Too bad you're wearing shorts tonight," I whispered into her ear. "Otherwise, we might have given it a go."

She turned around, staring into my eyes.

"We can always come back," she suggested, kissing me and continuing to sway against me. My breathing grew heavier and harder until I couldn't resist kissing her once again.

"You're right," I said as we pulled apart. "We have time for once."

"Or..." she said, brushing my hair out from my face.

"Or what?" I asked, and she smiled, a smile so beautiful it nearly stopped my heart.

"We can return to our very private and gorgeous suite, escape the heat and the noise... Is there music?" she inquired, leaning forward to nibble on my bottom lip.

"There could be," I replied, and that was all the convincing I needed.

From there on out, things only improved in our relationship. However, a few days later, when I woke up to the sight of her pleasuring me orally, I quickly realized that the day wasn't going to be as calm and relaxing as I had hoped. Nevertheless, as she took me deeper, any reservations I had were swiftly discarded.

My fingers gently intertwined in her hair, guiding her movements as I thrust my hips. Watching her lips and hands work so feverishly was a sight I knew I would never tire of. Our eyes locked, and as her lips curved into the sweetest, most beautiful smile, I struggled to hold back my release.

I climaxed into her mouth, observing as she eagerly consumed every drop, unable to contain my ragged breath as she crawled on top of me.

"Hey," she greeted, planting a kiss on my lips, and I couldn't resist turning with her in the bed, ensuring that I reciprocated thoroughly.

"I could get used to waking up like that," I remarked, and she smiled.

"You should because I'm going to be doing it more often."

I gently held her face, gazing into her eyes.

"Do you feel better?" I asked, and she nodded.

Over the past few days, she had been actively planning our itinerary, exploring the city's major landmarks, and I almost hadn't noticed how ill and frail she sometimes appeared.

But that was until we got back late the previous night. She'd finally succumbed and headed to the bathroom.

"It's fine," she reassured me. "I usually get a bit sick like this sometimes, so I'll be fine soon."

Because of this, we spent the rest of the evening in bed just holding each other.

"But now that she had woken me up in the most provocative manner possible, it was obvious it was leading to something else.

"I have our itinerary for the day," she announced, and my expression faltered. I would have tried to hide it, but in the state I was in with her, I felt comfortable enough to show my exhaustion.

"What's wrong?" she asked, looking at me, her lips slightly trembling as she tried to contain her laughter.

"I want us to just rest today," I confessed.

She stared at me, and I could tell she was fighting back her amusement.

"Is that what's wrong? You just want to laze around?" she inquired.

"Yeah," I replied. "I've enjoyed all the different locations so far, especially the hot springs, but do we have to take another flight today?"

"It's for the hot air balloon ride," she explained, and I closed my eyes.

"Let's postpone it until tomorrow. I feel like I'm working again," I suggested.

She laughed and then positioned herself on top of me.

"So, you're one of those people who laze around during vacations?" she teased.

"Lazing around is a vacation for me," I admitted. "I don't think I've done that in the past ten years without it being a business trip or something else."

She nodded in understanding.

"I think we might be here for a while longer, so we can take the balloon ride and do other activities, but today I just want to stay here and do nothing. Hopefully, with you."

Her laughter finally escaped, and I was a bit startled.

"What is it?" I asked.

"And here I was, trying to make this the best holiday you've ever had," she said playfully.

"Unexpectedly, that was your plan, even when you weren't feeling well," I replied.

"Trust me, I wanted to do nothing but lie down as well, but my family always did that when we went on vacations, so I wanted us to actually put in the effort to explore here. Honestly, I regretted not doing it the last time I was here, so I promised myself that I'd change that if I ever came back again."

"Well, you've been doing just that so far, but let's have a day lazing on the beach and eating greasy food."

"I have no objections to that," she agreed, turning around to rest comfortably by my side.

47

Lena

I was startled awake by the ringing phone. The calls had been reduced to a minimum during the first few days that we were here, so as I opened my eyes, I couldn't help but notice the difference. We both went straight to sleep after making plans for the beach, but since it was about midday now, I consoled myself that we could head over there in the evening.

"Hello?" I answered, hearing Kane's smooth and calming voice on the other end. He had gone into the other room to speak on his phone after it had rung earlier.

I closed my eyes again as he continued speaking, and then everything went silent.

It remained that way for a while until I felt his warm, comforting frame come over to me.

I accepted this warm embrace, leaning even further into it until he finally said what the phone call was about.

"That was Matthias," he said. "The company's general

counsel." I recognized the name as the lawyer who was close to Kane, so I wondered if the call had a social purpose.

"He just called to say hello?" I asked Kane, and he shook his head.

"Not exactly. He more or less called to let me know that your brother has been trying to reach us."

My eyes instantly snapped open.

"What does he want?"

"It's your brother, he wants us to buy his percentage of the equity," Kane replied, and I turned around to face him.

"My brother? What's happening?"

"It's the same offer he proposed earlier."

"Hasn't he already transferred it to your sister?"

"Yes, he has, but according to Matthias, the deal isn't officially ratified yet. When he saw that we were immediately kicked out, I think in a way, he got cold feet," Kane explained.

At his words, a sigh escaped me. I didn't know what to think.

"Are you going to accept?" I asked, noticing Kane deep in thought.

"Will she even agree to relinquish control?" I asked, and he fell silent, lost in thought.

"She might have been the one to even request it," he said, and our eyes met.

"Matthias said Dylan told him the deal wasn't ratified yet, but what if it was? It's a much better excuse to go with that Dylan pulled back, rather than admit that she ran into roadblocks she couldn't solve on her own."

I didn't know what to think about all of this. I felt relieved, but at the same time, I couldn't help but be disappointed because I had truly hoped that we would have more time to spend together here.

"What do you think?" he asked, and I met his gaze.

"I don't know," I told him. "Do you still want to stay here for a few more days?"

He laughed as he looked outside the windows.

"We haven't gotten to the beach yet or ridden in the hot air balloon. There's no rush, is there? We can take a day or two to specify the terms of agreeing to this and see if he will respond."

Kane nodded in agreement.

"And," I added, "in order for us to check if Kate is truly the one behind this, how about we ask her to relinquish a percentage of her equity? Perhaps 5 to 10 percent. This way, you hold the majority vote, and something as ridiculous as this doesn't have to happen ever again."

He considered my suggestion, nodded in agreement, and then made the call.

48

Kane

I had never been so conflicted. On one hand, I was eager to head back home after the terms of the deal had been changed, and on the other hand, I was tempted to let them stew for just a bit more as they wondered if I was going to accept the deal or not. Kate had reluctantly given up eight percent of her stake as stipulated in my terms, and although I could have easily pushed for ten, I decided to let her keep her dignity with it.

Now that I was returning, I couldn't wait to begin putting things back in order once again. The lawsuit had come in, but it was nothing I hadn't handled before. So, although I was dreading the stress it would bring, I was more grateful than ever that we had taken the much-needed rest.

Due to Lena's absence from the company at the same exact time as mine, there was no suspicion by anyone that we were together, and I truly didn't mind. As we headed back on the plane, I considered asking her, but I held off on it until we arrived back at her apartment. It was a Saturday, so the next day there was no work to prepare for, and the moment we arrived at her apartment, she invited me up.

"Want to stay the night?" she asked. "I think I've gotten quite used to you over the past week, so it will suck to sleep alone."

I loved hearing this, and she didn't need to ask twice, so my luggage was brought up as well.

"You can take it to my bedroom," she said. "I'll order some Chinese food for us."

I did exactly this and walked in to meet the clean, spacious room.

I was exhausted since I had slept very little the previous night, but I wanted to spend the evening with her, so I turned to head back out to the living room. Just before I turned off the lights, however, I noticed a box on her vanity and was about to pass by when I couldn't help but stop.

The instant I read the words; a heavy chill ran through me. I picked it up, and my eyebrows instantly shot up. I lifted my gaze and truly didn't know what to think.

She hadn't brought this up at all, so of course, things wouldn't go smoothly if I were to. But most importantly, her exhaustion and recent illness during the trip, despite how hard she tried to fight it, all suddenly made sense to me. I was beyond astonished, and not until I took the test stick with me to her in the kitchen did I truly even know how and what to feel.

49

Lena

Diana had so thoughtfully and to my surprise left us groceries before she left, so there was no need to order in. It would have been faster, but since we had all the needed ingredients for pasta, I decided to whip something up for both of us. This night felt special in many ways, almost like a new start, and I didn't quite know how to process it. But with him being here, us sharing a meal that I made, it felt personal and comfortable.

I kept looking towards the door, hoping he would come out and help. When he eventually did, I couldn't help but smile. However, when I saw the expression on his face, I was taken aback. I was rinsing a few vegetables in the sink when he emerged, so I had to put them down and face him in his solemn mood.

"Are you alright?" I asked, meeting his gaze. Then, I noticed that he was holding the pregnancy test box in his hand, and I almost gasped out loud. Thankfully, I was able to catch myself in time, or maybe it was the shock that kept me silent. All I could do was stare at him.

"Lena?" he called, seeking my attention.

"Where did you get that?"

He paused, and I leaned against the the kitchen counter, feeling particularly dizzy.

"On your vanity," he replied, confirming my suspicions. I nodded, realizing how careless I had been in forgetting to throw it out. In my mind, I cursed myself as my heart started racing.

Everything now came down to this moment, and I felt completely unprepared. I had pushed thoughts of this revelation aside, avoiding the dilemma of how and when to tell him. But now, it had come back to haunt me.

"Are you pregnant?" he asked directly, and I let out a heavy sigh.

"Yes, I am," I replied, those words being the hardest I had ever uttered. It felt like a weight had been lifted off my shoulders, yet as I looked at him and saw the confusion in his expression, the weight returned, even heavier than before.

"You weren't planning on telling me?" he asked, and his question terrified me.

At first, he seemed confused and somewhat shocked, but now he appeared composed, as if he had built an impenetrable wall between us.

"I was, I just..." I struggled to find the right words to explain the whirlwind of emotions that had plagued me since I found out.

"You just what?" he pressed, his tone demanding an answer.

"I was waiting for the right time. It's not exactly expected news. I was shocked too when I found out, and I needed time to process it all," I replied, hoping he would understand.

"When did you find out?" he inquired, and I contemplated my response. Finally, I decided to tell him the truth.

"Just before we went on the trip," I admitted.

"But... you drank alcohol with me at the restaurant on the beach."

"Not really," I reassured him. "I initially ordered something alcoholic but then switched to a non-alcoholic option before it was served with your wine. I mostly drank water. I didn't act any differently so that you wouldn't notice. Besides, you don't drink a lot, so there weren't many moments that required me to drink."

"And your illness?" he asked, and I nodded.

He understood because truly there was nothing left to say, and he headed over to the couch and took a seat. I turned off the pot of boiling water and joined him, although I chose to sit in an armchair a little distance away.

"So, what's the plan now?" he asked.

I had asked myself this exact question over and over again, and yet I couldn't say that I had found a response.

"I don't know," I replied honestly.

"It's unexpected. I didn't expect you to be ready for this. I mean, I know I'm not," I admitted.

"I'm ready," he said, and my heart nearly stopped. I turned to him, surprised by his words.

"What?" I managed to say.

"I said I'm ready," he repeated. "Why wouldn't I be?"

I looked at him, wondering if he was fully aware or at least expecting the challenges that would come with this. I knew, yet I didn't have the courage to bring it up.

"We're both financially capable of contributing to their care, but if it comes to having to do it alone, you know I'm capable as well. Of course, I'll never keep them away from you..."

"Wait," he interrupted me, and I could hardly hear him over the sound of my pounding heart.

"You want to do this alone?"

"It's unexpected," I told him. "And since I can do it alone financially, I'm not looking to saddle you with any..."

"Saddle me?" he asked, his voice filled with disbelief. My mouth snapped shut.

"We're in a relationship. This wasn't some one-night stand with a stranger," he pointed out.

After that, I didn't know what else to say.

"Okay," I finally replied, but he seemed even more perplexed.

"Okay?" he asked, seeking clarification. So I decided to be direct and explain myself.

"This was sudden," I said.

"So you've said." he responded.

"Exactly. I don't know what to do. I feel... great about having your baby, but our relationship is so new. We haven't even had time to properly establish our bond, and I thought that having a baby would happen a few years down the line. So now... I don't know how to feel or what to do. But what I do know is that I'm falling in love with you. Maybe I already have, but I'm also too logical to trust that. There are some things that only time can truly tell."

He stared at me, processing my words.

“You believe time is the true determinant of the success of a relationship?"

"In most cases, it is. With time, the other person's flaws

and unacceptable quirks start to appear, or they change so much that you don't recognize them anymore, and then you start seeing why you weren't a match from the beginning," I explained.

"Those telltale signs are never sudden," he pointed out. "We just refuse to acknowledge them until it's too late."

"You're right," I admitted with a nod.

"You think we won't make it?" he suddenly asked, and I was shocked by his question.

"That's a direct question," I replied, and he nodded.

"Yes, it is."

I looked at him, tears welling up in my eyes.

"I think we have a really good chance."

We watched each other in silence, and then he nodded.

"An alternative," I said. "We could just continue the way we are and resolve issues together as they come up, and if a year or so down the line we know better, then we'll do better."

"No," he replied, surprising me.

"What do you mean?" I asked, my eyes widening in surprise.

"I'm sure of you," he said. "And I want to do better now."

I stared at him, perplexed.

"You do?" I asked.

"In the face of this, yes," he replied. "And it's something that I have considered long before this. I just didn't think you were ready."

My eyes filled with tears as I processed his words.

"Yeah," I replied. "I didn't think I was ready either, but let's do it this way. Everything in life is uncertain, no matter how much preparation you have at first. But I know in my heart that I'm more than ready to take this step with you."

I stared at him, feeling my heart swell with joy and excitement. He stood up and came over to me, squatting down to be at eye level. I gazed into his eyes, unable to contain the overwhelming emotions inside me.

"I want you with all my heart, and I want the life we can have together," he said. "So, what do you say we take this year by year?"

Tears streamed down my face as I nodded, filled with a mix of emotions.

“Yes,” I whispered and then leaned forward to kiss him. The moment I did all my fears and worries seemed to completely dissipate.

It felt perfect, it felt right, and it felt true.

EPILOGUE

Lena

The meeting was about to start, and although I felt relatively calm, I couldn't stop glancing at my phone. I was going through the terms to be negotiated with my new assistant, Emma, for our division. As we finished reviewing them, I felt a sense of relief wash over me. This would be our first major contract for the division, and despite knowing our numbers were solid, I couldn't help but be nervous about whether the pricing should be adjusted lower for a first-time deal.

Eventually, Emma left to head to the conference room with the others, and I finally gave in to my impulse. I picked up the phone and called Kane.

"Hey," he replied almost immediately, and just hearing his voice had the effect of enveloping me in warmth.

"Hey," I replied, closing my eyes and taking a deep breath to calm my racing thoughts.

"Ready?" he asked, and I couldn't help but place my hand against my belly. It always reminded me of him and the life we were building together. I was showing a bit more now, but not enough for anyone to notice, which was a relief since our wedding was just this weekend.

"I feel like we should postpone this meeting until after the wedding," I suggested, hoping he would understand.

Kane laughed softly.

"I mean, what's a few more days?"

"In the business world, you know the answer to that."

"I know, I know. A few more days, or even hours, could mean success or failure."

"What is it?" he asked softly, concern evident in his voice. I looked around my office, contemplating my decision, and then decided to go to his office instead.

"I'm going to come over to your office real quick," I told him. "Are you busy?"

"About to wrap up a meeting now with Matthias, but you can walk in," he replied.

"Alright," I said, ending the call.

The walk to his office was a welcome distraction. As I passed through the lab, I checked in on the preparations for the meeting in half an hour. Seeing everything in order reassured me that I had done my very best in preparation. Our fragrance had been three months in development, with new scents I had established in LA. Now, we were offering it to P&G as they prepared to launch a new home air freshener brand.

Everything was in place, but it was the biggest deal I had ever been involved in, and the entire company had their eyes on me. Taking a deep breath, I continued my walk and soon arrived in Kane's office. His secretary smiled at me and, as usual, ushered me right in.

The first thing I saw when I walked in was Matthias's

smile, which had always struck me as peculiar. Kane had told me that he was just happy to see that Kane had found someone. Apparently, he had been almost convinced that no one would ever be enough, but since Kane had been with me, he had become softer and happier, and everyone benefited from it.

I was more than happy to see him as well, and in no time, Matthias got up and took his leave. Kane stood up and came over to me, and although my intention was to hug him, when I saw his gorgeous face, all I wanted to do was kiss him. My hand slid around his neck, and within seconds, our tongues were entwined in a passionate kiss.

He instantly surrendered to the kiss, and when I felt his arm wrap around my waist, I melted even more. The kiss seemed to go on forever, as if neither of us wanted to let go. Eventually, though, we had to break the kiss, knowing that I couldn't afford to miss my meeting.

The biggest smile was on his face as he pulled away and looked deeply into my eyes, and my heart just melted.

"What's wrong?" he asked, glancing at his watch.

I immediately got to the point.

"I had always heard that if you weren't ready to walk away from the table, you should never go into a negotiation."

He laughed at this and then nodded, pulling me towards the edge of his desk. After we settled on it, he pulled me between his thighs, ready to discuss.

"Yeah," he replied. "What's on your mind?"

"I am ready to walk away if they propose less than 38 million. But I don't think I'm ready to do so if they propose less than the 45 million, we're asking for."

"So..."

"I think I need you with me so that I don't cave because I feel like I just might," I said. He smiled, and then he kissed me once again.

"I'm so happy that you're coming to me with this," he said, and I pouted.

"You're happy seeing me weak?"

"Yes, for once. You never are. But here you are leaning on me, and it just makes me so fucking happy," I replied.

"But..."

"But" he smiled, "I am confident that you can handle this one completely on your own. And from my experience with huge deals like this, they will be willing to pay forty-two million, maybe not more than that, but it sure is a hell of a lot more than 38."

I stared at him and then nodded.

"So, you think my walk-away number should be 42 million?" I asked, seeking confirmation, and he nodded.

"Absolutely. Your scents are revolutionary, so don't sell yourself short, and this is just the start. It will set the value of your scents for all others to come."

"So, you really won't be sitting in with me?" I inquired again, still hopeful.

He shook his head and then pulled me close to him, pressing a kiss against my forehead.

"No," he replied.

I understood this and, in a way, I was relieved to hear it. It was just that I was getting so used to having him around these days that not having him to lean on was no longer something I shied away from.

But regardless just hearing him speak to me in this way was beyond wonderful.

I straightened my spine, gave him a kiss and headed out.

I was still a bit nervous but when the meeting started and I recalled his encouragement in my head, I was reminded once again that there was absolutely nothing to worry about.

The End

COMING NEXT - SAMPLE CHAPTERS

STRICTLY BUSINESS

Chapter One
Wyatt

I look at my watch and I'm surprised to note it's almost nine pm. The surprise is not because I'm still in the office – that's normal for me and it would be more of a surprise if I was home at this time. I am surprised because I thought it was much earlier than it is. Apparently, time flies when you're swamped with work, not just when you are having fun, although the two are often interchangeable for me as I genuinely love my job.

Ignoring the thought of dinner, I get back into work mode and I open the next email to be dealt with. It's simple enough. One of my graphic designers has sent a campaign to be finalized. I look over the designs. Overall, they are good, and I like them a lot, but I do have a few small tweaks that need completing. I note these down and send the new file back to the designer. The tweaks are small enough that some people would say that I was nit-picking, but I'm a perfectionist and my team knows that. I think they would be more concerned if I signed off on a campaign immediately than when I take the time to look over it and help them to strengthen it.

I'm about to open the next email in my inbox when my cell phone rings. The ring pierces the soft silence that has settled around me. I look around my desk, searching for my ringing cell phone, but it isn't there. It must be close because I can hear it trilling, the sound seeming to get angrier the longer I ignore it. I realize the sound is coming from the top drawer of my desk. I pull it open and take my cell phone out.

"Wyatt McAvoy," I mutter, as I swipe the screen.

"Craig West," an amused voice say. He laughs, then starts taking the piss out of me. "Wyatt McAvoy. What the hell, man? What happened to, yeah what's up?"

I grin at the sound of his warm gruff voice. "I couldn't find my cell phone and by the time I did, I figured it was almost ready to stop ringing so I just swiped quickly without looking at the screen," I say. "Now what could I have possibly done to deserve this pleasure?"

Craig is my best friend and has been since we started high school. We went through high school and then college together and even now, in our early forties, we are still close, so I find it a bit strange when Craig sounds awkward when he next speaks.

"Actually, I wanted to ask you for a favor," he says.

We regularly roped each other into doing things like helping each other move apartments or decorate rooms before we were making enough money to pay other people to do stuff like that. And even now, if either of us needs anything, we go to each other first. Which is why I find it odd that Craig sounds so awkward all of a sudden. It's not like this is unprecedented territory for us.

I wonder if he needs to borrow some money.

Of course, I'd be happy to lend him whatever he needs, but that's one scenario I never thought I'd see Craig in...ever.

"Go on," I say when it seems like Craig isn't going to say anything without me prompting him to speak up.

He sighs and I picture him getting his courage up. I'm starting to feel a bit nervous now. What can he possibly want from me that he's this reluctant to ask for? I sense it's about something more than just money.

"Could you possibly give Serena a job?" Craig finally says.

Serena is Craig's niece. I remember her well enough from before she went off to college. She was a plump little thing with a mass of mousey brown curls that were always in disarray, and she wore horrible wire framed glasses that were too big for her face, making her eyes look strangely bug like. But she was a sweet girl and she had always been polite to me. Considering she'd gotten into an ivy league college she must be intelligent too.

None of that mattered though. I had to say no, and Craig knew it. I felt bad to say no to him, especially after how awkward he had been about asking, but he too understood the score. He was awkward about asking because he knew I was going to have to say no.

"I'm sorry man. You know I love you, but you also know my number one rule of business – never mix business and pleasure, or in this case, friendship."

"I get that," Craig said, suddenly more confident. "But

this isn't you taking on a dud as a favor to me. It would be you taking on a great asset as a favor to yourself. I've seen some of her work Wyatt and she's good. Real good. And don't forget she's got a degree in business management and marketing from Harvard. In fact, the more I think about it, the more I think I am actually doing you a favor asking you to have Serena go and work for you."

I knew she had gone ivy league, but I had no idea where and I certainly hadn't known that her degree was actually relevant to what she would be doing here if I was to give her a job. My company, Smart Marketing Solutions, is, as the name suggests, a marketing firm. We take care of a company's branding and message, and we design ads for various social media platforms, ads for old school media like newspapers and magazines, and TV ads. We also have a team working on viral content for platforms such as Instagram and TikTok.

And I do need a new associate.

Since I just promoted my last associate to marketing executive which means she's off in the company on her own now working on her own portfolio. I need an associate to help with my workload because I have to run the company as well as take care of my personal clients. Could I take a chance on Serena? If there was anyone I would be willing to break my rule for it would be Craig, or his brother, Martin, Serena's father.

"If I did agree to employ her, and I'm not yet, I'm just talking hypothetically, she wouldn't get any special treatment. She would be treated like any other associate which is the bottom rung of the ladder," I say.

"Of course, I get that, and she does too," Craig says immediately. "She's not looking for any special treatment, she just wants someone to give her a fair chance. You remember what it was like leaving college with your degree and realizing it was next to impossible to get a foot in the door anywhere decent."

I do remember it. I remember it well. It was that struggle to find anything worth doing, which eventually led me to start my own firm. It seemed that was the only way in without knowing someone in the industry because the positions I saw advertised where always for someone with years of experience, something I couldn't get because no one would give me a chance.

"I know you're a bit reluctant to give her a chance because you know her," Craig adds into the silence. "But I guarantee, if she turned up for an associate position interview with that degree and her portfolio and you had no idea who she was, you'd be begging her to take the position."

I know he's probably right, and I can feel myself relenting. I suppose Craig is right in a way. It's as wrong to overlook someone just because you know them as it is to employ them purely because you know them.

"If I did take her on, you'd have to promise not to interfere and you would need to understand that if it's not working out, I won't hesitate to get rid of her, just like I would anyone else," I say. "And you would need to make sure Martin understands the same thing."

"I know," Craig replies. "But she won't let you down. I know she won't."

"Fine," I say with a sigh. "Tell her to be here at nine o'clock sharp Monday morning."

"Thanks Wyatt, you're the man," Craig says happily.

"Make sure she understands this though – knowing the

right person got her in the door, but only performing in her role will keep her on this side of it," I say.

"Got it. Thanks again. Catch you later man," Craig says.

He ends the call before I can speak, probably to make sure I can't change my mind. Should I change my mind? Probably, but I won't. I've said I'll give Serena a chance and I will, and I just have to trust that Craig is mature enough to not sever our friendship if Serena working here doesn't work out.

***

Monday Morning
Nine o'clock sharp

I take a sip of my hot then quickly scan over my schedule for the day. The next hour or so is the only time I have to return emails and phone calls because my day is completely full of meetings from around eleven o'clock. I could move a meeting or two if I have to, but I'm hoping that won't be the case because truth be told, I'd like to get these meetings done and out of the way. I put my hand on the receiver of my phone, ready to pick it up and call one of my clients, when there is a knock on my door. It can only be Ruth, my personal assistant.

"Come in," I call.

I look up as the door opens. Ruth is tall and very thin, to my mind to the point of being scrawny, but she considers herself to be fashionably slim. I can see the bones at the top of her chest in the skintight black dress she's wearing. The blunt bob she wears her sleek black hair in hangs close to her jaw, showing off her best feature, a swan-line graceful neck. I guess she wouldn't look out of place in the offices of Vogue.

"What's up?"

"It's kind of a strange one," she says. "There's a young woman here to see you. She says she's your new associate..."

"My new ..." I start and then stop when I remember I told Craig to tell Serena to come in today at nine and it's now, I glance at my watch, eight fifty-five. Good. At least she knows how to keep time. "Ok, send her in please."

"Wait, you mean it's true?" Ruth says, her eyes widening.

"Yes," I reply. "Sorry Ruth, I forgot all about it or I would have told you."

"Oh, that's ok," she says with a slight frown. "What about HR and stuff?"

I sigh. "You'll sort all that out with her later, won't you?"

"Right. Of course, I will. I'll send her in now."

I nod and turn to my computer. Knowing I won't have time to do everything I wanted to do now, I decide that the phone calls can wait. I will catch a cab to my first offsite meeting later on today rather than driving and get caught up on my way there and for now, I'll start on my most important emails.

I open the most important one and start typing my response. I'm almost done when there's another knock on my office door.

"Come in," I call. When the door opens, I don't look up. "Take a seat Serena, I will be with you in two seconds. I just need to send this email."

"Ok," she says.

I sense her moving towards my desk and sitting down opposite me as I finish up the email. Her scent wafts towards me – vanilla and something else I can't place? Whatever it is, it smells good. To my great surprise I find myself taking longer, deeper breaths to take in the unfamiliar, but delectable scent. Slightly unfazed, I finish the email, hit send, and look up at owner of the delectable scent.

She smiles and for a second, I feel like everything stops.

The beautiful woman in front of me is not the Serena I remember. The old Serena was a plump, quite shapeless girl, this Serena is...well, voluptuous, with delicious curves in all the right places. She is wearing a white blouse and a pin-stripped navy pencil skirt. Her breasts are round and full and I'm careful not to let my eyes linger over her flaring hips.

Where the old Serena wore glasses that dwarfed her face, the new Serena wears sexy, black framed rectangular shaped glasses that fit her face properly and draw attention to her huge, bright green eyes. Her hair is still curly, but it's a few shades darker and the frizz that used to sort of float all around her head has been tamed around her lovely face.

In short, I might as well just say it. Serena got hot. Like really fucking hot.

She has left behind that awkward teenage phase and turned into a beautiful young woman. It's a good job I don't mix business and pleasure and it's a really good job I don't go around fucking anyone related to my best friend too, because if I didn't have those rules in place, I think I could be in real trouble with this one.

I realize I'm staring at her. I force myself to smile and act like everything is normal.

"Hello Serena? It's been a while since I've seen you."

"Yes, it's been ages, hasn't it? I guess between my studies and your work we kept missing each other. How are you?"

"Good," I say quickly. "Now I don't mean to sound rude, but I'm kind of pushed for time so we'll have to get straight into it."

"Of course," Serena agrees smoothly. "And for the record, I don't think that was rude."

"Have a seat," I invite, waving my arm to one of the chairs in front of my desk. I try not to look as she slips into it elegantly.

"So, you graduated from Harvard?"

She nods. "With a degree in business management and marketing."

"And did that involve any sort of on-the-job training?"

"Yes, but ..." Serena says, then she shakes her head. "Nothing." It's obvious by her facial expression that she wants to say more, but she's not sure how I'm going to take it.

"Come on," I urge. "Spill it."

She chews her bottom lip. "I don't want to sound pretentious or anything, but I found the places Harvard sent us to for our placements weren't that great. Like, don't get me wrong, they were huge advertising agencies, and they would be good places to work, but as far as training went, they were too busy to really show us anything and all we did was sit around watching them or doing shit jobs like filing and making endless cups of coffee."

She pushes an orange file folder across the desk and smiles shyly.

"I took it upon myself to do some intern work at smaller firms through the holidays and I found those much more useful. I was even given some small projects of my own to work on."

I pick up the folder and flick through the sheets inside of it. It's good. Better than I expected, if I'm honest. I know Craig said he'd seen Serena's stuff and it was good, but he's biased and I'm not. But in this case, we agree.

"These are really good," I admit.

Serena blushes slightly and I can't help but notice how cute she is when her cheeks flush pink. My traitorous mind immediately and predictably flies into the taboo area. Would her cheeks would be that color when she's being fucked hard. I push that insane thought firmly away and focus on the file.

I come across a story board for a TV ad, for a soft drinks company, and I frown as I try to place why it is familiar and then it hits me. It's an actual TV ad that gets shown now and again currently. I know that advertising firm and now, and they must have moved heaven and earth to keep her and yet, here she is.

Now, I'm really impressed.

"Did you come up with all of this?" I ask Serena, nodding down at the story board.

"Not for the logos or the branding, but for the individual campaigns."

"Hmmm." I see that. I flick through the rest of the sheets in the folder, but it's just out of curiosity at this point. I have already seen enough to know that Serena is a good hire. The only thing is, the only opening I have right now is for someone to be my associate, but I'm too busy to do much with her today. I don't want her to think my firm is like one of those faceless firms that Harvard sent her to though where interns are largely ignored and don't learn anything.

I think for a minute, and I decide to take a measured risk. I lean down and open my third drawer down on my desk and pull out a thin file which I place on the desk. I close my drawer and smile at Serena.

"I think I've seen enough to know that you won't need hand holding a lot. Don't worry, I still plan on mentoring you and helping you to develop your skills. But today I am in back-to-back meetings and I'm not sure the next few days are any better. So, I'm going to give you the sort of chance most associates would only be able to dream of, but I think you can handle it."

She leans forward eagerly, her eyes wide with interest. "That would be amazing."

"I'm going to give you Hislop's stuff to work on. They are a brand-new start up and right now, they are selling a very niche kind of dog food. In time, they hope to branch out to other dog foods and then maybe to foods for other animals, but they aren't trying to run before they can walk, so right now, we're focusing on this one thing. They need a brand – logo, ethos, billboard campaigns, social media campaigns in preparation for a TV ad. Do you think you can handle that?"

Serena's face breaks into a wide smile and I notice how much it lights up her eyes, how the green sparkles and how ravishing she looks. I tell myself not to think like that, but how can I not? It's like saying there's a red box there, but don't notice that it's red though.

"Yes," she says. "I really do."

"Good." I push the folder towards her, and she picks it up and scans over the information sheets inside. She smiles again, her excitement at having her own project clear to see on her face. She looks back up from the folder and smiles at me.

"I can definitely do this," she says. "I promise I won't let you down."

I nod and return her smile.

"I'm sure you won't." I glance at my watch then I look back at Serena. "I really wanted to be able to spend more time with you on your first day, but I have to head out really soon. I will have Ruth show you around. You've met Ruth, right? My personal assistant?"

Serena nods.

"Good. For today, if you have any questions or if you need anything, just ask Ruth. Obviously, her speciality isn't marketing, but we have worked together a long time and I trust her opinion on most things, and I think she knows me well enough to know if I would approve something or not."

"Ok, that sounds great," Serena says with a smile.

"Perfect. Any questions?"

She shakes her head. "No. Not right now."For the first time since she came into my office, she looks down at her hands in her lap as she speaks instead of looking at me.

"Serena," I say gently. I wait for her to look back up at me before I carry on. "Please don't be worried about asking questions or speaking up. I like people who know their own mind and who aren't afraid to speak up ok?"

She nods. "Ok, then yes, I have a question. Well, actually, it's more of a favor to ask of you."

I frown. It's far too early for her to be asking for favors and I'm reminded once more that Serena is a family member of my best friend. Is she going to expect preferential treatment? Because if she is, she's going to be massively disappointed. Despite that, I am curious as to what she thinks it's acceptable to ask and I nod for her to go on.

"I was hoping we could keep it between us that we already know each other. I know I'm probably just being paranoid, but I don't want anyone thinking I'm only here because of that. I mean I get that at the moment, that is the only reason, but I want to prove myself with my work."

Ok, I admit I misjudged her. That's the sort of favor I can get behind. In fact, I am relieved she feels that way because I don't want to have to spend any time second guessing myself if people think I'm being too lenient on her, because if no one knows that we know each other, and I am too lenient, I have no doubt someone will let me know. It also means that if Serena is working with someone else, they won't give her an easy ride thinking that's what I would want.

"Yes, that's perfectly fine," I say with a smile. "It's always a good idea to keep work and personal lives separate."

Serena smiles gratefully. "Thank you."

"No problem. Right, if that's it for questions, I'll get Ruth back in here."

"No more questions for now, but I will have loads for later," Serena says.

I call through to Ruth and ask her to come back to my office. In less than a minute, there's a quiet knock on my door before it opens and Ruth steps inside. She closes the door quietly behind her and walks towards my desk. She doesn't sit on the other chair next to Serena, but perches at the edge of my desk. I find it very strange behavior, but I let it go. I don't want to undermine her in front of Serena on Serena's first day here.

"So, obviously you two have already met," I say. "But just to make it official, Ruth, this is Serena West, my new associate. Serena, this is Ruth Stainsby, my PA."

The women smile at each other. They both look a little uncertain, but I guess that's normal until they get to know each other a little bit.

"Ruth, I've just been explaining to Serena that I am up to my eyes with meetings and work for the next few days and I've asked her to go to you with any questions or needs she might have. If you could also check in on her now and again to make sure she's on the right track that would be a big help."

"Yes, of course," Ruth replies easily, a smile hovering on her red lips.

"Good. Serena will be working on the Hislop's campaign," I add.

"What? Alone?" Ruth asks, raising an eyebrow.

"She's more than qualified to do the work, but she won't be on her own will she? You'll be there to help her if she needs it."

Ruth gives a sidelong glance at Serena

I sigh. I don't have time for this, but I need to know if there is some sort of problem.

"What's wrong?"

"Nothing," she says.

"Then what's with the face?"

She looks away from me for a moment and then she looks down at the desk.

"I'm just not sure I should be the one looking after Serena. I've never done anything marketing related. Should she not be with one of the marketing executives?"

Well, I wasn't expecting that. This morning is definitely full of surprises. What I mistook for hostility on Ruth's part was actually self-doubt. I have never known Ruth to doubt herself so I can be forgiven for not recognizing it I suppose.

"Serena is more than able to hit the ground running on the marketing side. Anything she needs to ask you is probably going to be more system based, or maybe where to find something. But if you do take a look at the campaign now and again, you know my tastes and you know the brand's values. I trust you to know if I would be happy with the campaign at hand or not."

Ruth's smile widens and she looks up at me once more.

"Then consider it done," she says. She turns to Serena with the same happy smile on her face. "Are you ready for a tour of the building then?"

Chapter Two
Serena

I smile politely at Ruth as she offers me a tour of the building. She doesn't like me, you can tell that from a mile away, but I don't know why. She covered it well when Wyatt noticed something was off, but not well enough to fool me. I don't know what to make of her. I don't know if she's not a very nice person, or if the whole ice queen routine is just her work persona or something.

But I do know now that I will really have to hit the ground running here and be willing to work things out for myself though, because I really don't want to have to ask this woman for her help.

On the other hand, it's a shame Wyatt is going to be busy over the next few days because holy shit, would I be happy to have to ask for his help. My mind can't help but wander off in familiar directions.

I see myself walking into Wyatt's office, naked except for my bra and panties.

"Can you help me?" I ask in a husky voice that isn't my real voice, but I wish it was. "You see, I am almost at orgasm, but something is stopping me from getting there."

Wyatt stands up from his desk chair and comes around to the front of his desk and he beckons me to him. I eagerly oblige and he wraps his arms around me and pulls me close and kisses me. As he kisses me, he pushes my panties to one side and works my clit until I come, screaming his name, and soaking his hand and the cuff of his shirt sleeve.

Oops.

I have always had a crush on Wyatt for as long as I can remember. He was my cool Uncle Craig's even cooler friend, and he was handsome in a way that boys my age just weren't. But this is different now. This isn't like a crush; this is a serious attraction. I don't know how any straight woman could look at the perfection that is Wyatt and not have a serious attraction to him.

He's tall and broad shouldered and even when he's fully dressed, I can see his defined muscles pushing against his clothes, like even his body knows it is perfection and wants to be shown off. He has light grey eyes, and they stand out against his tanned skin and dark hair. He has a square jaw and cheekbones to die for, and the smattering of stubble he is sporting is so fucking hot I feel wet just looking at him. It's so hard to look at him and not imagine straddling him, riding his cock.

But I know I can't act on these urges. Wyatt has never shown the slightest bit of interest in me sexually, and I am not going to be that girl that throws herself at her uncle's friend and gets rejected.

Talk about tragic.

Especially now that I'm working for him. No, I will have to stick to craving for Wyatt from afar – that part hasn't changed since before I went away to college. I don't know how long I can be around Wyatt without acting on the lust I feel when I look at him though.

"Serena? Are you coming?" Ruth asks.

Give me two minutes alone with Wyatt and I would be, I think to myself. Of course, I don't say that and when I feel my cheeks turn pink from my dirty thoughts, I'm sure that my blush will be mistaken for embarrassment that I was off in a world of my own while Ruth was talking to me.

"Yes, sorry," I say, getting quickly to my feet.

Pre-order here:
Strictly Business

ABOUT THE AUTHOR

Thank you so much for reading!
If you have enjoyed the book and would like to leave a precious review for me, please kindly do so here:

Insufferable Boss

Please click on the link below to receive info about my latest releases and giveaways.
NEVER MISS A THING

Or
come say 'hello' here:

ALSO BY IONA ROSE

Nanny Wanted

CEO's Secret Baby

New Boss, Old Enemy

Craving The CEO

Forbidden Touch

Crushing On My Doctor

Reckless Entanglement

Untangle My Heart

Tangled With The CEO

Tempted By The CEO

CEO's Assistant

Trouble With The CEO

It's Only Temporary

Charming The Enemy

Keeping Secrets

On His Terms

CEO Grump

Surprise CEO

The Fire Between Us

The Forgotten Pact

Taming The CEO Beast

Hot Professor

Flirting With The CEO

Surprise Proposal

Propositioning The Boss

Dream Crusher

Until He Confesses

Printed in Great Britain
by Amazon

35713267R00202